I left the house the way I'd gotten in. Through the rear window. And my luck ran out, there and then. Three storm troopers were strolling by. They saw me at the same time I saw them. And they stopped dead, frowning at me.

They didn't know me. And if they didn't know me, I wasn't one of the people who had a right to be in the estate. It didn't require smarts to realize they'd cornered a trespasser.

They got their clubs in hand quickly and spread out just enough to block my exit. They had mean faces, and their brown shirts bulged with pumped-up beef. Wall-to-wall muscle. They closed in on me looking eager but deliberately taking their time.

I yanked the tire iron from my belt and let my own mean streak take over. . . .

Also by Marvin Albert:

THE UNTOUCHABLES

Published by Fawcett Books:

Stone Angel Series:

STONE ANGEL
BACK IN THE REAL WORLD
GET OFF AT BABYLON
LONG TEETH
THE LAST SMILE
MIDNIGHT SISTER
BIMBO HEAVEN

Gold Medal Class Westerns:

APACHE RISING
RIDER FROM WIND RIVER
THE REFORMED GUN
CLAYBURN
THREE RODE NORTH
THE MAN IN BLACK
LAST TRAIN IN BANNOCK

Tony Rome Mysteries:

MIAMI MAYHEM
THE LADY IN CEMENT
MY KIND OF GAME

THE ZIG-ZAG MAN

Marvin Albert

FAWCETT GOLD MEDAL • NEW YORK

In memory of Dr. Ira Epstein
A young man of many talents,
Physician, artist, musician—and friend.

"Reality is messy."

    —mathematician Benoit Mandelbrot

1

"Ten million is a lot of dollars," I said.

"Not to my father, it wasn't," Helen Marsh said bitterly. "The sort of money he had grows more millions all the time. Giving away ten to get me back in one piece would have been a very temporary loss for him. Replaceable in a year, two at the most."

She raised her left hand from her lap, where it had been hidden by the sun-faded wicker top of my patio table. I watched the effort it cost her to let me look at that hand. She placed it flat on the table and stared at it with loathing.

"Not like fingers," she said. "They don't grow back."

The hand had its thumb and two fingers left. Her little finger and ring finger had been chopped off with an ax. First one, and then, five days later, the other.

Eight years ago.

When Helen Marsh was ten years old.

"It wasn't the *amount* of the ransom money that bothered Daddy," she said, making "Daddy" sound like a dirty word. "What he could never stand was letting anyone beat him— at anything. *That's* what made him balk at paying for so damn long. Daddy had his pride, you see. It was a matter of principle for him. Not letting somebody use me to push him around. That's how he saw it. Pride and principle," she repeated, in a voice as sharp and brittle as a glass dagger. "That's why he let them do this to me."

Everything she said came out in short bursts. With a break after each to drag in a shallow breath for the next burst.

1

Paralyzing panic or rage can do that; but it's a short-lived affliction except for certain types of psychotics. Helen Marsh didn't strike me as psychotic. But what had happened earlier that day was shoving her perilously close to some sort of emotional brink. Or perhaps back toward one she'd spent eight years pulling away from.

Her back was to the horizon, where the glistening turquoise Mediterranean spreading out from the slope below my house merged into a golden-blue sky. She was almost as tall as I. About an inch over six feet. With long, streaky-blond hair and big hoop earrings and a lean, gangly figure in loose-fitting sweatshirt and dungarees. She had one of those small, perfect noses that women go to plastic surgeons for but seldom achieve. In a few more years she might turn out beautiful. But I doubted that she could see anything about the way she looked, beyond that ruined hand. I wondered if she ever would.

I watched her close the hand into a fist. The way she'd kept it when she had first arrived. That way the mutilation wasn't immediately noticeable, unless you were looking for it. Finally she put it back on her lap, where the table between us hid it, and worked at taking deeper, slower breaths of air. But she remained tense, almost rigid, her eyes narrowing on thoughts I could only guess at.

It was Arlette Alfani who'd brought Helen Marsh to me, after phoning from the offices of her law firm in Nice to make sure I was in. Arlette had led the way to my place in her sporty white Porsche. Followed by Helen Marsh's Citröen XM, driven by Ferguson, her bodyguard. After kissing me and making the introductions, Arlette had settled into a rattan chair by one end of the patio table, where she could quietly watch both of us while she smoked a Gitane.

Her short-cropped hair was a shiny black helmet in the bright late afternoon sunlight. She had on one of the loose-fitting summer-weight business suits that she wore when she was working to camouflage her lush figure. I'd become too intimately acquainted with that figure to be unaware of it if she'd been wearing a barrel. Just as I'd come to know so well those dark eyes of hers: prone to spark with hot fury or cool mockery at times, but with other moods that could stab me with abrupt desire or fill me with a tenderness that still surprised me.

At the moment, those dark eyes were all penetrating attention, weighing young Helen Marsh's every shift of tone and expression.

The girl glanced toward Arlette and then back to me. She drew a breath and said, "I make myself believe there really is a hell. I like thinking that's where my father is now. Forever. Like I was for that week."

I said, "Do you prefer scotch, bourbon, brandy, or vodka?"

"What?" she asked uncertainly, the unexpected question bringing her just a little out of her agonizing self-absorption.

"I could use a drink," I told her. "And I want you to calm down. Liquor sometimes helps."

"I—I usually take pills for that," Helen Marsh said.

"What kind?"

"Seresta—I used to need stronger ones, but the last couple years . . ."

"When did you take your last one?"

"Four hours ago. A little longer."

"That's long enough," I said. "What'll you drink?"

She looked at me, really studying me for the first time. Then she said, "Arlette did give me the feeling you're a take-charge kind of guy." Her tone didn't reveal if she approved or disapproved. Maybe she didn't know either.

I glanced at Arlette, who smiled a small smile. Anyone who tried to take charge of *her*, when she wasn't in the mood to play that kind of game, was in for a short, sharp surprise.

Helen Marsh said, "I like a brandy, now and then."

Arlette gave me a little nod and snuffed out her cigarette, got out of her chair, and went into the house.

Helen Marsh said, "I'll tell you what calms me better than either pills or liquor. Guns."

That got her my full attention.

"I started learning how to shoot when I was twelve," she said. "With a revolver, and a rifle, too. I got to be very good with both. I still am. The thought was, if those men who kidnapped me were ever caught and tried, I was going to wait outside the courthouse and kill them when they were brought out. It gave me something positive to look forward to.''

Saying it didn't make her smile. The notion apparently continued to feel reasonable enough to her. "Of course," she resumed in a dead-flat voice, "they never have been caught. But I still shoot at bottles and watch them smash and pretend they're the kidnappers I never saw. It does help. Maybe it's even kept me out of a nut house. Though God knows I've spent more time with shrinks than most kids.''

At eighteen that was how she still thought of herself—as a kid. Some essential part of her was still living inside a terrified, pain-shocked ten-year-old.

"There's a ravine in the woods a couple miles from my village," she told me, "where I go pretty regularly with Ferguson to practice shooting." Her tension in my presence was easing a notch. Arlette had told me on the phone about the girl's fear of strange men. Her kidnappers had been men, and since then she hadn't been able to handle being alone with one she didn't know.

Not that she was alone with me. Ferguson was there, close by in the shade of my olive tree, where she could scan all approaches to the patio without the sun getting in her eyes.

"Ferguson and I do everything together," Helen Marsh continued. "She lives with me, goes anywhere I go. She's much more than a bodyguard to me.''

Ferguson was from the Auvergne, in central France, but after divorcing the Scot she'd been married to she'd kept his last name because it gave her an exotic touch she liked. Her first name was Nicole, but everyone called her Ferguson.

She was in her late thirties, a freckled redhead with a hard-chunky build. The baggy linen jacket she had on over her blouse and belted slacks reached halfway down her sturdy thighs. It was kept unbuttoned for quick access to the pistol holstered under it on her left hip. As permanent bodyguard to a girl whose annual inherited income from a thriving American corporation almost equaled the yearly take of a top rock star, Ferguson never had a problem getting her permit to carry a concealed weapon renewed by the French government. Nor any difficulty about having that permit honored in other countries.

Helen Marsh looked at her with the first suggestion of a smile that she'd shown since her arrival, and switched from English to pretty good French: "Ferguson is my *friend*, my only friend. She is always so kind. Even when I am—being difficult."

"You're no trouble," Ferguson said.

"Yes I am," the girl said. She looked back to me and stuck to French: "Especially when I have the nightmares. Ferguson has to get in bed with me and hold me tight until I stop being afraid to go back to sleep."

Ferguson shrugged a little. "I would be doing the same with my own daughter, if she had lived. It is a substitute motherhood. No trouble," she repeated firmly. "It is good for me, too."

Helen Marsh was back to studying me—as much as she could without quite meeting my eyes. She reminded me of the wild robins that moved down to the warmth of my area every late autumn when the Alps rising behind the Riviera began to get too cold for them. One of them would usually pick my grounds for its winter base. When I'd start putting out food and water for it, I could glimpse it watching me from the trees near the patio: interested in my show of helpful friendliness, but nervously wary. The robin wouldn't fly in from its safe perch to test what I'd put out until I went back into the house and closed the doors to the patio. Gradually, as the days passed, it would come closer when I was outside. But never too close. Recognizing me and trusting me—but always tensed to dart away if I should reach out to touch it.

"Pierre-Ange . . ." the girl said hesitantly. "That's a weird name for an American."

"My mother is French. She wanted to make sure I never forgot that part of my heritage when I was back in Chicago, living with my dead father's parents during school terms. It was," I conceded, "a pretty effective reminder."

"Did people actually call you Pierre-Ange in *Chicago*?"

I smiled a little, remembering a few who had. "Never

more than once," I said. "After that they called me Pete. You can, too."

Arlette came out with a bottle of cognac and four brandy glasses on a Cinzano tray. It wouldn't have taken her that long to gather those. Arlette knew where everything in my house was as well as I did. She'd been stalling in there, giving Helen Marsh a bit more time to settle in with me. Like the robins.

Ferguson registered the number of glasses and said, "None for me, thanks. I don't drink on duty."

"Are you ever off duty?" I asked her.

Ferguson just smiled.

Arlette set the tray on the table and poured a good amount of cognac into one of the glasses. She held it out to Helen Marsh. The girl took the glass and started to put it down on the table in front of her.

"No," Arlette told her, and put some of her unique blend of good-humored warmth and inner steel into it, "first drink some."

The girl took a small sip, and Arlette said, "More than that." She didn't sit down until Helen Marsh had her second sip. I took the bottle from Arlette and poured for both of us. We raised our glasses in a silent toast and looked pointedly at the girl. She sighed, and then downed a third sip while we had our first. When we put our drinks down, she was beginning to look a few degrees removed from the near-hysteria caused by what had happened to her that day in Paris.

I began to question her, careful not to spook her into withdrawal as I quarried her memories for any potentially useful detail, taking her once more over the whole story, back to what had happened when she was ten.

2

I DID KNOW MOST OF THE BASICS. FROM THE EXTENSIVE NEWS coverage of the story eight years back, and from what Arlette and Helen Marsh had already told me. I even knew some things about the girl's father. Harley Marsh had been a man whom people who knew him best loved to hate. Their opinions of him had made juicy quotes for everything from gossip columns to the financial pages. According to all accounts, he'd been a vicious, suspicious, conscienceless son of a bitch.

When he'd died, last year, there'd been no mourners.

One thing nobody faulted him on was his business acumen. Harley Marsh had had an unerring instinct for a competitor's jugular, and always stuck in the knife with perfect timing. Buying up companies he'd undermined, Marsh had built a Washington State lumber firm into a diversified corporation involved in construction, real estate development, canning, and aeronautic technology. Along the way, he'd regularly and ruthlessly shed business associates, wives, and children.

He didn't discard friends, because he never had any. Loyalty was something he expected and extracted from others, often brutally. Friendship he considered a cringing pose of the weak: those afraid of retribution if they betrayed others. Harley Marsh had been too sure of himself to fear retribution.

Helen was the youngest of Marsh's four children—each by a different wife. Her mother had died shortly after she was born, and her father had installed Helen and a nanny in a

Seattle apartment he never visited. Marsh had stashed her sister and two brothers out of his sight in the same way. Making sure his kids didn't get to know each other well enough to later team up against him. One of his many preemptive strikes against any possible retribution in this life. He didn't believe in a next life; but just in case, one of his many former attorneys had quipped, Marsh had probably prepared blackmail dossiers to be used against God and the Devil.

"I don't remember ever getting to meet my brothers and sister until his funeral," Helen Marsh told me. "And by then—we found we just didn't have much to say to each other. Just four strangers—and the corpse of a man none of us knew."

When she was eight years old, Marsh had gotten her shipped off to an international boarding school for young girls, in northwest Germany. It was isolated in the farmlands between the town of Schleswig and the North Sea: far distant, it seemed, from the dangers and corruptions of a chaotic modern world. There the students were force-fed languages, comportment lessons, and the other courses that would prepare them for entry into the best Swiss finishing school by the age of fifteen. The students were from all parts of the world, but the school's fees, forty thousand dollars per annum, guaranteed a certain kind of exclusivity. The little daughters of wealth were safely insulated among their own kind, with no chance of meeting kids too far below them financially.

"There *were* status differences," Helen Marsh told me. "There were kids that were just rich, and others that were fabulously rich, and some brats took the difference seriously. But outside of missing my nanny at first, I was happier there than back in Seattle. At least I was with other kids. The school bunked us three to a bedroom, and I got to be real friends with the two I was put in with. One was the daughter of an Arab prince, and the other's father was a dictator in Central America."

Helen Marsh was smiling to herself when she spoke of her roommates, but the smile slowly dissolved as she said, "I really loved those two girls—but I was jealous of them, too. *They* got to see their fathers, now and then.''

Harley Marsh never visited the school and never arranged for Helen to come to him during school holidays. She was not the only student there who had to learn to live with that. There were always some other little girls with parents prepared to pay a substantial supplement in order to be spared the inconvenience of having their offspring around between school terms. And there were teachers willing to remain at the school to supervise them, for an addition to their normal salaries.

The summer when Helen Marsh was ten, there were two teachers and five other girls living in the school. They were all asleep the night the kidnappers came.

Helen's roommates had returned home for the summer, and she was alone in the room they shared. It was early next morning before it was discovered that she wasn't there. A teacher making the rounds to wake the girls up for breakfast assumed at first that Helen had awakened earlier and was wandering around the school. When she wasn't quickly found, both teachers and the remaining students prepared to search the grounds outside. It was then that one of the school's side doors was found to be unlocked. Someone had expertly cut a pane of glass out of the door, reached through, and opened it from inside.

A teacher immediately phoned to the police in Schleswig. Before they arrived, the phone in the school's office rang. The voice of the caller was male, and unmistakably German. The teacher who took the call thought his German had a Bavarian intonation.

What the voice had to say was brief: ''We have Helen Marsh. So far she has suffered no harm. Inform her father that I will contact him later about the ransom to be paid if he wants his daughter back alive.''

A subsequent police check with the telephone company revealed that the call had come from Holland: from a coin-operated long-distance phone booth at an Amsterdam post office.

The next call was to the main offices of Harley Marsh's

corporation in Seattle. It was made at seven in the evening, European time—in Seattle, it was ten in the morning. The man calling said he wished to speak to Harley Marsh about "his daughter's future welfare." The switchboard operator who took the call reported that the man spoke English with some kind of foreign accent. She passed the call on to the corporation's chief resident attorney, who thought that the accent was either German or Dutch.

The caller identified himself as representing the people who had kidnapped Helen Marsh, and said he wanted to speak directly with her father. The company attorney told him that was impossible at that time, but that he had been authorized to speak for Harley Marsh about this matter. The kidnapper, sounding angry, demanded that Marsh be told to prepare ten million dollars in used, unmarked bills—fifties and hundreds—and await further instructions about delivering the ransom.

The attorney told him that his own instructions were to say that Harley Marsh would not pay a penny in ransom money to anyone. But that if his daughter was not immediately released, unharmed, he would spend a great deal to insure that the kidnappers were hunted down and punished.

The reply to that was ice-cold: "Tell Mr. Marsh that if the hunters come anywhere near us, his daughter will be killed. And the next time I call, I will expect to speak to him directly." The caller hung up without listening to the attorney's response.

This call, too, was traced to Holland: this time a phone booth down in Rotterdam.

The next morning, farther south across the Belgian frontier, a package the size of a candy box was delivered to a Brussels newspaper by a man who left it on the reception desk and immediately walked out without a word. Nobody could later describe him accurately: beyond the fact that he was short and wore a bushy red beard, perhaps a fake. The package was addressed to the paper's editor. The receptionist passed it on to the editor's secretary, who opened it and began to scream.

Inside, well wrapped, was a child's finger.

With it was a typed message, in excellent German:

This finger belonged to Helen Marsh. We deeply regret the necessity for such an extreme measure. But Mr. Harley Marsh, though he is one of the wealthiest men in the United States, refuses to pay a penny to save the life of his own daughter, or even to discuss the matter with us. Can he really he so hard-hearted, so lacking in normal parental feelings? Please inform Mr. Marsh that this is how the rest of his daughter will be delivered, in small pieces, unless he responds to us more reasonably, more humanly.

Over the next few days, the news media all over the world headlined the story and printed the full text of the kidnappers's letter. One British tabloid front-paged a photo of Helen Marsh's severed finger next to a picture of her father in one of his frequently surly moods, over the words "YANK TYCOON WON'T PART WITH PENNY FOR DAUGHTER'S LIFE." Its inside-page coverage ran under the continued headline "STINGY MULTI-MILLIONAIRE." Other tabloids, including some in the States, got harsher than that, narrowly skirting libel suits. TV panel shows munched on the story at length, and few of the comments about Harley Marsh were pleasant. A respected news anchorman informed his audience, poker-faced and without further editorial comment, that Marsh had recently paid over twelve million dollars for an oceangoing yacht intended for business entertainment—and had spent almost twenty million in renovating his corporation's headquarters building. The inference to be drawn by the public was clear: Harley Marsh valued these things more than the life of his little girl.

The kidnappers waited silently for three more days. Long enough for the unfavorable publicity to reach saturation point, but not long enough to let it die down. Then the member of the gang who handled its telephone contacts called Seattle again. This time he was put through to Harley Marsh.

And Marsh told the caller, "I'll pay you *one* million. That's my only and final offer. Take it or leave it."

The caller hung up without another word.

Two days later, another package the size of a candy box was delivered—this time to a television station in Hamburg. Inside it was another of Helen Marsh's fingers. Along with an audio cassette and another typewritten message. The cassette held only Marsh's voice, coldly making his one-million-dollar "only and final" offer for his daughter. The typewritten message was addressed this time to Marsh:

My dear Mr. Harley Marsh—

Again you have forced us to commit an act that we prayed would not be necessary! How can you be so heartless? A man of your great wealth haggling over what your daughter is worth to you! Offering us a payment that is ridiculously below what we asked of you, and refusing to budge from that! Surely this is beneath you? But *we* are not heartless, and we do not wish to cause further pain to a   child   that   we   apparently   care for more than you do. We *will* budge from our original demands—though surely that sum is a small one to someone like you. We will accept only five million U.S. dollars. And that, Mr. Harley Marsh, is *our* final offer.

Two days after that, Marsh paid the five million.

One of his ex-wives told a reporter, "If I know Harley—and I certainly do, to my regret—it was strictly a practical business decision on his part. All that nasty publicity. Harley didn't want people to start cutting down on buying his company products. A loss like that would mean more to Harley than losing the kid. He's not what you'd call a nice man."

The payment was delivered by one of Marsh's European lawyers, who followed to the letter the kidnapper's last telephoned instructions. Driving at night along a series of dark, deserted country roads in the German state of Schleswig-Holstein, with the ransom money in two suitcases.

The instructions had repeated a warning. If the person who picked up the money was seized or followed, Helen Marsh would be dead when she was found. So no police were anywhere around when a flashing light beside one of the dark roads signaled the spot for the lawyer to toss the two suitcases out of his car and drive on. Next morning the kidnappers' spokesman called the police and told them where they would find the girl. Less than two hours drive south of the school from which she'd been snatched. In a packing case beside a road outside the historic old city of Lübeck.

She was rushed to a Lübeck hospital, alive but unconscious and in terrible condition. Her mutilated hand had become badly infected. She was filthy and suffering from dehydration and the dangerously heavy dosages of sedatives administered to her during her captivity. And she was in traumatic shock. It was almost three months before she came out of that sufficiently to speak with any coherence.

When she could, the police found what she had to say interesting. But the trail was three months cold by then. Nothing she told led to catching or even to identifying her kidnappers.

They never even found out where she'd been held captive.

3

"DID YOUR FATHER CARRY THROUGH ON HIS THREAT TO spend a fortune having the kidnappers hunted down?" I asked her.

"I don't think so. I don't know for sure, but I think he decided it would be too much bother for a man with more important matters to take care of. Just wrote off what he'd paid them and got his mind back on business. If his mind was ever on anything *but* his businesses for more than three minutes while I was being chopped up."

She snatched up her glass with a shaking hand and gulped down the cognac left in it. Then she brought the hand with the missing fingers up from her lap and looked at it again. The hand that probably represented her self-image.

Arlette pulled her chair around the table until she was sitting beside the girl. She reached out quickly and grasped the mutilated hand. Helen Marsh tried to yank it away but found she couldn't. When she stopped trying, Arlette relaxed her grip, but Helen Marsh let her continue to hold her hand, making no further effort to pull away. She leaned against Arlette, the tension in her gradually loosening, and she briefly bent her head to brush it against Arlette's shoulder. When she straightened a bit, she looked close to tears. But the tears didn't come.

I waited until I was sure she was composed enough: "You said you never saw any of the kidnappers, start to finish."

She nodded. "That's right. I was asleep when they came into my room, at the school. It was the flashlight that woke

14

me—but not all the way. I wasn't alarmed at first, didn't even open my eyes enough to see who it was. The teachers used to make bed checks at unpredictable times. I thought that's what this was. Until a big hand clamped down over my eyes. And another hand over my mouth. Then I felt a needle being stuck in my arm, and right after that I passed out.''

Her voice had begun to quiver. She broke off and got it back under tight control before continuing: "When I came to, I was on a narrow mattress on the floor of what turned out to be a bathroom. My right wrist was chained to the bottom of the toilet, but with enough play in the chain for me to move between that and the mattress. *Feeling* my way, because I couldn't see anything. There was this burlap bag over my head, so I couldn't. Tied under my chin. I was warned not to try pulling it off, because if I saw them, they'd have to kill me. It had a small hole in it so I could breathe and be fed through it. Not that I ever got to eat or drink much. They kept me in a drugged sleep most of the time.''

She paused and looked at the way Arlette was holding her hand. When she spoke again, it was with a steadiness that cost a great deal of effort. "When they chopped off my finger—the first one—the pain brought me out of that drugged sleep. All the way and screaming my head off. They stuck another needle in me and put me under again. And they must have given me an extra-heavy shot before they took off my other finger, because I didn't feel them do it.''

Ferguson came over to the table and poured some more cognac into Helen Marsh's glass. The girl looked up at her and complained, with her first, frail attempt at humor, "You're all trying to get me drunk.''

"Sometimes it is the best medicine," Ferguson said, and went back to her position by the olive tree.

Helen Marsh took a small drink, letting her left hand continue to rest in Arlette's.

I said, "You told the police the kidnappers were three men, and they always spoke Italian to each other.''

"I'm pretty sure there were only three. And quite sure it was Italian. That was one of the languages I was learning at the school. Along with French, and German, of course. But

I didn't hear them speaking Italian to each other much. Just when I was coming out of the drugs, the first time. After that, they didn't talk to each other when they were near me.''

"What were they talking about, the time you did hear them?''

"About why I hadn't come out of what they'd injected into me yet. This was before they realized I *was* coming out of it. They were worried they had given me too much dope. One of them said if I died without waking, they'd gone to all the trouble for nothing. But another one thought even if I died, nobody else would know, and they could just go on as planned. They said some other things I didn't get. I'd only had Italian for two years—and I was groggy and disoriented. And only ten years old, for Christ's sake . . .''

"They all spoke Italian,'' I said, "but one of them spoke it with a strong German accent.''

Helen Marsh nodded. "When I came to enough to start crying and asking what happened to me, he was the one who talked to me. In English, like I had, but with that German accent. He told me not to worry, that I'd be back with my friends at school soon—if I behaved myself. He asked my name and I told him, and then he asked who my parents were, and where they lived. I told him about my mother being dead, and who my father was. . . .''

That told me what it had already told the police, eight years ago. The kidnappers hadn't slipped into the school to take Helen Marsh, specifically. They'd simply grabbed the first girl they came on. Any of the young students at that school had to be from a very rich family. Any one of them would serve their purpose.

And once they knew which one they had, they wouldn't have had to do any research to find out all they needed to know about Harley Marsh and what he was worth. The first news coverage of the kidnap would have given them that— well before that phone call to Marsh's headquarters in Seattle.

I said, "You told the cops the one with the German accent seemed to be the leader.''

"That was the impression I got—but perhaps just because he was the only one of them who ever talked to me."

"And you think he's the one you came across in Paris today."

"I don't *think* it," Helen Marsh corrected me firmly. "I *know* it. I was up there with Ferguson for a couple of days. Staying at the Ritz. We were checking out late this morning, to catch our plane back down here. This man entered the lobby and came over to the registration desk. I heard him tell the desk clerk he had a suite reserved for ten days. That voice—I could never forget that voice."

"With the German accent."

"He spoke to the clerk in French," she said, looking uncomfortable about it. "I—I didn't catch an accent."

Ferguson said, "Sounded like perfectly normal French to me. But it was a United States passport he gave to the clerk at the desk. If he is American, though, he must have spent a great deal of time here in France, with some language lessons to back it up."

Helen Marsh gently removed her hand from Arlette's. This time Arlette let her do it. The girl automatically started to put her hand back under the table. Then she stopped herself, closed the hand into a fist, and put it down on the table. But turned so that I could not see where the fingers were missing.

I didn't consider telling her the obvious. That the mutilation of her hand was a very small affliction compared to the disfigurements and crippling deformities that so many others had to live with. I assumed she must know that. Knowing it didn't prevent her from continuing to experience it as the central fact of her life. If she had lost those fingers in an accident, it would have been different. But the missing fingers were only the physical evidence of the way she'd been knocked out of kilter when she was a child. The real damage was inside, where what had been done to her was still going on.

She looked at me and said, "He could have *faked* that German accent he used eight years ago."

"That's a possibility," I said.

"But he's still got the same *voice*."

"It *was* eight years ago," I said. "And you were only ten years old at the time, and stupefied by drugs."

She shook her head stubbornly. "I've heard that voice in too many nightmares—the ones that hit when I'm awake, too—to be wrong about it. I'm certain this was the same man. But you, you think I'm obsessed with what happened to me, and the obsession's worked inside me and screwed up my head."

"What I think," I told her, "is that you have an entirely reasonable desire to find out if this man at the Ritz was really one of the kidnappers. You want me to check on him, learn who and what he is—and where he was when you were kidnapped."

"I want more than that," Helen Marsh said. "I know he was one of those men. I want him caught and forced to tell who the other two are. I want the three of them *punished* for what they did to me."

"I assume you mean *legally* punished."

"Do you think I'm really going to go out with a gun and shoot them? I'd *like* to kill them, sure. But I'm not crazy— or not *that* crazy, anyway. I want them put in prison, for the rest of their lives. Maybe then I can begin getting over what happened to me. Once I know they're suffering for it."

She wasn't the first victim I'd known who carried that kind of burning hunger. To strike back. Somehow. Anyhow. I'd seen it in rape victims, and the parents of murdered children. Unable to purge themselves of their ordeal as long as the criminals who'd inflicted it on them did not pay the penalty they deserved. But the law these days didn't pay much attention to the emotional needs of the victims.

"What you want," I told Helen Marsh, "requires digging up solid evidence. Proof that will stand up in court. You want a lot."

"Arlette thinks you can do it," the girl said. "I trust her judgment. I don't think she'd let it be influenced by the fact you two happen to be lovers."

I quirked an eyebrow at Arlette.

She said evenly, "I always level with my clients."

I sighed. "There's no such thing as a private life left in

this world." I looked back to Helen Marsh: "What you're asking for could involve me and my Paris partner in a full-time investigation over an unpredictably extended period. Spreading to a number of other countries and involving extra help from some of the big, pricey agencies. It could cost you a small fortune. And you might wind up very disappointed by what we find out."

"I won't be disappointed," Helen Marsh said flatly. "Because I know I'm right about that man. And one thing I don't lack is a fortune. I can spend as much of it as it takes to get this done."

"Within reason," Arlette said, giving me her strictly business tone and look.

"Things have come to a sad state when lovers bargain over money," I told her.

"I'm not the one who holds the final reins on that, *chéri*. After her father's death, trustees were appointed to control disbursement of Helen's income until she reaches the age of twenty-one. Since she lives most of the time in this area, the trustees selected our law firm to handle legal and financial matters for her in France. I phoned them after Helen came to our offices this afternoon, and explained the situation. And that Helen's physical and mental health are involved. They'll approve all fees and expenses—within reason."

Helen Marsh told me, "Don't let that bother you. If the damned trustees get tight-fisted, I'll chip in more. From what I stash away out of my allowance payments."

"It won't come to that," Arlette said. "They *will* accept our decisions on what constitutes reasonable costs. Just as they accepted our recommendation of Pierre-Ange to direct the investigation." She took a check from her shoulder bag and gave it to me. "This makes it official."

The check was from one of the special client accounts of Bonnet, Bonnet & Alfani. The two Bonnets were a husband-and-wife team who'd started the law firm two decades ago and made it one of the best on the Côte d'Azur. Though Arlette was very junior to them, she had achieved a full partnership. The check was signed by her and cosigned by Helen Marsh. The amount was more than adequate for a starter.

I put the check on the table, set my brandy glass on it, and said to Helen Marsh, "Okay—what name did this man at the Ritz use when he registered? And what does he look like?"

"I'm afraid I didn't catch the name. And I can't give you much of a description. Hearing that voice knocked the pins out from under me. I got so dizzy, I thought I was going to faint. When I looked at him my eyes blurred. I thought I was suddenly going blind. All I saw was, he's tall, and sort of old."

Ferguson said, "The name he gave the desk clerk was Benjamin Hulvane. He's almost exactly the same height as Mademoiselle Helen. Thin, and about seventy years old, I'd guess. But vigorous-looking. Hair originally black but mostly gray now. Recently barbered. Narrow face, short straight nose, thin lips. He was wearing a beautifully tailored suit, gray pinstripe, silk, I think. Black shoes of that soft leather-like gloves. And horn-rimmed glasses that prevented me from seeing the color of his eyes."

I gave her a look, and she said, "That's part of my job. Checking out the people around Mademoiselle Helen. I did give *him* special attention, when I caught her reaction to him. I didn't know what was the matter, but I had to help her walk out to our taxi. She didn't tell what it was about until we were on the plane flying south."

"My first reaction," Helen Marsh said, "was just to run away. And hide. But by the time we landed at Nice, I knew that wasn't what I needed to do."

I asked Ferguson, "Did this Benjamin Hulvane catch her reaction to him, too?"

"I am almost certain he did not. He was concentrating on getting the formalities over with so he could get up to his suite. He looked tired, jet lag perhaps."

Arlette had her strictly-business expression back in place. "One more point, Pierre-Ange. I assured the trustees you'll do the investigation in stages. Just a preliminary check first. Calling it quits if anything shows this man can't be one of the kidnappers."

"Sure. Goes without saying."

But Helen Marsh didn't like it at all: "The only thing the

trustees want to do is humor me a little. Just go through the motions and then pat me on the head and say, 'There there, little girl, it was just your imagination overworking.' What the *hell*—he won't be walking around dripping evidence he's a kidnapper! He must have done a damn good job of covering up his tracks by now.''

"Uncovering those tracks," I told her, "is the job you're paying for."

After she and Ferguson headed up the hairpin drive to their car, I took the check inside the house and phoned the Côte d'Azur airport. Next I telephoned the Paris apartment-cum-office of my partner, Fritz Donhoff. What I got was his answering machine. I told it the essentials of the case, and the estimated time my plane would arrive at Orly Airport.

When I went back outside, Arlette was standing by the outer edge of the patio, sipping her cognac and watching small orange clouds chase each other across the evening sky. A warm rising wind was ruffling tendrils of her raven hair and flicking the darkening sea with tiny whitecaps.

"The only Paris flight I could get a reservation on isn't until ten tonight," I told her. "That gives us a couple hours here to prove we're the lovers the whole world seems to know about."

Arlette turned to me with one of her heart-clutching smiles. "Not this evening, Josephine," she said ruefully. "I have three trial preparations waiting back at my office. And they all have to be ready by first thing in the morning."

We did manage some passionate hugs and kisses before she left. Which only made me more sharply conscious of what I would be missing, up there in Paris. Exactly as she'd intended.

4

THE NEXT MORNING WAS NOT PARIS AT ITS BEST. MURKY light and a damp, fitful wind. Black puddles left over from a prolonged rain the previous night. No rain today as yet, but no sky either. Above the Left Bank of the swollen Seine, the upper half of the Eiffel Tower was obliterated by the city's low ceiling of thick, dirty mist.

A few blocks in from the Right Bank, the top of the Napoleon Column in Place Vendôme almost touched the bottom of that dark gray overhang. In spite of the gloom, the sedate elegance of the vast square shined through as strongly as when it was built in tribute to Louis XIV—whose statue had subsequently been removed and replaced by the column. France has great respect for accomplishment, and Napoleon did manage to get more Frenchmen killed than King Louis.

Place Vendôme continues to pay tribute to solid accomplishment; as well as extracting tribute from it. Eleven international banks and the greatest concentration of luxury jewelry boutiques in Paris occupy the ring of dignified buildings surrounding the *place*. The jewel on the ring is the Ritz Hotel, a bastion of self-assured wealth.

I had driven my Paris car, an inconspicuous Renault 5, to the *place* early enough to find a legal parking spot that gave me a view of the Ritz entrance. I sat behind the wheel, waiting and watching. The banks opened for business; and later the boutiques. At regular intervals I got out of my car and put another coin in the parking meter. Then got back in and waited some more. By ten-thirty a Rolls, a Bentley, two Mercedes sedans, and a Jaguar were parked in an illegal cluster in front of the Bank Sepah of Teheran, near the Ritz. Their chauffeur-bodyguards stood by the cars exchanging chitchat while their bosses were inside doing heavy business. None of the meter maids ticketing other vehicles went near them. I continued to wait and watch. I'd taken the precaution of having an extra-big breakfast, but by eleven I was thinking about lunch.

Twenty minutes later, Fritz Donhoff strolled out of the Ritz directly behind another man who carried a briefcase and a furled umbrella.

The doorman, after a word from the other man, signaled to the taxi station. Fritz scratched his cheek and looked up at the sky as though he'd only come outside to check on the weather. Notifying me that the man he'd followed out was the one who was registered as Benjamin Hulvane and whose voice had freaked out Helen Marsh.

Hulvane looked to be about the same age as Fritz. In his early seventies. Perhaps a little younger. They were pretty much the same height. But Hulvane looked skinny that close to Fritz's thickset figure.

A taxi arrived, the doorman opened the back door, and Hulvane climbed in. As the taxi pulled away Fritz shook his head at the doorman and went back into the hotel. To see what he could find out, with the help of his pet criminal locksmith, inside Benjamin Hulvane's suite. I turned my Renault out of its spot and tailed the taxi.

It is impossible for one person to shadow someone closely for any length of time without being noticed and eluded, if the quarry is checking for a tail. Even if the quarry is not wary, it is difficult not to lose him after a while. An efficient tail job requires a team of alternating followers, some on foot and others in cars, all connected by instant radio communication.

But sticking with Benjamin Hulvane as long as possible, and seeing what he got up to, was only a secondary purpose of this tail job. The primary purpose was to warn Fritz to get out of that suite if Hulvane headed back to the hotel; or if that became a possibility because I'd lost him.

I was still with him when he got out of the taxi on Place du Châtelet. He walked toward Rue St. Denis. I went after him on foot, leaving my car parked halfway up on a sidewalk. "Reasonable expenses" has to include the occasional hefty ticket for parking violation.

Someone had applied gobs of lipstick to the eroded mouth of the stone lion guarding the Tour Saint Jacques. A few blocks farther, in Rue St. Denis, organ music from the ancient church of St. Leu and St. Gilles penetrated the thickness of the moth-eaten red-plush curtains covering the entrance of the windowless, brightly lighted porn shop across the street.

The man I had followed there was near the rear of the shop, studying the titles in three stacks of eight-by-ten photocopies of French, German, and English hard-core books. I drifted to the opposite wall and stood with my back to him, scanning the videocassettes on the shelves: occasionally selecting one and making a show of slowly reading its vividly descriptive blurb.

The shop had opened for business only fifteen minutes ago. So far, Hulvane and I were the only customers. The shop's lone clerk sat behind his counter next to the entrance curtains, carefully going over figures in a loose-leaf ledger. At irregular intervals he marked his place in the ledger with his pencil and glanced up at the high, tilted mirrors strategically placed around the walls to help him make sure customers weren't trying to steal the merchandise.

I was using one of those mirrors to keep my man under surveillance.

Paris hotels don't come classier than the Ritz. About the only thing Fritz had been able to learn about Benjamin Hulvane last evening was that the suite he'd booked for ten days was costing him some two thousand dollars per day. So he was a man who liked the best and could afford the best. But now here he was on sleaze street, with its lineup of shabby buildings and rock-bottom hookers and creepy back rooms with half-hourly rates.

It might indicate nothing but an aberrant yen for an occasional dip in the gutter. Up to that point I hadn't seen Hulvane do anything to suggest that he might harbor more dangerous quirks. Maybe by now Fritz was discovering something that did, inside Hulvane's suite.

Ferguson had described him well. There was nothing frail about his lean build. There'd been energy to spare in the way he'd walked, and there was banked strength in the way he held himself now. Circumstantial evidence of regular, strenuous exercise stemming the sands of time.

His sinewy hands had the same sunlamp tan as his narrow, deeply furrowed face. It was a harsh face. Cold, clever eyes and compressed lips. The frames of his glasses were gray, supplementing the gray of his hair and the softer grays of his jacket and slacks. His necktie was black, like the briefcase and furled umbrella he'd put down beside him. The briefcase was a nonreflecting leather. The umbrella had a discreet gold band.

There was a hard confidence to the man that his perusal of the pornographic book collection didn't diminish one iota.

But there was something repellent, too, that I couldn't locate in his face or manner.

Scientists claim that we are still close enough to our animal origins to smell danger in another animal, though we can no longer recognize where the warning is coming from.

I told myself I was letting Helen Marsh's utter certitude influence my judgment too much.

A new customer pushed in through the entrance curtains. A plump middle-aged man in a plastic raincoat, with a rain hat tugged low over his brow. He glanced at me, then at Hulvane, then back toward me. I put a cassette box back on the shelf, took down another, and did a job of appearing engrossed in its heated prose.

The newcomer walked past me and came to a halt beside Hulvane. He pulled a volume out of the middle stack and leafed through it. He and Hulvane appeared to ignore each other, the way browsers do in that kind of place. The position the new man had taken blocked my view of both their faces. If either said anything to the other, it was too low for me to hear.

The newcomer returned the book to the top of the middle stack. He wandered over to the fetish corner and stared without expression for a while at its assorted combinations of leather and chains. Then he turned and walked back to the shop entrance. The clerk asked him quickly if there was something special he'd be interested in seeing. But the man was through the curtains and out into the invisible street before the question was finished. The clerk resumed his study of the ledger. The muffled music from the church organ across the way continued to mix with the shop's pervading odor of disinfectant.

Hulvane picked up the volume the other man had put on top of the middle stack. Even with the reversal of letters in the mirror, it was easy to read the short title crudely printed on its spine: *Dolly, Esclave*—vintage French S & M from the 1930s. Without bothering to look through it, Hulvane took it with his briefcase and umbrella to the front counter. He showed the book to the clerk without letting it out of his hand.

I hadn't seen the other man slip anything into the book, but that was obviously what had happened. At that stage I didn't know enough about Hulvane to make even a wild guess at what it might be.

The clerk told him the price, took his money, and asked if he wanted it wrapped. Hulvane shook his head and put the volume inside his briefcase. He closed it and left, carrying the briefcase in one hand and his umbrella in the other.

I gave it a count of five before going after him. The clerk was into his offer to come up with anything special I might desire when I stepped out into Rue St. Denis and let the curtains close behind me.

The city's dense cloud cover had begun to leak while I'd been inside. A soft, steady drizzle. Hulvane had opened his umbrella to protect himself from it as he walked away. That made it easier to keep him in sight, and harder for him to look back without the movement of his umbrella warning me. I altered my appearance while I followed him. I'd been bare-headed and wearing a brown nylon bomber-style zipper jacket when I went into the shop. I took off the jacket, turned it inside-out, and put it back on. Now my jacket was dark blue. I got a cap of the same color from its pocket and put it on. That's usually all it takes to disguise yourself during a walking tail. Unless your quarry is suspicious he might be followed and is extra-alert. So far, I hadn't caught any sign of that from Benjamin Hulvane.

If that was his real name.

He was going in the opposite direction from my car. If he got lucky and found an available taxi in this rain, I wouldn't be likely to find another on time. But it seemed I was the one having the luck. Every taxi in sight at the next few intersections was taken. When Hulvane reached the Metro station at Porte St. Denis, he stopped and took a long look around. I backed into a doorway and stayed there until he closed his umbrella and disappeared down the stairs into the Metro.

The platform of the number eight line was crowded. I kept part of the crowd between us while we waited for the subway train to come. When it did, I got into the car next to Hulvane's and pushed to a position where I could keep an eye on him through the end windows of the two cars. He got off at the Bastille stop. I climbed the Metro stairways a circumspect distance behind him.

The rain hadn't let up. The sky looked like laundry water after it's washed a load of grimy overalls with heavy-duty detergent. The wet stone of the Place de la Bastille reflected splashes of gold and streaks of red and green, from shop signs and traffic lights. People who'd gone out unprepared hurried past holding plastic shopping bags over their heads. Hulvane had opened his umbrella when he climbed out of the Metro station.

It gave me a split-second warning when he suddenly turned and looked in my direction.

His gaze slid past me without pause as I turned to study the nearest taxi stand with a disgruntled frown. There were no taxis. Just a dozen grim-faced would-be passengers who looked like they'd been waiting there a long time. When I did my give-up shrug and turned around, Hulvane was on the other side of Rue de Roquette, vanishing into the Passage du Cheval Blanc.

I beat a red light across the street and went in after him.

5

THE CHEVAL BLANC WAS AN OLD, COBBLED PASSAGE MEandering through the interior of a large business block. It was full of workshops and other small business enterprises. It was dingy-utilitarian; nothing pretty about it except for some flowers in window boxes of upper apartments. The backs of sooty stone buildings loomed above the passage on both sides, and in places it was covered over by second- and third-floor connections between the buildings. Even on sunny days it got little sunlight. On this gloomy early afternoon it was already dusk in there.

Side passages and quirky courtyards led off from it, named in order after the months of the year: *Janvier*, *Février*, *Mars*, *Avril*, *Mai*. . . . Hulvane was turning into the Cour de Mars when I entered the main passage.

By the time I reached it he was no longer in sight.

It was a crooked, cramped little courtyard. Part of it was roofed over by the bottom of a couple cross-passages that were double-decked, one above the other. Under that, a large orange cat was snoozing on the corrugated tin roof of a low outhouse. Hulvane wasn't in there answering a call of nature, because the outhouse door was padlocked.

There were open doorways to inner staircases to my left and right. The left one was dark, but the other was lighted inside. Most of the common-use light bulbs in places like this were on short-time switches. Energy conservation. Lower electricity bills. The cat on the outhouse roof raised

its head an inch and squinted at me as I went past to
the lighted staircase.

I heard a heavy door bei.. shut just above me and to the
left when I stepped inside. I started a quiet climb up the
worn-down wooden steps. The stairway light snapped off.
Leaving me surrounded by darkness and a smell of dry rot.

My hand found the flaking iron railing of the banister, and
I felt my way up the rest of the stairs to the landing above. I
turned left into a narrow corridor, trailing the fingers of one
hand along a greasy wall. My other hand reaching out ahead
of me into the dark. After only a few careful steps, the tips
of my outstretched fingers came against the end of the corridor. I brushed my fingertips around lightly. They were
touching a wooden door. Not the kind of door that showed
a streak of light at the bottom. And its keyhole, I learned
when I crouched down, wasn't the kind you could see
through.

I felt my way back through the short corridor and down
the stairs. When I stepped outside into the little courtyard I
looked up to my left. At the double-decked cross-passages.
Both were almost entirely walled by large windows. The top
cross-passage was dark. But there was light on inside the one
under it. The light leaked through the closed slats of venetian
blinds that covered the interiors of the grimy windows. I
couldn't see even the moving shadows of anyone inside.

Avoiding puddles of rainwater between uneven cobbles, I
returned to the court entrance. The orange cat didn't show
any interest in me at all this time.

On both sides of the entrance were small signs with the
names of the little businesses inside. A battery distributor.
A delivery service. A wig maker. A rapid laundry firm. A
violin teacher. And something calling itself Vanité Photo.
Each sign told where its firm was located inside. The directions for Vanité Photo fitted where Benjamin Hulvane had
gone.

I went back into the courtyard. The lower of the double-
decked crossover passages was still lit inside its venetian
blinds. Both stairway entrances were dark. I stepped into the

one on the left, deep enough to become part of its darkness, and watched the one that Hulvane had used.

It was a long wait. Long enough for me to start wondering, not for the first time, if I *was* just humoring the obsession of a badly disturbed girl who happened to be rich enough to afford pointless humoring. An obsession about a man's voice she had only heard before when she was just ten. And heavily doped. But which she claimed to remember so vividly she could still distinguish it from all others. Though the man had spoken then with a strong German accent, and no longer did.

Hulvane *had* done a couple of odd things since leaving the Ritz. But so did a lot of people; and that didn't connect them to an eight-year-old kidnapping.

It was forty-five minutes before the other stairway light went on. I moved back a step, deeper into the darkness of my own staircase entry. Hulvane emerged from the one across the courtyard, carrying his briefcase and umbrella. He pressed a button on the umbrella's gold-banded handle and it snapped open. Raising it against the drizzle, he walked past me out of the court. I leaned out of my doorway and saw him turn left into the main passage—away from the entrance we'd both used coming into the Cheval Blanc.

The rain was keeping the Cheval Blanc's foot traffic sparse. Following Hulvane through it, I saw that the only people between him and me were a couple of workmen lugging a wrought-iron gate along the main passage. They turned left into a narrow side passage, and then there were none. I lagged farther behind Hulvane. He turned right into another side passage that led out of the block's interior to the wide, heavily trafficked Rue du Faubourg St. Antoine.

Hulvane strolled along the street, stopping several times to look at the display windows of furniture stores lining it on both sides. Apparently in no hurry to get anywhere in particular. Never looking back in my direction.

He crossed an intersection and continued his window-shopping stroll along the next long block. At the end of it he turned left into Avenue Ledru-Rollin. I moved faster to reach the corner before he disappeared on me. He was still in sight: walking up the avenue not far ahead of me, keeping to his leisurely pace. But as I slowed my own pace Hulvane made another left turn, into a drive-in gateway.

I lengthened my stride again. Most of the big blocks in this neighborhood were riddled with interior passages, courts, and alleyways—and this was one of them.

What Hulvane had turned into was the Passage de la Bonne Graine. It was very short and Hulvane was no longer in it. Unless he was behind one of its few locked doors. I went through la Bonne Graine swiftly. It ended at the crossway of Passage Josset. Hulvane wasn't in this one's long stretch to my right. I took the much shorter stretch to the left. Before that dead-ended, there was a wide opening to my right leading into Passage Lhomme.

There Hulvane was, continuing his leisurely stroll in the rain.

I slowed down and followed him again. But I didn't like it. The Passage Lhomme cut through the rest of this block, leading back in the direction from which Hulvane had come: toward the block containing the Cheval Blanc passage. I began to have an uneasy feeling that Hulvane knew he was being followed. But he hadn't looked back to check for a tail; not once since he'd come down that stairway and left the Cour de Mars. That bothered me, too.

I couldn't buy Hulvane in the role of an aimless, innocent stroller.

But my half of this morning's job was still to stick with him as long as I could. That didn't get canceled by the possibility he'd spotted me on the way to Place de la Bastille, recognizing I was the same man who'd entered the porn shop after he did.

Passage Lhomme was definitely upscale after the Cheval Blanc. It had more space and didn't have that walled-in look. The thin rain fell on trees and a little garden with a children's swing and tall flowers in decorative pots. The workshops and other commercial enterprises looked prosperous, and the ivy-covered apartment buildings above them had been kept in good condition. Benjamin Hulvane strolled past an antiques shop, paused to look into the window of an art gallery. He paused again to admire an exterior spiral staircase, of wrought-iron recently painted a dark red, that led up to a roof garden. Then he walked on to the far end of the passage, and out into Rue de Charonne.

I followed Hulvane across the busy street and we entered the middle of the block on the other side, via the Passage Thiéré. We were still upscale: pricey cabinetmakers' workshops, a couple of bright new restaurants, a pharmaceutical laboratory, more art galleries. It ran straight through the block, but Hulvane turned out of it long before the other end.

We were abruptly downscale. A driveway passage with missing cobbles and dingy back walls on either side. A factory with a thin black smokestack rising high above a courtyard that was crowded with parked cars, vans, and small trucks. Hulvane walked between the parked vehicles toward a low building attached to a higher back wall.

Its side walls were of stone with no windows. But its slanting roof was of reinforced glass, and there was a wide display window in the front wall. A sign painted on the front window said the place was a club teaching several versions of the martial arts.

Hulvane opened the door beside the front window and went in. I found a spot among the parked vehicles where I could see inside the club's single large practice room.

There were seven young people in there—five men and two women—going through their motions wearing Oriental practice costumes. Their teacher was Oriental, too: a short man with a spare build. He issued commands as his seven students twirled and launched hand and foot strikes that they hoped would prove lethal if they ever got caught in a desperate encounter. Most of them were graceful enough; but none showed evidence of the hair-trigger reflexes and follow-through power required for any kind of hand-to-hand combat. If you've got that in you, it can be brought out and trained to a peak. If you don't, it can't be injected into you by any school. The students were getting a good workout, though; well worth their time and money.

I watched Hulvane carry his briefcase and furled umbrella

over to the teacher and say something with a polite expression on his narrow face. The teacher shrugged and gestured toward a side wall. Hulvane went over there, leaned his back against the wall, and appeared to become engrossed in how the practice session was conducted.

I shifted between parked cars until Hulvane and I were out of each other's line of sight. The martial arts studio had no rear exit. He couldn't leave without passing me.

My new position had an extra. It gave me a clear view of the two women students, across the room from Hulvane. I watched them twirl, strike, and kick while I waited for Hulvane's next move. Both women looked like they had been doing these kinds of exercises regularly for a long time. They had limber bodies in marvelous shape.

So did the young men; but I have always had a personal preference for marvelous shapes of the female variety. Call it a quirk. My friend Jean-Marie Reju, the best bodyguard in Europe, would have found it a foolish quirk, but we'd long ago agreed to disagree on that point.

I enjoyed the show for some ten minutes before Hulvane came out of the place, raising his umbrella against the drizzle. I made no move to hide myself from him. I'd decided it was time to see how he might react to my blatant presence.

What I got was no reaction at all. Hulvane went by without a glance in my direction, heading back toward Passage Thiéré. No more of the leisurely stroll, though. Long, fast strides. Nothing wrong with his legs. Good blood circulation, undiminished by age.

I strode after him. But I didn't get far. He turned in to the main passage, and I was a few steps from it when two men came into it, side by side, blocking my way.

They were shorter than I, but their shoulders were as broad as mine. Both about thirty, with blunt-featured faces and almost identical expressions of assured authority. They were dressed almost alike, too. Designer jeans, heavy black shoes, and zipper jackets of expensive leather, one brown and the other black.

The brown jacket was unzipped all the way, giving me a glimpse of the pistol holstered under it. The guy with the black jacket took a police card from his breast pocket and showed it to me: inspector from the extra-tough B.R.I.— *Brigade de Recherches et d'Intervention*. *"Bonjour, monsieur,"* he said with routine politeness as he put his card away. "Your papers, if you please."

I gave him my wallet, opened to my I.D. You don't start an argument with French cops. They can lose that routine politeness abruptly.

Black Jacket read my name aloud: "Pierre-Ange Sawyer . . ."

I nodded. "What's the problem?"

It was Brown Jacket who told me: "There have been too many break-in burglaries in this quarter recently. We got a phone call about you from a worried resident. Suspicious loitering."

"Not loitering," I said. "Working." I gestured at the identification cards Black Jacket was studying.

Black Jacket said, "According to this you are a private investigator, Monsieur Sawyer." He glanced at Brown Jacket, who said, "That could be a fake. Even if he *is* a private detective, it doesn't prove he's not working for the burglary gang, looking over buildings for break-in possibilities."

"I have an old friend in the B.R.I.," I told them. "Commissaire Robert Gojon." Though it wasn't quite accurate to call Commissaire Gojon a friend, we had known each other for some years. A professional relationship with its ups and downs. "He'll vouch for me."

"We will check with him as soon as we get there," Black Jacket promised, and he stuck my wallet in his side pocket. "Our orders are to bring you in for questioning."

"You're making a mistake," I said, keeping my tone mild. "And interfering with my work. Commissaire Gojon won't like it."

"In that case," said Brown Jacket, "Gojon will reprimand us, and we will apologize to you."

"Please, monsieur," Black Jacket said, with a stern edge sliding into his polite tone, "we would rather not take you to our car in handcuffs. That would be embarrassing for you. And for us, later, if what you've told us is true.''

I sighed, shrugged, and gave them a resigned nod. ''Might as well get this over with.''

Benjamin Hulvane was gone from the Passage Thiéré. The three of us walked back through it: Black Jacket beside me and Brown Jacket close behind.

By then I was certain they weren't the police.

B.R.I. inspectors called my contact there ''Commissaire Gojon'' or ''the commissaire.'' He commanded respect. None of them would dare to refer to him as just ''Gojon,'' the way Brown Jacket had.

And everyone in the brigade knew his first name was Jean-Claude. Neither of these two guys had reacted in the slightest when I'd called him ''Robert.''

But I went along with them, compliantly.

They were counterfeit cops.

But the gun the one behind me had let me see was very real.

6

THEIR CAR WAS A FOUR-DOOR FIAT. IT WAS NOT A COMFORT to find it waiting for me on Rue de Charonne, named after the ancient ferryman of the dead.

Black Jacket opened the rear door and then went around the car, sliding into the front behind the wheel. Brown Jacket motioned for me to get in back. He had his right hand on his belt buckle, close to his pistol, but not making a point of it. My docile acceptance of the situation, with my certainty that Commissaire Gojon would straighten it out quickly, had relaxed them a bit. Maybe enough.

I climbed in and slid partway across the backseat to make room. Brown Jacket lowered his head and started to climb in after me. When he was halfway in I rammed the heel of my right shoe against his near shinbone. With enough follow-through power to kick the leg out from under him and bring him tumbling forward toward me. I drove my elbow up as he came down. The point of his chin and the point of my elbow connected with an impact that jarred through my chest and snapped his teeth together with a crunching noise.

He sprawled across my knees with his hands fumbling aimlessly past my lap, clutching fistfuls of air. He wasn't all the way out, but his brains were too occupied with trying to unscramble themselves to pay any attention to my grab at his gun.

Black Jacket was twisting around in the front seat, unzippering his jacket hastily with one hand and reaching inside it with the other. But he was awkwardly positioned, and the

37

zipper slowed the try for his gun. I had the other man's pistol out and aimed at his face before he could complete the try. He blinked into the gun's dark muzzle, looked unhappy, and brought his hand out empty.

"Face forward," I told him quietly.

He did so. I snicked the gun's safety on and hammered his mastoid bone with its grip. He leaned sideways, his sagging head leaving the world behind for a while as he fell across the front seat.

Brown Jacket was made of sterner stuff. He spat out some blood and a broken piece of tooth, and tried to shove himself up with one hand while his other grabbed for my wrist. I chopped the gun across his temple, and his arms went limp on him and he rolled just enough for me to club the back of his neck. He spilled off my knees and landed on the floor across my ankles, joining his partner in slumberland.

I dragged my feet out from under his huddled weight. One of his legs was sticking out of the open back door. But none of the pedestrians hurrying past in the rain seemed to notice. They had their eyes straight ahead and their minds on reaching shelter. I leaned over the front seat and removed my wallet from Black Jacket's pocket. Then I settled back and did a fast search of Brown Jacket's pockets. But he wasn't carrying identification.

There was no time for more than that. It was getting too long since Hulvane had shaken me off. By now he could be almost back to the Ritz, if he'd gotten lucky and caught a taxi.

I climbed out of the car and slid the pistol out of sight under it. Then I did a swift hike back to Place de la Bastille and the nearest public phone booth.

I dialed the number of a phone booth behind the Ritz Hotel. Eugene Nardi, Fritz's pet locksmith, answered promptly.

"I lost the man," I told him. "A while ago. Get Fritz out of Hulvane's suite, quick."

"He's already out and gone," Eugene said. "Fritz told me to tell you he'll be having a late lunch—in a *bookstore*. He said you would know where he means."

* * *

I'd already begun to look forward to lunch before starting to tail Benjamin Hulvane around Paris. After taking two Metro trains back to my illegally parked Renault, and driving to Place de la Concorde, I was famished. I left the car where it was certain to attract another whopping parking ticket, to add to the one I'd found waiting under the windshield wiper back at Place du Châtelet. My growling stomach had no patience left for traffic-crawling in search of a better spot.

I walked into W. H. Smith's Bookshop on Rue de Rivoli and climbed the carpeted stairs to its English Tea Room. A very British-looking place, and Fritz Donhoff was finishing a very British lunch. Poached eggs on toast. With creamed spinach and baked beans. And a pot of tea. Fritz gets outlandish moods at times.

My own mood was raging hunger. But succor was not far off. A mouth-watering aroma of hot steak-and-kidney pie wafted my way from the kitchen. Add side dishes of potatoes, peas, and salad to that, with a demi bottle of rosé, and I just might live. I took a seat facing Fritz and gave the order—in French, because in spite of the restaurant's name and ambience, none of its waitresses spoke English. Ours hurried off to the kitchen in response to some urgency she detected in my face and tone. I reached across the table, snagged Fritz's last piece of toast, and wolfed it down.

His baggy eyes regarded me with a mixture of parental disapproval and tolerant affection. Fritz had long ago decided it was his duty to fill a void created by the death of my father before I was born. "I take it," he said in that warm middle-European voice of his, "that our Mr. Hulvane did not stop off somewhere to eat."

"He didn't, so I couldn't. Is Hulvane his real name?"

"I didn't find anything in his suite to indicate it isn't," he told me calmly, and then neatly refilled his teacup from the pot without losing a drop.

Calm and neat also fitted the way Fritz looked. A thick mane of silvery hair, flawlessly combed as always. An old-fashioned velvet suit that fitted his large frame becomingly. His shirt cuffs peeked out of his jacket sleeves just enough to show their pearl cuff links. The opal stickpin was perfectly placed in his conservative necktie.

His fleshy Bavarian face wore its habitual blend of kindly interest and matured competence. I'd seen that expression combine with the rumbling warmth of his voice to charm women of all ages and inspire trust in normally mistrustful men. I had also seen his expression and tone change, ever so slightly, and scare the hell out of some extremely tough characters.

The strength of Fritz's big body hadn't been sapped too much by age. Except for his legs. Those hadn't held their own against time as well as Hulvane's seemed to. That was why he'd originally decided he needed a partner. The strenuous legwork some jobs entailed was getting harder for him.

"What *did* you find in Hulvane's rooms?" I asked him. "Don't expect an account of my day until I'm fed."

"One of his two suitcases has a hidden pocket under its lining. Hulvane's passport and airline ticket are in it."

"Nothing else?"

"No. Otherwise, both suitcases had been emptied, their contents arranged tidily in closets and dresser drawers. One of the suitcases was purchased in Munich. The other doesn't have a shop label. According to labels on Hulvane's clothes, they were purchased in many different cities. Munich, again. Also New York and Rome, Paris and Miami, London and Caracas, Venezuela."

Fritz reeled off the city names without consulting the notebook he always carried. I was sure he hadn't forgotten any. Fritz could pretend senility when it suited him to play old and feeble. But the steel-trap memory hadn't acquired any rust.

"The passport," Fritz said, "confirms that his name is Benjamin Hulvane. No middle initial. It lists his birthplace as California, and his birth date as two years later than mine."

Our waitress returned with my meal. As she transferred it from her tray to the table in front of me, Fritz took a sip of his tea, frowned a bit, and then looked up at her with his warmest smile: "I'm afraid I have allowed my tea to grow tepid. Would you mind, my dear, if I asked you to bring me more, really hot?''

The waitress almost blushed. "But *of course*, monsieur," she told him fervently. Quickly putting his teapot, cup, and saucer on her tray, she went off to the kitchen with a saucy movement of her pleasant derriere. I had already tucked into my steak-and-kidney pie, and my mouth was too full to comment on Fritz's way with women.

"Hulvane's passport is a fairly new one," he resumed. "Issued only one and a half years ago—in New York. And New York City is what Hulvane has marked in as his present residence in the United States." Fritz recited an apartment address on an expensive stretch of Manhattan's upper east side. This time he took out his notebook, afterward, and checked to make sure he'd given the address correctly. He had.

Looking a bit smug about it, he put the notebook back in his pocket and said, "There is no foreign residence listed, nor has Hulvane written anything in the space for person to be notified in case of death or accident. The customs and immigration stamps in Hulvane's passport show he has traveled quite a bit during the past year and a half. Always to and from New York. Rome once, Caracas two times, and this is his third trip to France. The previous two were for longish periods: three weeks the first trip, five weeks the second."

The waitress returned with Fritz's tea service. She stayed by the table watching him fill his cup. The tea was steaming hot. It would have boiled my tongue, but that was the way Fritz liked it. He blew gently on its surface, took a practiced taste, and beamed appreciation at our waitress. This time she did blush.

I finished the last of my late lunch as she went away. I added a flavorful swallow of wine to the delicious aftertaste of the steak-and-kidney pie, and leaned back a contented man. Hunger adds to the pleasure of a good meal—when it fades to a dim memory.

Fritz took a heroic sip of his scalding tea. His baggy eyes watered a little. But his voice was unaffected: "Hulvane's airline ticket is round-trip, New York–Paris–New York. Via the Concorde—as one would expect of a man who can afford ten days at the Ritz. His return flight is booked for nine days from now.''

"New York seems the logical place for our next inquiries. Hulvane's home base.''

"I have already arranged to get preliminary inquiries under way,'' Fritz told me. "I phoned Jacob McKissack about it.''

Jake McKissack was in charge of international operations for one of the biggest security and investigations firms. It was staffed by former FBI and Treasury agents and fueled by extravagant fees from businesses and individuals in the megabuck bracket. We'd only been able to afford McKissack's firm a few times in the past. But it did deliver, in certain areas. There were few secret business or government files that its well-connected agents couldn't get to.

I looked at my watch. Just after three in the afternoon. In Europe. In New York it would be a few minutes past nine in the morning. Jake McKissack seldom got to his firm's Manhattan headquarters before nine-thirty.

"You called him at home,'' I said, and began to smile at Fritz. "Probably got him out of bed.''

He nodded and smiled back. "I made the call immediately after leaving Hulvane's suite. I believe it was seven in the morning, for him. Woke him out of a sound sleep.'' Fritz didn't like the big business agencies much.

"McKissack must have loved that.''

"He didn't seem to mind, after I told him we have a new client who won't be drained dry by the monstrous prices he charges.''

"McKissack wouldn't mind being dragged off the most beautiful woman in the world, if it meant money for his firm.''

"A rather vulgar way to put it. But the point is undoubtedly correct. He assured me they will get us as much background information on Benjamin Hulvane as possible in the next twenty-four hours. Including whether he has or had a bank account that was considerably enriched eight years ago.

And whether Hulvane was in Europe when Helen Marsh was kidnapped. That will entail their checking the passenger lists of all international airlines during that year. McKissack warned me he will increase the charges for the man-hours that will require, because of the speed with which we want the information.''

Fritz refreshed himself with another drink of tea. He frowned a bit. Which meant its temperature was already down to a heat normal people could tolerate. He put down his cup, still frowning, and said, ''Now you can tell me what *you* discovered about our Mr. Hulvane.''

I told him, in detail. Starting with my following Hulvane from the Ritz to the porn shop. Ending where he'd shaken me off by using a couple thugs pretending to be cops. Fritz gave the details his undivided attention.

''It would seem,'' he said thoughtfully when I'd finished my account, ''that Hulvane wished to do more than simply losing you.''

''Sure. He wanted to get me someplace where he could find out *why* I was following him. The guy that started to get in the back of the car with me—as soon as he had the door shut he would've pulled out his gun and used it to keep me quiet. While they took me to wherever Hulvane was supposed to be waiting to interrogate me.''

''We have to assume that, by now, that pair has informed him you are a private detective.''

''Which'll make him even more nervous. About who I'm working for. And what I or my client knows about him. He's mixed up in something dirty.''

''Perhaps,'' Fritz said, with a caution that was automatic with him. He would have made as good a scientist as he had a German police detective and a French private investigator. No conclusions before you had the proof. ''But dirty or not, what Hulvane is up to now need not have any connection with the kidnapping of Helen Marsh.''

''Probably not, this long after. What it does tell us is that he's not someone we can rule out at this point.''

"Benjamin Hulvane," Fritz agreed quietly, "does not appear to be a normal citizen."

"*Not normal* is carrying understatement a bit too far, Fritz. Even for you. Hulvane spotted me shadowing him, and didn't show it. That means he's experienced at checking his back trail—because he's put a lot of time into shady activities. And he knew how to get in touch, very quickly, with a couple of thugs who could snag me with a phony police I.D. That spells criminal connections, and criminal intent."

"Probably," Fritz conceded, and gave it more thought. "There was one other bit of information I got from Hulvane's passport. The dates on its entry and exit stamps indicate that he has spent as much time, over the last one and a half years, in Venezuela as he has in the United States. So Caracas might be another logical place for some preliminary inquiries about him. I don't believe Jacob McKissack can be of much help there. But you, I recall, used to have a contact who might be able to."

I still did. I went to the phone booth on the landing outside the tea room and called him.

7

"I HAVE SOME INFORMATION FOR YOU, SEÑOR FARA," I TOLD him after the Venezuelan Embassy's switchboard put me through to his office. "Hot information."

"If it is no better than last time, I won't be interested."

"It is *much* better. Can I see you? As soon as possible today?"

"Not here. I'm about to leave the building for a business meeting."

Alonzo Fara's English was as lousy as my Spanish; so our telephone conversation was in French, which he spoke almost as well as I did. He had to, or he wouldn't have been given this foreign posting. The United States is the only country in the world whose representatives abroad—from ambassadors down to junior CIA officers—can't speak the language of the country they're sent to. Making them totally dependent on local informants. Who deliver a crafty mélange of truth and fabrication, knowing their American paymasters can't check it out themselves.

In addition to French, we were speaking double-talk—for the benefit of the embassy people who monitored all of its phone calls, in and out.

Interpreted, I had told Alonzo I needed information from him. In a hurry. He'd told me he wasn't interested unless I was able to pay more than the last time I'd needed his help. I'd said the money would be good and I wanted to meet as soon as possible today. He'd assured me he could leave the embassy quickly.

45

He usually could. Alonzo was listed by his embassy as an assistant to Venezuela's trade delegation. Everybody knew he was actually an intelligence officer. Mainly concerned with keeping an eye and ear on the doings of agents in France from countries bordering his own: Colombia, Brazil, Guyana—and the island-nations of the Caribbean that washed Venezuela's northern shore. His job—or his conception of it—didn't require too many hours of any day. And it paid him fairly well.

But not enough for the life-style he'd come to enjoy in Paris. Which inclined him to supplement his official income with whatever extra cash came his way quietly enough to go undetected by his embassy. He never met the sources of this income at his office, for the same reason that he never talked openly to them on his office phone.

I said, "I'll meet you anyplace you say. Where is your business meeting?"

"I can meet you at four," Alonzo told me. "For a few minutes. In the Sorbonne. Outside the *bibliothèque* at the top of the stairs, just after you come in from the Cour d'Honneur."

"Fine." I hung up the phone and went back to Fritz and told him what I'd arranged with Alonzo.

"I'm going home," Fritz said. "There may be messages from people I asked to try finding out something about Hulvane. And I want the camera shop there to do a fast job for me." He brought his Minox out and bounced the tiny camera on his thick palm.

"You tricky devil," I said admiringly. "You managed to get a shot of Hulvane."

"Two of them," he told me, with a certain amount of pride. "One when he came through the lobby past me this morning. The other of his passport photo."

I glanced at my watch. "I've got time to drive you home. And from there I can walk to the Sorbonne in less than ten minutes."

We paid what we owed and left lavish tips for our waitress. Fritz stopped to thank her effusively before leaving. Tenderness toward women was not something he put on only when it was useful. They responded so nicely because they sensed that in him.

Outside, the rain had stopped and the solid cloud cover showed promise of breaking up. I plucked the parking ticket from under my windshield wiper and tossed it into the glove compartment with the first. Fritz got into my Renault and I drove him across the river, up to Place Contrescarpe.

He got out there. The photo shop we used was just around the corner from the *place*, and the house where Fritz and I had adjacent apartments was around another corner. I drove in a third direction and put my car into the garage where I usually kept it. That left me almost fifteen minutes for a leisurely stroll to my rendezvous.

I made it with time to spare. The covered terraces of the bistros on Place de la Sorbonne were crowded with university students comparing homework and arguing scholastic points over their coffees. The rigor of French educational demands etched their faces with a gnawing anxiety they couldn't shake off even when flirting with each other. Failure to excel now would blight the rest of their lives.

I went into the Cour d'Honneur and passed its tribute in stone to Robert de Sorbon, the man who founded the university more than two centuries before Columbus discovered America. The statues of Louis Pasteur and Victor Hugo watched me enter the central building. Inside, I climbed the curving marble staircase. Alonzo wasn't there yet. I waited for him on the landing outside the library's high, closed doors, and looked up at the three giant *fin-de-siècle* paintings on the walls around me.

The same woman had posed for all three. In the one called *Science*, she had on a hooded cloak and seemed to be mourning. In the second painting, titled *Dream*, she wore a gossamer see-through gown. The third was called *The Song of the Muses Raising the Human Soul*. In that one she was nude. I was backing up for an all-encompassing view of her three-stage striptease when Alonzo came up the curving stairs.

"Lovely, isn't she?" he said, scanning the three huge pictures with pleasure, squinting slightly.

"They had models in the old days," I agreed, "who knew how to stir an artist's blood. And you know how to pick odd places for a business meeting."

"I had to come here anyway. My daughter is now a Sorbonne student. I pick her up at this time every day, to take her home." Fara gestured at the library doors. "She waits for me in there. Concentrating on her studies, one hopes—not engaged in idle conversation with some loutish male student."

I gave him a curious look. "Your daughter is old enough to attend the university, but she can't find her own way home?"

"I don't trust her not to tarry along the way. She is very young and vulnerable, and the young men of Paris these days . . . Well, I don't believe in exposing my daughter to too many temptations."

I didn't ask why he didn't have his wife pick up their daughter. I knew the answer to that one. His wife was a beauty and he didn't trust her, either, out alone among the temptations of Paris. He phoned several times each day to make sure she stayed in their spacious apartment when he wasn't with her. "Doing," he'd once told me, "whatever married women with a maid do at home to pass their time."

Alonzo knew all about the temptations of Paris. He was a handsome man of fifty-one, and vain about his looks. His double-breasted suit was artfully cut to minimize the debut of a middle-aged spread. Which he tried to control by vigorous exercize—mainly in the bedrooms of pretty Parisiennes.

Nobody ever claimed that Latins have shaken off the double standard.

Getting out my notebook, I printed "BENJAMIN HULVANE," tore out the page, and gave it to him. He put on his glasses to read it. He was supposed to wear glasses all the time, but he couldn't tolerate the way their lenses interfered with women getting the full impact of his beautiful eyes.

He took the glasses off as he looked up from the name. "This doesn't mean anything to me. Should it?"

"Not if it doesn't. Hulvane is a native American citizen,

but he has spent some longish periods in Venezuela during the past year and a half. Perhaps before that, as well. I'd like to know if your colleagues in Caracas have any information about him.''

"That would require expensive overseas telephone calls. Which I cannot charge to my embassy. And payments to certain Caracas friends, for the time and trouble involved in their searching for the information.''

"Have I ever failed to pay you back for your expenses?''

"No,'' he admitted. "But what *else* will you pay me, this time?''

I named a fair price for his making the try. "Plus a reasonable fee for whatever you get from Caracas, based on how interesting the information is.''

"I did not find the fee too satisfying the last time, Pierre-Ange,'' he reminded me.

"I warned you at the start that the client was low on funds. This time the client is quite wealthy.''

"Ah . . .'' Alonzo folded the name I'd given him and tucked it in his pocket. "In that case, I will get on it as soon as I have my daughter safely at home.''

He would also, I knew, write up a formal report for his embassy. Stating that the information I'd given him was something the Venezuelan intelligence services already knew about, so he'd only had to pay me a small amount. That amount would be tacked onto his official expense account, together with his taxi fare for our meeting.

We shook hands, and he went into the library while I went down the stairs, after a last look at the three wall paintings.

When I reached the Place de la Sorbonne, I turned into the student-filled Brasserie Ecritoire and went down its rear steps to the cellar. The phone booth was next to the toilets. I checked through the phone book, found Vanité Photo, dropped in a franc and dialed its number. Intending to hang up as soon as anyone picked up at that end.

If someone was still there, I wanted my talk with them to be face-to-face. It had to be from there that Hulvane had contacted the hoodlum pair who'd tried to grab me. I waited through ten rings of Vanité Photo's telephone. No response.

I hung up, retrieved my coin, and walked back toward Place Contrescarpe.

When I reached it, I came to an abrupt halt. Fritz Donhoff sat at a table inside the terrace of one of the four bistros, La Chope, watching for me. I went in. But I didn't need to get close enough to read his expression in order to register the warning in his presence there.

We hadn't forgotten that Hulvane's worry about why I'd tailed him wouldn't have ended with the failure of his two thugs to bring me in for interrogation. They would have given him my profession and my name. And my apartment was in the phone book.

The way we'd arranged it, Fritz was supposed to be out on Place Contrescarpe only if there was serious trouble waiting for me.

8

THERE ARE TIMES WHEN CONCERN ABOUT LIFE OR DEATH—
especially your own life or death—is stronger than worry
about getting caught violating some finer points of the law.
In my trade that occurs more often than in most.

I had a legal permit to own the compact Beretta pistol I
took out of its secret compartment in my garaged Renault.
What I didn't have was a license to carry it around outside
with me. French law is tougher on that fine point than the
laws in most American states. Nevertheless, I holstered the
gun to my belt under my jacket, with a load jacked into its
firing chamber, before Fritz and I started back toward our
house.

The garage was two blocks in the opposite direction from
the *place*, and going there first had cost us time. But there
was no rush. The men Fritz had heard inside my apartment—
at least two, he thought, but couldn't rule out there being
more—weren't likely to go away. They'd be settling down in
there, waiting for me.

Our apartments were above the ground floor of a four-
story stone house that was built in the 1600s, restored in the
1920s, and split up into fairly modern apartments with large,
high-ceilinged rooms after World War II. The two we owned
took up all of our floor and were laid out identically, sepa-
rated only by an inner wall except at the stairway landing.
Entry to the front of the house from the street was through
an open courtyard that could be watched from our living

51

room windows. So that approach wasn't the healthiest, present circumstances considered.

At Place Contrescarpe we angled away from the house: down the undulating slope of ancient Rue Mouffetard. From there, a covered alley cut between and under the close-packed houses of our block. At the end of it another alleyway took us to the back door of our house. Fritz went in first. If any of those waiting in my apartment had come out for a look down the steps, it was me they'd be looking for. Fritz wouldn't mean anything to them. Not yet.

Fritz nodded without looking back at me. I stepped in and silently closed the back door. The ground floor had a hallway from there to the front door. Fritz walked through it to the stairway. He was a heavy man, but he could move with no more sound than a gliding eagle when necessary. He looked up the stairs and nodded again. When I joined him he climbed the steps just as quietly.

On the landing above, he gave a third nod. I went up after him with my hand inside my jacket, ready on the Beretta's grip.

Our doors were on opposite sides of the small landing. Fritz took out keys to unlock his. I looked at the two locks on mine. Neither showed telltale scratches. The people inside were not amateurs.

I followed Fritz into his big living room. Like mine, it also served as library and office. We went through it into the dining-kitchen. It had been in there that Fritz had heard the first sounds from my place, through the separating wall. I waited while he pulled a cabinet drawer all the way out and reached into the space behind it for his pistol. It was the same model Beretta as mine. I had another hidden in my own apartment. But I couldn't count on getting to it before the people in there noticed me. Therefore the gun from my car.

Our house guns weren't breaking any law. "Protection of domicile" permitted us to have them—as long as we didn't take them out of the house. Fritz had been tempering that rule with his own commonsense survival instinct much longer than I had.

We left the kitchen via a short corridor that led past the

bathroom to Fritz's bedroom. He had left the door to its closet wide open, the clothes on his hangers pushed to either side, forming an opening between them. The interior walls of his closet, like my own, were covered with intricately flowered wallpaper that concealed the low door we had installed between our two closets. I drew my gun and snicked off its safety before stepping into his. Crouching, I worked the little hidden lever that unlocked the low door in the closet's back wall.

Fritz had done the same, after the sound from my apartment had reached him in his kitchen. It was from here that he'd heard a man's voice, somewhere near the other end of my place, too soft to make out the words.

I opened the door about two inches. We had made sure it was constructed to open and shut silently; and we maintained it that way. Through the narrow opening, and the hangers of clothing I kept in Paris, I could see my own closet door partly open. And a slice of my bedroom. I didn't hear any sound in there except the faint ticking of the apartment's electricity meter.

Glancing at my watch, I looked back at Fritz and raised three fingers. He looked at his own watch, nodded, and went off toward the front of his apartment.

I opened the door enough to slip through into my closet. Closing the door carefully behind me, I went under my hanging clothes and straightened up just inside the partly opened door to my bedroom. I stepped into the room with my finger on the Beretta's trigger. The bedroom was empty, and so was the short corridor leading toward the front of the apartment. Still no sound of the trespassers.

And then there was: a faint *click* from the other end of the apartment. Like a glass being set down on wood. I froze in position, looking in that direction. There were no further sounds. I looked at my watch. Two minutes to go. I went slowly through the corridor. Nobody in the bathroom. Nor in the kitchen—but the liquor cabinet was open, and a bottle of scotch was missing from it. A couple glasses I'd left on the sink's drainboard that morning were gone, too.

I waited until there was only thirty seconds left. Then I

eased my way across the kitchen to the wall beside the opposite doorway. I tilted my head just enough for one eye to see into the living room.

They were between me and the apartment's entry door, their backs to me. The same pair, Brown Jacket and Black Jacket, sitting in the easy chairs on either side of the coffee table. My bottle of scotch was on the table, with the two glasses. This time each man had his gun out and ready, waiting in the hand resting on one chair arm. They were close enough for me to see the dark lump I'd made behind Black Jacket's ear.

I waited. The last seconds of the three minutes slid by. There was an authoritative knock at my apartment door.

The pair lurched to their feet, pistols aimed at the door.

On the other side of it Fritz barked, "Police . . . Open up!"

It was decades since he'd been a cop, but he hadn't forgotten how to sound like one. It was a tone the two thugs were experienced enough to recognize. They lowered their pistols and looked at each other in consternation. Neither came up with anything to say. They were caught in a trap, with the police outside the door, no other exit from the apartment that they knew of, and prison in their futures.

On the other side of the door, Fritz's cop voice sounded again, this time as though giving orders to one of his junior inspectors: "Use the skelton keys."

He didn't need anything like that, because we had keys to each other's apartments. But the hoods didn't know that. When Fritz's key turned the first of my two locks, Black Jacket looked around hastily for someplace to get rid of his weapon. He dumped it in the wicker wastebasket beside my desk and swept a newspaper off the desk to cover it.

But Brown Jacket was still staring uncertainly at the door, gun lowered but still in hand. Either he was a slow thinker or he was thinking very fast: about the chances of shooting his way out of this, cops or no cops.

When a key was inserted into the second lock, he started to bring his pistol up.

I stepped out of the kitchen and snapped, "Drop it or I'll blow your brains out."

Melodramatic as hell, but it's usually a stopper. It did stop Brown Jacket from bringing his pistol all the way around to bear on me when they both twisted in my direction. But it didn't make him drop it. He hung on to his reluctance to do so even when he saw my Beretta aimed at his chest. Mulish stubbornness—not shared by his partner, who just stood there with his empty hands hanging, looking gloomy and making no move toward the wastebasket.

The door behind them was flung all the way open and slammed against the wall. They spun toward it and saw Fritz with *his* gun aimed at them. I repeated my "blow your brains out" warning. Fritz didn't say a thing. He just shifted his gun until it was dead center on Brown Jacket, and his expression was not the one that charmed women and made men feel comfortable with him.

I watched Brown Jacket's fingers force themselves open. His pistol thudded on my thick carpet.

Fritz stepped into my living room and kicked the door shut behind him. "Against the wall for a frisk," he said with that heavy cop voice. "I imagine you both know the position."

9

THEIR PISTOLS AND THE PHONY POLICE I.D. WERE ON MY desk. Also a professional set of lockpicks. I'd been careful not to get my fingerprints on any of these, and not to smear theirs. I hadn't found any other weapons or identification on them.

They lay facedown on my living room floor, arms and legs spread-eagle, their noses touching the carpet. An arrangement that prevented any desperate moves. We'd made them remove their jackets, shoes, and socks, and their trousers and undershorts were down around their knees. All of which was calculated to add strong feelings of exposed vulnerability to their helpless positions.

Fritz sat in a chair near their bare feet. I leaned against the desk looking down at their heads. We kept our guns in hand. I still thought of the pair on the floor as Brown Jacket and Black Jacket, because they wouldn't give their names. We hadn't pressed them on that. I didn't much care what *their* names were.

I said, "Who sent you after me? And why?"

Neither answered.

Fritz said, "You two obviously cannot look forward to lenient sentences for first-time offenses. Although judging by performance, you don't seem to have learned much from past experience. That means you are both stupid. But not too stupid to know you'll be spending most of the rest of your lives in prison—*if* we take you in."

Brown Jacket turned his head to look back toward Fritz.

"You're not cops," he rasped. "You're too old, and he's just a *private* detective."

"Nose *down*," Fritz told him, hard and cold.

Brown Jacket's nose went back into the nap of the carpet.

I said, "We can call the cops, if you really want them. Commissaire Gojon *is* an old friend."

"The commissaire," Fritz said, "will be amazed and delighted by the number of crimes you two have managed to commit in one day. Criminal possession of lethal weapons. Attempted kidnapping of my friend. Passing yourselves off as members of the police. Possession and use of a forged police identification. Illegal, armed entry into this apartment. With intent to kill . . ."

"We weren't going to kill anybody," Black Jacket blurted, without raising his nose from the carpet.

"Of course not," I said. "You broke in here and waited for me to find out if I wanted to rent the apartment to you. Or maybe to see if I'd like to buy your guns."

"Intent to kill," Fritz repeated.

"We were just supposed to take you someplace," Black Jacket said. "Like the first time, in the—"

"Shut up," Brown Jacket snarled at him.

"Take me *where*?" I said.

No answer.

"It seems," Fritz said, "that you two would rather we turned you over to the police. They will be especially interested in your posing as police detectives. The best attorney in the world won't be able to wiggle you out of that in combination with all the other crimes you committed today. If you don't die in prison, you will be much older than I am when they let you out. And in much worse health. But that is your choice to make."

"If we tell you," Black Jacket asked, "you just let us go? Without—" He was stopped by a growl from his partner.

"Where were you supposed to take me?" I asked again.

No response.

"Call the commissaire," Fritz told me.

I picked up the desk phone and began to dial.

"*Wait*—" Black Jacket said.

"Where?" I demanded.

"A place in Passage du Cheval Blanc . . ."

I put the phone down. "Which place?"

"It's—"

"Shut *up*!" Brown Jacket snarled again.

Fritz leaned forward and touched the muzzle of his gun to the bare sole of Brown Jacket's left foot, close to the heel. "You are under the impression that you are tougher than your partner. When in fact you are merely more stupid. Perhaps it will help you to understand the extent of your stupidity if I put a bullet through your foot exactly *here*. All the small bones in there—you would be a cripple the rest of your life."

Brown Jacket's foot twitched away from the gun. I could see beads of sweat popping out on his forehead.

Fritz slid the gun up the inside of Brown Jacket's leg. "Perhaps you would prefer having the bullet make you a eunuch."

"Don't!" Brown Jacket bleated.

The gun returned to the sole of his foot. "Then stop being so stupid," Fritz said. "Answer my friend's question."

"And don't lie," I said. "We know too much, already, for you to get away with it."

"Vanité Photo," Brown Jacket said shakily. "That's the place we were supposed to take you. In the passage."

"Who told you to take me there?"

"Guy that owns the place . . . Genoud's his name. Jacques Genoud."

"That's your first lie," I said. "I warned you we know too much for that."

"It's the *truth*! I swear it!"

"It *is*," his partner affirmed quickly. "Genoud—he's the one asked us to bring you to his place. Both times."

"I know who wanted me brought there," I said. "Tell me about *him*—and it wasn't Genoud."

"I don't know who you mean. Genoud's the one called us. We've done stuff for him before—and some other people he knows. We do the job and don't ask questions. Genoud said to be in Passage Thiéré, gave us time to get there. He described you and said you'd be coming out of that side court.

Right behind a tall, skinny old guy carrying a briefcase and open umbrella . . .''

"That old guy," I said, "is the one we want you to tell us about."

Brown Jacket spoke up again: "We don't know anything about him. Just what Genoud said. That you'd be coming out after him—" He made an abrupt whining sound when Fritz's gun muzzle pressed deeper into his bare sole. "I swear it! All we know is what Genoud told us to do."

"Do both of his feet while you're at it," I told Fritz. "If they're going to keep lying, I want them to have something to remember us by, all those years in a cell."

"He's *not* lying," Black Jacket chipped in fervently. "We never saw that old guy before. Or since then, either. Jacques Genoud didn't say his name, or anything else about him. Just he'd be the one coming out into Passage Thiéré ahead of you."

It was possible. They were too ready to talk now, to be holding back on that. I asked, "*Why* did Genoud want you to bring me to Vanité Photo?"

It was Brown Jacket who was quickest to reply, and I didn't think he was trying to cover up anything. Just eager to spill his guts. "Genoud didn't say why. Not that first time, and not after you got away from us and we called to tell him about that. He was sore, but we gave him your name, and that you're a private detective, and he said he'd call us back. When he did, all he said was to come here and try bringing you to his place again. And," he added miserably, "not to mess up again."

We continued questioning them for some time. Their answers came pretty freely after Brown Jacket's obstinacy broke down. But not much of what they had to say was of use.

They told us their names, but those didn't mean anything to us. They knew little about Jacques Genoud, beyond his having hired them a few times before. They were not inquisitive. Minding their own business, which was supplying short-term heavy menace for anyone who paid for it, was all that concerned them. They didn't know where Genoud lived.

And my check of the phone book didn't turn up a home number under his name. If he had one, it was unlisted.

Genoud had always made contact with them at Vanité Photo. A passport photo shop they believed was a cover for various enterprises that slipped back and forth between illegal and somewhat legal. One of those, they'd heard, was concerned with pornography distribution. They couldn't be certain about that. Genoud was also a contact for anyone in need of forged papers of any kind. This they were sure of. They'd gotten their fake police I.D. from him.

Whether any of this information on Jacques Genoud had any connection with Benjamin Hulvane, I had no way of knowing at that point. We let them pull up their pants and put their jackets, socks, and shoes on before locking them in my living room closet. They wouldn't suffocate in there, but it wasn't the most comfortable place for two people to have to spend much time. The closet was not a spacious one. But that was their problem. Fritz and I adjourned to a part of the kitchen from which we could watch the closet door, but not be overheard by them if we kept our voices down.

"Say Hulvane contacted this Jacques Genoud yesterday about some forged papers he wanted," I said.

"No evidence of that," Fritz said.

"Just *suppose* he did. The fake papers would be what was passed to him today at the porn shop. Sometime after he left there, he spotted me following him. And wanted to know why. He knows Genoud can get hold of heavy workers like those two goons in the closet. So Hulvane goes to Vanité Photo and has Genoud contact the goons. But Hulvane doesn't want the goons to know anything about him. He wouldn't be around when they deliver me to Genoud's place. They handcuff me to something and go away. Then he comes out of the woodwork to interrogate me. With Genoud or without him. It all fits."

"It could," Fritz said, "*if* your first supposition is correct. Even so, it doesn't tell us much about Hulvane that we didn't already believe. Criminal connections."

"I think it's time for me to go see if I can find out more than that. In the one place we know about."

Fritz nodded. "You might even find Hulvane there, waiting for those two to bring you in. I'll keep an eye on the closet, and not let them know you are gone."

I did a fast change into dry clothes and left the house to get my car and head for Vanité Photo. The first hint that that job might have complications I hadn't anticipated came when I stepped out of our front courtyard.

There was a black Peugeot 405 parked across the street, several cars down, with its engine idling. When I emerged from the courtyard, it pulled out with squealing tires and sped away. I caught a very brief glimpse of the man driving it.

I couldn't be sure, but it could have been Benjamin Hulvane.

If it was, he already knew the pair Genoud had hired for him had failed again.

❄ **10** ❄

THE RAIN HADN'T RESUMED, BUT THE AIR FELT LIKE A sponge soaking up what had fallen earlier, and the splits in the cloud cover hadn't opened enough to save Paris from premature twilight. Inside the Cheval Blanc, it was night. Along the main passage artificial light shined out of all the workshops still operating. But not in the Cour de Mars. And not behind the venetian blinds of the overhead passage that housed Vanité Photo. High above there was the glow of life in some back windows of a building that towered over the passage. But down there in the crooked little court it was dead and dark. The orange cat had abandoned the outhouse roof and gone off to somewhere less spooky.

My Beretta was back in its belt holster under my jacket. I got it out before stepping through the door to the stairway on my right. Another situation where safety took precedence over legality.

The timer-button for the stairway light was at the foot of the steps, but I didn't touch it. The pencil flashlight I'd brought from my car made a less blatant advertisement of my presence. With that in one hand and the gun in my other, I went up the stairs and along the short corridor. The flashlight's thin beam showed me a business card tacked to the wooden door at the end. It was old and gray, with the name and phone number of Vanité Photo on it. Nothing else. Genoud's company wasn't exactly advertising for attention, either.

I put my ear to the door and listened. No sounds inside. I

rapped my knuckles against the door. No response. I did my Fritz Donhoff immitation: pounding the door and barking, ''Police—open up!'' Fritz wasn't the only one who'd been a legitimate cop and could still do the voice.

Still no response. Not from inside Genoud's place, and not from anywhere else in the building.

I tucked the Beretta in the front of my belt, where I could get it back in hand quickly. I put the little flashlight between my teeth, with its beam aimed at the door's single lock, while I took out my own set of pro lockpicks. Selecting the one that looked right for the job, I went to work. The lock wasn't an easy one. It took almost five minutes before several interior dead bolts snapped open in unison. Nobody used all that time to shoot at me through the door.

Stuffing the lockpicks in my pocket, I brought out a thin surgeon's glove and worked my left hand into it. I put that hand on the doorknob, snicked off the pencil flash but kept it gripped between my teeth, and took the Beretta out of my belt. Then I went in, very fast, crouching low and angling away from the door.

That didn't trigger any reaction, either. I hit the floor on one hip and snatched the flash from my teeth. I rolled it away from me across the floor in the same instant I snapped it on. Nothing . . .

Shutting the door, I picked up my light and flashed it around. I was in a large room that looked as though it had once been factory space. Not much had been done to change it since then. A stark room, barely furnished. A metal desk and a swivel chair. Several straight-back chairs, one against a whitewashed wall facing a camera with a strobe light on a tripod. Two file cabinets and some framed photographs on the wall beside them. Two floor lamps and a desk lamp. I left them off. Their light would show outside, through the closed blinds. My little flashlight wouldn't.

The room had once been longer. An unpainted plywood back wall had been installed across it, with an opened door of the same material. I found two smaller rooms beyond that. One used for storage of cardboard boxes. The other a photographer's darkroom. No back exit.

Returning to the main room, I stuck my gun back in its holster and transferred the flash to my right hand. I locked the front door from inside with my gloved hand. When I searched the place that was the only hand that touched anything. I started with the back rooms. The darkroom had no photographs in it at the moment. The boxes in the storage room contained erotic and pornographic pictures, dozens of copies of each pose.

In the main room I found the camera on the tripod empty, the file cabinets filled with photocopies of hard-core books. The framed photos on the wall showed the same man with different women. Each woman was young and good-looking. The man was neither. He fitted the description the two goons had given us of Jacques Genoud: short, fat, in his mid-sixties but with a full head of dark hair and an equally dark Mongol-style mustache.

I used my lockpick set again to open the desk drawers. There was only one thing in any of them of interest. A thin pack of calling cards held together by a rubber band. They had Jacques Genoud's name and a Paris phone number—not the one on his desk. I used that phone to call Sylvane Buongiorno, a friend of mine who was a junior executive in the telephone system, and caught her just as she was preparing to quit work.

Sylvane called me back six minutes later with the address that went with Genoud's unlisted phone number.

I parked on the Quai d'Austerlitz a short distance after the railroad station and walked it from there.

The view across the Seine was of the Bercy district—where the city's past was being obliterated by long rows of blank, boxy office and apartment buildings. Filing cabinet architecture. Maximum storage of working population in minimum space. Even Fritz Lang's *Metropolis* hadn't matched Bercy's new lack of soul. His robot goddess had too much personality to be at home among those monotonous slabs of concrete and glass.

On my side of the river, Erector Set functionalism hadn't yet raped much of the Quai d'Austerlitz. Most of its old conglomeration remained. Riverside warehouses and moored barges and big commercial showrooms. Brick and stone houses of human scale. Bistros with names like Café La Marine and Rendezvous de Les Mariners to remind you that Paris is connected to two seas and an ocean via a thriving commercial network of European river and canal traffic. The address I was looking for was a few steps past Rue Robert Fulton, inside a wide driveway.

I stopped outside the driveway for a wary look around. I didn't see Hulvane or the car he'd been driving—if that had been him I'd glimpsed outside my place. The only people in sight were a group of workmen carrying a life-size green and gilt papier-mâché elephant from a truck into a showroom called Le Monde Sauvage. I slid a hand inside my jacket, touched the comfort of the pistol on my belt, and walked into the driveway.

Jacques Genoud's address was a small, nicely maintained house. The driveway went past it and dead-ended at a printing plant that had closed for the night. The house was two-story, with recently painted gingerbread decorations around its peaked roof. Its ground floor was a three-car garage. A wooden outside stairway, also recently painted, went up to a narrow balcony surrounding an upstairs apartment.

The garage doors were closed and padlocked. Preventing me from seeing if there were cars in it now. But lights were on inside the upstairs apartment. I drew out the Beretta, held it down against my thigh, and climbed the stairway.

I passed the apartment's door and moved quietly along the balcony, peeking into its windows. All of them had their venetian blinds down, but with the slats open so I could see in. Maybe Jacques Genoud never bothered to close them. There were no other buildings around with windows that looked into his. My tour of Genoud's balcony gave me a look into his living room, a study with leather-bound volumes in a bookcase wall, a bedroom with a four-poster bed, a bathroom, a dining room, and kitchen.

All the rooms were painted a dazzling white. Much of the furniture was also white. It gave the apartment a look of immaculate purity. Genoud probably needed that, after a day of the sort of work he did at the office. The chastity of the place was enhanced by its lack of any trace of messiness. No shoes left out of the closet, no newspaper dropped on a sofa or chair.

And nobody in any of the white rooms, as far as I could make out through the blinds. But the lights *were* on. And I could have missed something. There were corners in two rooms that were hidden from my vantage points outside.

The tour of the wraparound balcony brought me back to the apartment's door. I put the thin glove on my left hand and pressed the bell. It chimed inside. No one responded to it.

The lock on this door was an easy one. It opened after less than forty seconds work. I went inside and shut the door behind me.

There was nobody in the living room except Marshal Pétain, and he was in an ornate frame on the wall above the large white sofa. The frame was gilded, and the picture in it was an oil painting. Pétain in his eighties, after he surrendered France to Hitler and became the puppet head of the French government during the Nazi occupation. He was wearing his famous marshal's cap, thick white mustache, and that expression of grandfatherly benevolence. A staggering number of French Jews who believed his promise that they were safe with him in charge were shipped to concentration camps and tortured for prolonged periods before being slaughtered. Including children too young to believe or disbelieve him.

I moved on into Genoud's study and looked around at the wall of leather-bound books, the white desk and its white telephone.

I *had* missed something.

There was blood on the telephone.

It was still wet, and there was a little pool of it under the telephone, leaking off the back edge of the desk.

I moved around the desk, stiff-legged.

Jacques Genoud was on the floor behind it. I recognized him by the dark Mongol mustache. Most of the hair I'd seen in his framed office photos was a wig, and it had fallen off.

Without it he was much older. Late seventies. The darkness of the fringe of genuine hair around his bald pate was, like the mustache, the result of a dye job.

He was on his back with one knee bent up and the other leg twisted beneath it, his head turned to one side. He wore a plaid shirt, dark slacks, and bedroom slippers. One of the slippers had pulled off his heel and hung from his big toe. There was a sharp hump on the instep of the bared foot. One of the metatarsus bones had been broken badly at one time, and hadn't been tended to properly.

The hilt of a dagger protruded from Genoud's heart. Only the hilt. All of the blade was inside him. The dagger was one of those expensive items you can buy from souvenir shops that pander to people nostalgic about Hitler's truncated Thousand Year Reich. An SS officer's ornamental dagger with a death's-head on the pommel.

More of Genoud's blood smeared the leather and steel of a swivel chair shoved against the wall by his fall. Much more was soaking into the white bearskin rug under him. His eyes were open and seemed to be regarding this soiling of his pristine retreat with a remote sadness.

◉ 11 ◉

"AND GENOUD IS *ALL* I FOUND IN THERE," I TOLD FRITZ. "Not a hint of any of the businesses he was mixed up in. Nothing connected to Hulvane."

"I don't imagine you stayed there long enough for a detailed search," Fritz said.

"I wanted out," I admitted. "Hulvane could have hung around, watching for me to show up so he could make a call and have the cops there while I was inside. And I don't need you to tell me the case for Hulvane murdering Genoud is thin."

We were back in my kitchen keeping our voices down so the goons in the living room closet wouldn't hear. Fritz was heating water for a pot of herb tea. "Thin, and totally circumstantial," he said, "but probably not wrong. I used the phone in your bedroom to check with my contact at the Ritz ten minutes ago. Hulvane isn't back in the hotel. He hasn't returned once since leaving it this morning."

"He's been too busy with me. It *was* him I spotted outside here. Watching to make sure Genoud's goons brought me out when I came home. He didn't see me arrive and then he saw me come out alone. Hulvane's got to be smart enough to figure I got help and the goons got snared. And that they might tell us about Genoud if we sank some teeth into them. He made a fast call to Vanité Photo, told Genoud to get out of there and meet him at his home."

Fritz nodded and poured boiling water into my teapot. "Hulvane was already worried by what you may know about

68

him. But perhaps he became more concerned about what else you might find out. If so, he would have a strong motive to cut off the potential source of such information.''

"Or to have it done for him. I don't picture Hulvane strolling around Paris carrying a Nazi dagger on him.''

Fritz added a small handful of herbs to the pot. "Perhaps the dagger belonged to Genoud. He may have kept it on his desk. In which case Hulvane only had to pick it up and use it on him.''

I shrugged. "Or somebody else brought it there for the purpose. Either way, it comes down to the same. Hulvane murdered Genoud, in person or by proxy.''

"That is a serviceable supposition,'' Fritz acknowledged in a neutral tone, appearing to give more thought to putting the lid back on the pot neatly. "Until we learn something further to prove or disprove it. The police may come across some facts that do that for us.''

I went to the bedroom and phoned Commissaire Gojon and told him about the two gunmen we'd caught in my apartment. Their names meant more to Gojon than they had to me. "Those two have been in and out of prison since they were teenagers,'' he told me. "More time in than out.''

"Not very clever of them,'' I said.

"Neither one is a big brain,'' Gojon agreed.

My guess was that they'd been the only ones Genoud had been able to get hold of, as quickly as Hulvane wanted the job done.

"But what they lack in intelligence,'' Gojon added, "they make up for in viciousness. Who hired them to come after you?''

"They say it's somebody named Jacques Genoud. I never heard the name before.'' I made a point of adding, "I've looked in the phone book, but he isn't listed.''

"We know a little about Genoud,'' Gojon said. "He has a business called Vanité Photo that we've become interested in lately.''

"Vanité Photo—that's where this pair were supposed to take me. I never heard of that, either. But that's what they told us.''

"They seem to have told you a lot," he commented dryly.

"Fritz and I threatened them a bit," I admitted. "Not that we would have carried out the threats."

"Of *course* not."

"You won't find a mark on them, Commissaire."

"I'll be there," Gojon said phlegmatically, and severed the connection.

Fritz was sitting on my living room couch, sipping from his cup of tea and ignoring a peevish voice calling from inside the closet: "When are you letting us go, for Christ's sake? It hot in here!"

"Be patient," I called back. "Just a half hour more."

Commissaire Gojon made it to my apartment a few minutes sooner than that. He had three of his inspectors with him. The usual types: narrow eyes and wide shoulders. I indicated the pistols, lockpick set, and phony police I.D. on my desk. Gojon eyed the last item with special interest, smiling a thin smile. He instructed one of his inspectors to put it and the other items in separate plastic evidence bags, carefully. Fritz took the other two inspectors over to the closet and unlocked its door.

Black Jacket and Brown Jacket stepped out. Their expressions of relief dissolved when they saw Gojon and the inspectors. They didn't need an instruction booklet to identify them as real cops.

Brown Jacket called me a *sale con*.

Black Jacket glared at Fritz as the inspectors handcuffed them. "You promised no cops if we told you everything!"

"No," Fritz corrected him, "we said we would call the police if you didn't talk. We didn't say we wouldn't if you did."

They were still cursing us when the inspectors removed them, along with the bagged evidence, from my apartment.

Commissaire Gojon remained behind, looking at me thoughtfully through his black-rimmed glasses. He had to look up for that, because he was smaller than me. Smaller than most of his inspectors, too. And he was handicapped by an upper-class background that made him shy away from the intimidating manner his inspectors could deliver at will.

But there was an inner toughness none of them could match. They knew it, I knew it, and he knew it.

"Well now, Sawyer," he began mildly, "what does Jacques Genoud have against you?"

"I don't know, Commissaire. I told you on the phone, I don't know the man or anything about him."

"You do realize I will be questioning Genoud about this."

"I hope so. I'd *like* to know why he sent those two after me. They claim they don't know, either. But perhaps you can get more out of them than we did."

Fritz had sat down on the sofa and lit a small cigar, taking slow puffs while he watched Gojon and me, his eyes going back and forth between us as though he were at a tennis match and waiting for it to get interesting. Gojon looked at him and asked, "Do you have anything to add to that, Monsieur Donhoff?" Gojon always used the polite "Monsieur" with Fritz; something he never did with me. He had always been impressed by Fritz's years of experience and solid reputation.

Fritz appeared to give Gojon's question some thought. "No, Commissaire, I am afraid I do not know anything more than my partner does about this matter."

Gojon switched his attention back to me. "You haven't the faintest idea of what might underlie this attempt against you."

"Not the faintest."

"Make a guess," Gojon said acidly. "What are you working on at the moment?"

Fritz picked up the ball at that point, and I let him carry it along: "We are working for a reputable firm of attorneys, Commissaire. One of their clients received grieveous injury from persons unknown in the past. The firm has retained us to look into the matter, quietly, and see if we can discover the identity of these persons and help to bring them to justice. As far as we know at this point, this Jacques Genoud has no connection with our case."

"Who is the client involved?" Gojon asked him.

"I am sorry, Commissaire, but we are not at liberty to divulge that. The terms of our employment include our keeping that information confidential. It would be a breach of our legal contract with the attorneys involved to betray that.''

Commissaire Gojon kept his temper without any visible effort. One of the advantages—along with the disadvantages—of being so well-bred. "What is the name of this firm of attorneys, Monsieur Donhoff?''

Fritz told him that. "You may wish to ask *them* for their client's name. I believe, however, that their interest in the client's security and privacy would prevent them from giving you the answer. You could, of course, attempt to bring the full pressure of the law to bear. On them, and on us. But I really do not advise it, Commissaire. The client is extremely wealthy, and undoubtedly able to exert more influence within the government than you. This client's counterpressure could have an unfortunate influence on your future career.''

"I don't like being threatened, Monsieur Donhoff," Gojon told him soberly.

Fritz tapped cigar ash into the ashtray and replied just as soberly: "It was not intended as a threat, Commissaire. Merely a friendly warning, I assure you, from one who wishes you well.''

They looked at each other in silence for a long moment. I didn't see either of them blink, but Gojon finally turned back to me. "I don't expect you to go traipsing back to your place in the sunny South before I've finished talking to Jacques Genoud. You do understand that, Sawyer.''

"I'm more anxious than you are to find out why this Genoud character threw those two hoodlums at me," I told him. "I won't be leaving Paris until I hear from you on it. Though I must say, the weather along my stretch of the Mediterranean *is* much more pleasant than up here. You should come down and try it, Commissaire.''

"I assume you don't intend that as an invitation to your Riviera home.''

"I assume you wouldn't accept the invitation if I gave it, Commissaire. Am I wrong?''

He gave me that thin smile and left to join his waiting inspectors and their two prisoners, without bothering to answer the question.

* * *

Fritz's answering machine had a message. It was from one of the people he'd asked to check into the name Benjamin Hulvane. So far they'd all come up empty. This one had too, it turned out. He was a Belgian detective assigned by his government to Interpol's new headquarters in Lyon. There was nothing in the criminal files of its International Central Station there on Hulvane, from any of the 146 countries whose police forces were members of Interpol.

I left Fritz holding the fort while I went out to pick up the rush order he had given our local photograph shop. Eight postcard-size blowups of each of the two pictures he'd taken at the Ritz. The photos were still damp, and I had to pay triple the normal charges for the speed of the job. But it was worth it. The copy of Hulvane's full-face passport picture was perfect. The profile head-and-torso shot Fritz had snuck of Hulvane going past through the Ritz lobby wasn't bad either, considering that the subject was in motion and the print was considerably enlarged from a tiny negative. Anyone who knew Hulvane would recognize him from the two pictures in combination.

I went to the office services shop across the street and faxed both photos to McKissack's agency in New York. Then I did a stroll of the immediate neighborhood around our apartment house. Circling the block. Touring alleyways. Visiting every bistro, looking into each shop, scanning building windows.

It took me twenty minutes. If Hulvane was around again, I failed to spot him. Nobody was paying abnormal attention to our house, front or back.

Fritz hadn't gotten any calls in the half hour I'd been out. We went into my place and checked my answering machine. No messages. I switched off the machine and divided the photographs with Fritz. Four copies of each picture for him, four of each for me. My phone rang.

It was Alonzo calling with early results from his friends back home in Venezuela: "Your Mr. Benjamin Hulvane owns a large luxury apartment in the most exclusive residential neighborhood of Caracas. He bought it fifteen years ago. He spent much more time in Venezuela in the past than he has recently. He had a business there. Exporting extract of tropical plants from South America to perfume-processing firms in Europe. His company prospered for some years, but then went under about nine years ago because of competition from Third World countries with even lower labor costs. India, Egypt, Morocco, and Turkey. However, Hulvane apparently came out of the company's failure with sufficient funds to retire and continue to live well."

"He's not involved in any new business there?" I asked.

"At least no legitimate one. And so far, my friends haven't learned of anything illicit, either."

"Was he in Venezuela eight years ago?"

"My friends in Caracas didn't come through with the dates of his visits. I can call now and ask them to check those out, if you wish."

"I do. And if Hulvane was there eight years ago, have them check into whether he made any flights to Europe." I gave Alonzo a spread of four months that interested me in particular. Before to after the kidnapping of Helen Marsh.

He promised to pass that on. "Another thing my friends have already discovered, from employees at Hulvane's apartment building. He kept mistresses in Caracas. I mean one at a time, over the years—not several at once."

"Hulvane is not as young and vigorous as you," I pointed out.

"Yes. That may also account for the fact that he does not seem to have kept any mistress for the past two years."

"Have your friends see what they can find out about him from the ex-mistresses," I said. Discarded mistresses can be as valuable a source of unpleasant facts about a man as ex-wives and elbowed-out business associates.

"I have already told them to do that. I have also told my friends that the compensation for any truly valuable disclosures will be quite generous."

"You told them right," I assured Alonzo.

* * *

Commissaire Gojon phoned less than an hour later.

"Your Jacques Genoud is dead," he told me. "Murdered."

"Any idea who shot him?" I asked.

"I didn't mention that Genoud was shot."

"It's the first thing *anyone* thinks of if you say somebody was murdered," I said in as bored a tone as I could manage. "You know that, Commissaire. So don't try to trap me into a confession. I didn't even know him, and I didn't know he was shot. It was just the first image that popped into my head."

Gojon was silent for a couple seconds. Then he said, "Genoud wasn't shot. He was stabbed to death."

"Well, that is a great relief. Lets me off the hook. I thought he was shot—lucky wrong guess."

Gojon didn't bother tearing that apart. "According to the two men we removed from your apartment, they were locked in that closet for almost two hours."

"Less. Just seemed that long to them."

"Long enough, in any case," Gojon said flatly, "for you to go to Genoud's home, kill him, and get back before phoning me."

"Is that when Genoud was murdered?"

"It falls within the time span for his death estimated by the medical examiner."

"I was here the whole time that pair was in the closet," I said. "In my apartment. With my partner, Fritz Donhoff. We were trying to figure out why this Genoud that I never heard of would send them after me. And what to do about it. Whether to question them some more or leave that to you."

"They say they didn't hear you."

"Fritz and I did our talking in the kitchen. Quietly."

"They say they called out a number of times, asking to be released. And it was always Monsieur Donhoff who answered. Never you, except the last time."

"Fritz has more authority in his voice than I do, Commissaire. Most of the time I let him handle shutting them up. I *was* here, the whole time. Fritz will vouch for that. Anyway," I added, "I don't know where this Genoud lived. So how could I—"

"Don't play games, Sawyer," Gojon cut in. "You could have found out."

"With all due respect, Commissaire, you are the one playing games. You don't seriously regard me as a suspect. If you did, you wouldn't be talking to me over the telephone about it. You'd have sent a couple inspectors around to drag me in for one of your personally supervised hard-edge interrogations."

There was another silence at Gojon's end. He was giving me time to say more. I didn't. He said, "The weapon that killed Genoud is unusual. A death's-head SS dagger."

I allowed a short silence at my end. "Was Genoud a Nazi fan?"

"After the liberation of Paris, he was accused of criminal collaboration with the Gestapo's agents in occupied France. But he never came to trial. The charges against him were dropped and forgotten—for reasons I haven't been able to discover."

"You know why," I said. "Too many higher-ups in the postwar government had been collaborators. They squashed charges against as many small-fry collaborators as they could. Because if they didn't, the small fry would have squealed loud and long about *their* wartime activities."

"Yes," Gojon said. I could hear the sharply repressed anger in that single word. Not directed at me, this time. Maybe at the persistence of corruption in high places. Or at the indications that avenging angels had folded their business on this planet and gone off to work in someplace less hopeless.

"More recently," he told me, "Genoud's name began turning up in the rumor mills. Among other things, there was suspicion of his associating with young neo-Nazis."

"Any specific group?"

"Not that we heard of. There is no shortage of new Nazis here in France, as you must be aware. We probably have more than Germany now. But our groups are less closely associated with each other."

"Except they all like Le Pen and his Front National."

"Of course. After all, it was the record company Le Pen used to own that supplied so many of them with their collections of old Nazi songs. But that doesn't help us to keep track of them or infiltrate them."

"And the fact that a lot of cops dote on Le Pen," I said, keeping my tone as respectful as I could, "can't help much, either."

Commissaire Gojon didn't reply to that. It was a subject we'd discussed before. He wasn't in a mood for more of it.

I said, "If Genoud was mixed up with Hitler worshipers, he could have done something to make them sore. They're all violently unstable personalities."

"Sawyer, I don't need you to do my guesswork for me."

"What do you need?"

"This mysterious case that neither you nor Monsieur Donhoff care to divulge—in your work on it, you may come across some indication of who murdered Genoud. Or *why* he was murdered. It would hurt my feelings, badly, if I discovered that you failed to inform me of such findings. Rather promptly."

"Sure," I said. "Count on it."

I PHONED ARLETTE. SHE WASN'T AT HER APARTMENT. I tried her office but she wasn't there, either. That nasty little worm of jealousy that lurks in everyone's gut tried to rear its suspicious head. I stepped on it, hard, and Fritz and I went out to dinner.

I drove us all the way to the Ile de la Grande Jatte, in the middle of a bend in the Seine between Neuilly and La Defense. The Café La Jatte had become the latest "in" spot for show-biz and sports celebrities, top models, and prominent government and business types. *Très chic*—but comfortably relaxed about it. I didn't feel wrong in loafers, jeans, denim jacket, and one of the light silk scarfs—worn cowpoke style—that I prefer to constricting neckties.

Fritz, of course, was just his usual distinguished self. I could see other patrons trying to guess who he was—figuring he might be so important his P.R. staff spent most of its time keeping his picture out of the news media. We got a good table.

At the next table a husky movie star was dining with one of the new-wave fashion models—the ones with curves and Brigitte Bardot faces. Her gaze drifted our way as we ordered. Fritz gave her his appreciative smile. She smiled back. Deep dimples. Her escort turned his head and fixed me with a scowl from his most recent gangster film. I wished he was right: I wouldn't have minded being the object of her straying affection. When the actor realized his error, he dropped the scowl and gave Fritz a friendly smile and nod. In show biz you never knew: Fritz might be the money behind some big-time production company.

Our dinners proved to be worth the trip, and the wine was perfect. We took our time with both. When we rode back to our Mouff quarter, I drove slowly around our block before putting the car in its garage. Fritz and I did another precautionary prowl of the block, on foot, and entered the house with the same wariness. No new ambush awaited us. Just a message on my answering machine, asking me to call Barry Raxe.

He'd left his apartment number. I didn't need that. I already had his latest address and phone number in my book, and his present position on the ladder to success in my head. But Raxe didn't know that.

Three months ago the State Department had moved him from Washington to the American Embassy in Paris, where he had the title of chief security officer. An innocuous title for what Barry Raxe was doing now. Directing the State Department's intelligence operation in Paris. He had risen from a humble Detroit cop to that position via a calculated series of short, quick-kill goals. I had been one of his quick kills.

Once upon a time, Barry Raxe and I had both been investigators assigned to France by a Senate committee looking into connections between American overseas businesses and corrupting foreign influences. I got kicked out of that job, with extreme prejudice, when it was learned that I had deliberately destroyed evidence against an aging French gangster, enabling him to retire from criminal life without going to prison. A bad thing to do, I admit. I haven't always been a good angel. And I owed this particular gangster. When my mother had been very young, during the war, he had saved her from the Gestapo. The fact that he also happened to be Arlette Alfani's father didn't enter into it. I didn't meet her until later.

I'd have gotten much worse than being booted out of the job if I hadn't managed to blackmail a senator on the committee to go easy on me. But I didn't walk away from the experience smiling.

It rankled, and Barry Raxe was the nub of what rankled. All the time he'd been acting like my good-buddy coworker, Raxe had been checking into all my activities. It developed that he did that with all his coworkers, at every rung in the ladder. One secret of his upward climb. Sometimes he used their work to jump the gun on them, announcing the results before they got around to it. Taking all the credit for a job well done. Me—he turned in. It earned him a promotion to a solid job in Washington. And now he was in Paris.

I'd kept track because sooner or later . . . Later, I told myself, was better. Revenge, like most wines, gets tastier with age behind it.

I dialed Barry Raxe's apartment.

His wife, Sheila, answered. I'd always liked her; and I didn't think she liked what her husband had done to me—or to others in his zealous climb. But she hadn't balked, not to the point of breaking with him. Sheila was nice, but she was practical. Barry Raxe was not a lovable man. She had married him because her ambition was to eventually become one of Washington's wives-of-influence. Sheila was convinced that her Barry might in time become a deputy assistant under secretary of state.

That was her raison d'être for their marriage. His was Sheila's continuing income from an inheritance that, while not enormous, was substantial enough for him to live, dress, and entertain in a style that would cause his superiors to regard him as a man of distinction ripe for advancement.

Sheila was startled by my call. "Peter—my God! It's been so long. . . . Where are you calling from?" Her voice had gotten up-tight, thickened by a lingering guilt by association.

"I'm right here in Paris, Sheila. How've you been?"

"Well, fine. I didn't . . . I mean, how are *you*?"

"Just fine, Sheila. Barry left a message for me to call him."

"He *did*? I didn't know. I . . . We were just getting ready to go to bed. Barry's in the shower. Shall I tell him to call you back some— Oh, here he comes. . . ." She must have put her hand over the phone, because I didn't hear anything more until she said, "Peter . . . ?"

"I'm still here," I assured her.

"Just hold on a sec. Barry's going to talk to you from the phone in his study."

"Nice talking to you again, Sheila. Take care of yourself."

"You too, Peter. I wish . . ." She didn't say what she wished, and a couple seconds later she'd lost the chance to, because her husband picked up his study phone and said: "Okay, Sheila, I've got it. You can hang up now. Go to bed."

I heard her hang up, and then Barry Raxe's well-remembered friendly voice sounded in my ear: "Hey, Pete—how're you doing?"

"Swell."

"Everything's going good for you?"

"Sure, Barry. Making money and having fun."

"I'm really happy to know that, Pete." Raxe repeated "Really happy," with solid sincerity. "I worried about you after . . . well, what happened with the Committee. Worried you might not be able to pick yourself up again, after that hard a fall."

He was nervous, but working through it toward something.

"No problems left from it," I assured him.

"Great. Tell you the truth, Pete, I sometimes felt real bad about . . . what I had to do, that time."

"I made a mistake and got caught at it," I said blandly. "My fault. You did your duty—everyone said so."

"Yeah, but . . . You're really not sore at me?"

"Do I sound sore? Did I act sore, when it happened?"

"No. That's the truth, you took it like a man. I guess that's why you're doing all right again, you have guts and style. And luck, too; that's always important, right? You have all that going for you, there's no reason one mistake has to ruin a man's life forever. As long as he's careful not to make another bad mistake."

There it was. I said, "What bad mistake are we talking about, Barry?"

"I don't know the details," Raxe said. "It's just something I heard, and want to warn you about. You hear a lot of strange things in my present position. I guess you don't know, but I'm chief security officer at the embassy now.''

''Congratulations.''

''Thanks. Well, what I heard is, you're doing something nasty—and maybe illegal—to a well-off, respectable American citizen who is over here on business. His name is Benjamin Hulvane. It seems you have been spying on his dealings, for some rival company. Industrial espionage, that's the nice way to put it. Some call it stealing company secrets.''

''What's your connection with Hulvane?'' I asked Raxe.

''I don't know the man. I got a call from someone in New York. A very important person. Who asked me to tell you to drop whatever you're doing with this man Hulvane.''

''Who is the V.I.P. that called you?''

''I can't tell you that, Pete.''

''How high would you stamp the security rating on that, Barry—secret or top secret?''

Raxe forced a chuckle. ''Classified, let us say. The only thing in it for your ears is what I told you. Whatever your job on this Benjamin Hulvane is about, drop it. For your own good.''

''If I don't?''

''Why be difficult? You really want to create a problem for yourself, when you don't have to?'' Raxe's uneasy camaraderie was giving way to an itch to flaunt his growing power a bit. He let me register a note of quiet threat: ''The IRS has some real mean snoops stationed at our embassy here. They can play rough, when they get on the case of an American working abroad.''

''I'm square with the IRS right up into this year,'' I said. ''I pay taxes on all my income to the U.S.A., as required. Including on my earnings abroad, even where I'm also taxed by another country.''

''Yeah, but you're a small, independent operator—and small businesses are always vulnerable. You must deduct a lot of business expenses from your income.''

''All legitimate deductions.''

"But suppose one of those rough IRS snoops decides they are *not* legitimate," Raxe said. "Suppose he disallows most of your business deductions—going all the way back to when you started operating as an independent. Add the late penalties and interest over all those years to what you'd wind up owing the IRS, and you'd be out of business. You'd never be able to work your way out from under a debt that enormous. It's a hard world, Pete, and IRS investigators aren't known for having kindly hearts. Their job is to stick it in you, deep as they can."

"I seem to remember," I said, "that you were one of them, before the senate committee hired you."

"That's why I know so much about what they can do to a guy. And it ain't easy for anybody to fight back, unless you're a rich corporation. Which you're not. An IRS judgment's one time when the accused has to prove his innocence, not the other way 'round. What can you do, hire lawyers and go to court? The IRS has lawyers it pays all year, anyway. They can drag out the case for years. A small businessman doesn't have the kind of money to pay lawyers all those years."

"You do paint an unpleasant picture," I said mildly.

"A word from me to the IRS guys at the embassy," Raxe said, "could stop the investigation before it got too far."

"Or could start it," I said.

"It doesn't have to happen, Pete. That's why I'm warning you ahead of time. The message loud enough and clear enough for you?"

"Yep."

"Good," Raxe said, and I could hear him relishing the power-bite in his own voice. "Then I can tell the man who asked me to help that you'll climb off this Hulvane's back and stay off?"

"Sure," I said. "Count on it."

After we hung up, I filled Fritz in on the conversation. Then I went out, got my car, and drove to Barry Raxe's apartment.

◈ **13** ◈

BARRY AND SHEILA RAXE LIVED ON THE SMALLER OF THE two islands that were the original Paris and remain its true heart. The Ile Saint-Louis, one of the city's better addresses. They had a large third-floor apartment in a solid seventeenth-century building on Quai d'Orléans, at one end of the island. Its casement windows and balcony looked out upon the river, the tree-lined Left Bank on the other side, and the Gothic intricacy of Notre Dame Cathedral's east section on the adjacent Ile de la Cité. I estimated that a sizable portion of Sheila Raxe's monthly income was going into that high-prestige view.

I put my finger to their doorbell and leaned on it for several seconds. I couldn't hear it ring inside. The interior walls on Ile Saint-Louis are thick, and so was their apartment's tall, shiny mahogany entrance door. About ten more seconds passed after I took my thumb off the button. Then the little spy-hole in the door opened and Sheila's blue eye peeked out at me.

It took her a moment to register my friendly face. The spy-hole closed, locks were manipulated, and she pulled the door open. She'd put on a bathrobe and bedroom slippers. There were new anxiety lines around her eyes, and the touch of gray I remembered in her hair didn't show anymore. Otherwise she was much the same. A small, thin, delicately pretty brunette, forty now.

"What in the world are you *doing* here at this hour?" she demanded sleepily as I stepped into the oak-paneled vestibule with her. "We were in *bed*, Peter. Barry took a *pill*—he's had trouble sleeping and—"

"I'm sorry to disturb you, Sheila," I said. "But something urgent came up, and Barry ought to know about it."

At that point he appeared, coming out of a door down the hall behind Sheila, fighting to swallow a yawn and belting a brocade robe around a figure that had gotten portly. His hair was mussed and there wasn't as much of it as the last time I'd seen him. Raxe was the same age as his wife but looked a decade older because of the deep trenches in his face and their crisscross wrinkles. That wasn't new, but the fleshiness that emphasized it was.

"Something urgent came up," I repeated for his benefit, "and it can't wait. It's about Louise Doyle."

The doped look vanished from Raxe's pale eyes. His mouth opened for a gulp of steadying air, and then closed quickly when Sheila turned to him with a questioning look.

Raxe smiled at her. "It's just a security matter I've been trying to straighten out. Louise Doyle is an elderly American who has gotten herself into a spot of trouble over here. I asked Pete to see if he can help her, through his French connections. I can't tell you any more than that, honey. Pete shouldn't have mentioned her name in front of you."

He was still pretty fast on his feet, and not a bad actor. If his smile was a bit strained, that could be blamed on the sleeping pill he'd taken. Louise Doyle was a bouncy young foreign service officer doing her first assignment for the State Department at the Paris Embassy. According to my own embassy snoops, Raxe had been spending odd hours in Louise Doyle's little studio apartment over the past couple months. Probably instructing her in some of the nuances of her new career.

Sheila nodded at her husband and said, "Oh."

I smiled at him and said, "Sorry. Her name just slipped out. Have to be more careful about that."

Raxe told Sheila to go back to bed. "This won't take long."

"You do need your sleep, remember," Sheila reminded him. "If you shake off the effects of that pill, you'll have to take another. And then you won't be worth much in the morning.''

"I'll be there in a few minutes," Raxe promised her.

Sheila looked at me with a rueful smile. "Well, it *is* nice seeing you again—even at this time of night.''

"I'll make it a more reasonable hour next time," I told her. "So we can have a long talk." I didn't bother checking out how Raxe took that.

Sheila went off through the hall to their bedroom. Raxe opened a door to his study, off the vestibule, flicked the light switch inside, and gestured me in, his fixed smile still firmly in place. I went in and sat down on a leather-padded armchair beside a wide desk. Raxe closed the study's heavy door firmly. When he turned to face me his smile was gone, but the strain wasn't.

"What the *hell* do you think you're doing here, damn it!''

"Who is the guy in New York that asked you to scare me off Hulvane?" I asked him gently.

"I told you on the phone, I'm not at liberty to divulge that to you," Raxe snapped. "That stands."

His study was furnished with dark semiantiques from the eighteenth century. The ceiling beams were older and darker. But there were colorful modern prints on the paneled walls, signed. The Persian carpet looked like the genuine article. His desk was a flattop, with nothing on it but a gold fountain pen and an opened leather-bound diary with its visible pages blank. The chair I'd chosen felt solid and comfortable. I stretched out my legs and looked at my shoes and decided they could use a shine.

"Your wife's probably almost back to sleep by now," I said. "I'd really hate to go in there and disturb her again."

Raxe put his back to the door and glared at me. "You're attempting to blackmail me."

"Uh-huh."

"You're a vicious son of a bitch."

"Yeah. You remember that, the next time someone asks you to scare me with the threat of an income tax investigation.''

"That can still happen to you," Raxe warned coldly. "If you get me mad enough at you."

"No it won't," I told him. "If you try to get one started, it won't get off the ground. One of the IRS investigators at the embassy is an old friend."

"Which one?"

"I'm not at liberty to divulge that to you," I mimicked him. None of the IRS people were among my embassy contacts. But Raxe believing it meant he couldn't ask any of them to do a job on me. He might pick the wrong one, and I'd get tipped off and hit back.

"There's a dozen other ways I can dump trouble on you," Raxe told me, but his sense of unassailable authority was showing signs of unraveling at the edges.

"Who called you from New York?" I asked again.

"Do you really *want* to wreck your life with another bad mistake? I did warn you about that, on the phone. One last chance—back off and drop it. And I'll try to forgive and forget you coming here and trying to lean on me."

I sighed. "Seems I do have to go in there and explain to Sheila about Louise Doyle." I stood up and took a step toward Raxe and the door behind him.

"*Wait . . .*" Raxe brought both hands up to his chest and pushed his palms toward me. Like a traffic cop, but with less assurance.

I sat down again, crossed one leg over the other, and waited patiently.

We both knew Raxe couldn't afford a break with Sheila at this critical stage of his career. Most of the people who reached his present level in the power structure would stall there, for the remainder of their working lives. There was a drastically shrinking number of positions above it. The competition for those—against other climbers as determined and tricky as Raxe—got murderous. Without Sheila's income, he would have to give up this impressive apartment, lose the new Mercedes he hadn't finished paying for, and end his openhanded entertainment of the bureaucracy's high command. They would stop thinking of him as having the potential to be one of them, and regard him as just another mid-level civil servant.

"You seem to be implying there's some improper relationship between myself and Miss Doyle," he said stiffly. "That's simply not true. The only contacts between us have been concerned with our foreign service work. I would flatly deny any rumor to the contrary. And I would certainly bring legal action against anyone who attempts to spread such a rumor."

"I got it from a guy working for SIDE in Paris," I lied, using a tone usually reserved for hospital visits to the terminally ill. SIDE was Argentina's Secretariat of State Intelligence. "He was doing a routine check on Doyle, just to see if she might be vulnerable in some way, and he saw you going in and out of her studio apartment. He knows who and what you are, of course. So he installed an audio and visual surveillance setup inside her place for a few days. One of those tiny spy cameras in her TV, and bugs in strategic spots around the room. Turned on by remote control when you were in there with her. The cassettes SIDE's agent got from that are juicy."

Raxe's silence got heavy enough to crush the Eiffel Tower into a flatiron. His shoulders sagged. He sat down on the edge of a chair facing me, put his knees together, and clasped his hands on them like a subdued schoolkid. There was nothing visible left of his power complex. In its place was a cringing meekness that was as put on as his good-buddy act.

"Relax," I told him, "the agent isn't with SIDE anymore. I reckon you know about Argentina's recent economy move, cutting its intelligence operations down by half. He was one of those who got fired. That left him out of funds—and out of any loyalty to his former employers. I bought the cassettes from him. They're the only copies, so you don't have to worry on that score. They're in a bank vault now. With instructions, naturally, about where to send them if anything unpleasant were to happen to me."

"This is your way of getting even with me," Raxe said. "Your revenge for what I did to you."

"No, not at all," I told him. Truthfully. It was just a little sip. The rest could wait in the bottle, gathering more age. I wanted Raxe higher up the ladder before I kicked it out from under him.

"The thing with Louise Doyle, it's nothing serious," he told me. Reaching out for man-to-man understanding of normal sexual skirmishing. "I was just playing around a little. Everybody does it, you know that. Doesn't mean a thing—doesn't change my dedication to my marriage. But Sheila—she wouldn't understand that, if she found out. She'd be hurt by it."

"Wouldn't do your career much good, either," I commented sympathetically. "Higher-ups learning you're prone to doing things that could be used for blackmailing you." With no change of tone, I said, "Tell me who called you from New York. Or maybe there wasn't any call. Maybe you were acting on your own. A personal favor for Benjamin Hulvane."

"No—I told you the truth, Pete. Hulvane's name doesn't mean a thing to me. I did get a call about it. . . . Listen, you've got to promise me you won't tell him you learned it from me. He's very well connected. It could hurt my future."

"I won't squeal on you."

"Promise?"

"Absolutely."

Raxe sucked in a deep breath of air. He held it in, and then slowly let it out, like a balloon deflating. "His name's Brent Poole."

I let the name sink in, and it surfaced with a few basics attached to it. "Used to be with the Justice Department. One of its sharpest prosecutors. Made his reputation nailing two Mafia big shots on narcotics conspiracy charges."

"That's him. He quit Justice after winning the second of those conspiracy cases. Shifted into private practice. He's partners in a prestige law firm based in New York now. But he's still got plenty of very high level friends in Washington. That's where Poole could help me—" Raxe paused to drag in a breath of air before finishing it "—or could hurt me."

This case was gathering old men. Hulvane was only two years younger than Fritz. Genoud had been about four years older. Judging by the length of Brent Poole's career, he had to be in either his late sixties or early seventies. I wondered if their ages had any significance. No way of knowing, at the moment.

I said, "Stop worrying, Barry. I did give you my promise."

"I just pray to God you mean it."

"Why does Brent Poole want me to get off Hulvane? What's Hulvane to a man like Poole?"

"He didn't explain anything. Just asked me to do it—as a favor. You know how it goes—doing favors for the powers that be, that's how you move up in this world."

"Or down," I said. "Did Poole specifically ask you not to mention his name to me?"

Raxe thought about it. "I got a definite feeling he didn't think there'd be any reason for me to."

I speculated on what the connection might be between a Brent Poole and a Benjamin Hulvane. Gave that up as fruitless until I had more information. Got to my feet.

Raxe jumped up from his chair. "That's it? We're all square now?"

I raised a hand. Raxe flinched, thinking for a second I was about to slap him. I reached out and patted his cheek. "That's all, Barry. Live, love, laugh, and be happy. Prosper."

I found Fritz waiting up for me, in my apartment. It was almost one A.M., and he was in his pajamas and bathrobe, ready for bed. But with a bit of news to deliver first. He withheld it until I'd filled him in on my meeting with Barry Raxe, and he agreed to pass on Brent Poole's name to McKissack in New York. Then he gave me his own news.

Fritz had checked with the Ritz again.

Hulvane still hadn't returned to the hotel.

◼ **14** ◼

I SNATCHED THE GUN OFF MY BEDSIDE TABLE BEFORE COMing fully awake, and I was sitting up with it in my hand by the time I knew what had jolted me out of my sleep. Someone was entering my bedroom.

I twisted toward the sound, ready to fire and roll off the bed at the same time. Morning light filled the bedroom windows. Fritz was outlined against one of them as he came out of my closet, fully dressed for a new day. He was carrying a small paper sack from Perruche, the best of the Contrescarpe *boulangeries*. He came to a halt when my gun pointed at him, but his expression remained tranquil.

I lowered the gun, drew a shuddering breath, and swallowed a couple times to help ease my heartbeat back down to normal.

He'd had to use the secret door between our bedroom closets because there was no way to open my front door from the outside. We'd both agreed to lock the manual bolts on the insides of those before going to sleep. Hulvane could always decide to send in a second team. Maybe smarter than the first had been.

I put the gun back on the table and looked at the travel alarm clock beside it. Two minutes past eight A.M. I had planned to sleep until nine.

"What's happened?" I croaked.

"Two phone calls," Fritz said, and he walked away toward my kitchen. Experience had taught him how difficult it could be to explain anything complicated to me before I'd had some morning coffee.

I could smell him making it while I took my hot-and-cold shower. It was ready on the table when I trudged into the kitchen cinching the belt of my terry cloth bathrobe. Fritz had poured a cup for me and another for himself. He took a small, fresh-baked *tarte aux pommes* from the *boulangerie* bag and put it on a dish beside my cup. Nothing for himself, which meant he'd already had his breakfast. A big one—because that was one of the German habits he'd never shucked off. When I was in the States I usually breakfasted heavily, too. But in France I mostly went with the light French breakfast. Probably the animal in me, instinctively adapting to changes in terrain.

I cut an orange, ate it, and added milk to my coffee before settling down across from Fritz. He waited until I'd eaten all of my tarte and finished half of my coffee before he spoke again.

"The second of the calls I mentioned was one I made. To the Hotel Ritz. Hulvane isn't there. He did not come back at any time last night."

"Making sure he's not tailed again." I took another swallow of coffee. "For a while, anyway. He's got to go back there sooner or later. He's got all his stuff in that suite. In the meantime, we have his background to work on."

"That background," Fritz said, "turns out to have some rather odd aspects to it."

"Okay. Tell me."

"It was a phone call from Jacob McKissack that woke me," he said. "At seven this morning. Seven o'clock on the dot."

I grinned. "Using the time difference between here and New York to get even for your doing it to him yesterday."

Fritz nodded. "And at almost exactly the same time. I must admit I admire that little detail."

"Details are McKissack's strong point. What did he have to say?" I finished the rest of my coffee while Fritz told me:

"Firstly, the photos you faxed to him yesterday were shown to the doorman at Hulvane's apartment building. Who definitely identified the man in them as Benjamin Hulvane. The second thing McKissack had to say is that we already owe him a great deal of money. He's sending us a bill with all the details, but he wanted us to know the total owed at this point.''

Fritz gave me the total figure. I whistled, softly. Fritz shrugged. ''It is high, but probably justified. McKissack had quite a number of his agents working on Hulvane's background all of yesterday and very late into the night. In both New York and Los Angeles.''

I poured myself more coffee as Fritz began feeding me the info all those McKissack agents had turned up.

Benjamin Hulvane had been born in Ventura, California. His parents had owned a small general store. They'd had a second child, a daughter a few years younger, but she'd died of mastoid infection when she was eleven. Leaving Benjamin Hulvane an only child. He'd been a student at the University of California during most of World War II. Majoring in languages. Of which German and Italian were his strongest.

''Ah,'' I said.

''Yes,'' Fritz said. ''Our Benjamin Hulvane was an exceptionally bright student. The government postponed drafting him until he graduated—with honors—near the end of the war in Europe. The army gave him officer rank. Lieutenant. Because of his command of German, he was sent to the American Zone of Occupation in southern Germany immediately after the war. He was assigned to the U.S. Army's Criminal Investigations Department. Which was under the OMGB—the Office of Military Government for Bavaria, headquartered in Munich. That is where Lieutenant Hulvane was stationed.''

''Your old hometown,'' I said.

Fritz had no comment on that. Munich was a sore subject. Fritz had been a young police detective there before the Nazis took over. Even if he could have stomached them, they wouldn't have tolerated him. Fritz had called them slime too openly, too often. So he'd fled to Paris, and joined the Free French underground during the German occupation. After the war France had made him a citizen, as a reward for his services, and he'd been working out of Paris as a private investigator ever since.

Most of the friends he'd left behind in Munich had been exterminated by the Nazis before the war was finished. Most of the enemies he'd left behind had survived the war, but died of natural causes over the following decades. There were very few left—of both friends and enemies.

"Lieutenant Hulvane's duties for the OMGB," Fritz continued, "involved searching for and interrogating Germans suspected of either having committed war crimes or being active in the black market that was Germany's chief industry for some years after the war. Apparently he carried out those duties well. There is nothing against him noted in his military records. He took his honorable discharge from the army in 1947—in Munich. He left Munich a few months later. But it was almost ten years more before he returned to the United States, and settled in New York. McKissack's people haven't found any indication that he ever returned to California, even for a brief visit."

Nor had they been able, so far, to find out where Hulvane had been during that decade between leaving Munich and returning to the States.

"What about his parents?" I said. "Didn't they hear from him? Letters—phone calls?"

"That brings us to another oddity about our Mr. Hulvane. He had always been a devoted son, according to friends of his parents. Wrote to his father and mother regularly while he was stationed in Germany. But that stopped after he left the army. He sent them a short letter saying he needed to spend some time off alone, to find himself. After that, nothing. For ten years. His parents tried to get in touch with him. But he had left Munich and couldn't be located elsewhere."

"All this from friends of his parents?"

"Yes."

"I guess that means the parents are no longer around."

"They are dead," Fritz confirmed. "Shortly after Hulvane settled in New York, he sent them a telegram. Excusing his long silence and promising to visit them soon. A few days after receiving that telegram, they were killed in an automobile accident. While driving at night. Their car swerved off a hill road and plunged into a gully. The car was badly smashed, and so were their bodies."

"I get a creepy feeling," I told Fritz, "that Hulvane may have paid a short visit to California, after all."

"Considering what we've learned of him here," Fritz said mildly, "I wouldn't rule it out entirely. But we don't know of any reason why he would want his parents dead. And if he *was* responsible, it is more likely he had someone else do it for him. The California police sent a wire late the next morning to Hulvane in New York, notifying him of the fatal accident. He wired back—the same day, from New York— sending money for the funeral of his parents, and regretting that the press of business prevented him from attending it in person."

I found that my cup was empty again. I didn't refill it. Fritz and I looked at each other in sober silence for a bit. Then Fritz told me what McKissack had turned up on how Hulvane made his living in New York:

"He seems to have retired six or seven years ago. From a one-man office he ran as a New York branch for that perfume company in South America. Before that, for a few years after he returned from Europe, he had another small business. As an international art dealer. In partnership with a New Yorker named Lawrence Tuck. It went broke, apparently."

"Have McKissack's people questioned Tuck about Hulvane?"

Fritz shook his head. "Tuck hasn't been in America for the last four years. Since he was released from an alcoholic rehabilitation center in Maryland. He moved to Italy and hasn't returned. Tuck's mother was Italian, and some of her family is still there. It seems he went to live with them, at least temporarily." Fritz handed me a small file card. "This is his last known address."

On the card he had neatly written down Lawrence Tuck's name and an address in Genoa.

"No phone?" I asked.

"None," Fritz said. "Another negative: McKissack's agency hasn't found any flight to Europe that Hulvane made from the United States eight years ago. But . . .'' he added pointedly, ''Hulvane's name does turn up for one overseas round-trip flight that year. To Caracas. A lengthy visit. He did not return from Venezuela for almost three months. Those months encompass the time when Helen Marsh was kidnapped.''

I said it again: ''Ah.''

''Worth checking out,'' Fritz agreed.

Alonzo Fara wouldn't be leaving home for his office for another forty-five minutes. I had plenty of time to call and make sure his friends were pushing hard enough on flight records from Caracas to Europe. I asked Fritz if McKissack had been able to find out this soon about anything that might connect Hulvane to Brent Poole, the former Justice Department hotshot now in private practice.

''Not as yet. But McKissack already knew one thing of potential interest. Poole's law firm represents, among other big businessmen, a number of important underworld figures frequently charged with connections to both the Mafia and South American drug dealers. Including several against whom Brent Poole was preparing cases when he was still with the Justice Department.''

It wasn't surprising, nor unusual. Poole wouldn't be the first lawman investigating large-scale narcotics traffic to switch sides. Cops did it, and so did district attorneys and federal prosecutors. The enormous fees that big dope merchants could pay out was a lure hard to resist. And the ones the dope kings tried most to lure were the ones who were their toughest enemies.

Nothing illegal about it. Foreign countries keep recruiting Washington's top administration officials to help them thwart administration policies. Legitimate big businesses long ago made it standard operating procedure. If you can't beat an opponent, hire him.

''McKissack says,'' Fritz told me, ''that he'd have to proceed very cautiously and delicately if we want more than that on Poole. His law firm is extremely powerful. McKissack doesn't want Poole and his partners getting angry at him. I told McKissack to hold off on that, and other aspects of the case, until we are certain we're going further with it.''

I agreed with that. I'd have to see Helen Marsh again, first. And Arlette. To give them what we'd gotten so far—and what we hadn't. After that, it would be up to them to decide whether we called it quits or moved ahead on all fronts— until we found out who and what Benjamin Hulvane really was.

Because at this point we surely didn't know the answer to that.

Hulvane's profile was getting murkier instead of clearer.

❈ **15** ❈

FRITZ WENT BACK TO HIS APARTMENT TO SEE IF THERE WERE any new phone messages on his machine. I was going to my own phone when it rang. I picked it up, and Alonzo was at the other end.

"Telepathy," I said. "I was just about to call you."

"So you are anxious? Good. My friends in Caracas have come through with three items of value. Great value." He paused dramatically.

"I'll decide how valuable," I told him. "Just give it to me without the flourishes."

"One of my friends there located a woman who used to be Mr. Hulvane's mistress, at the time his business exporting perfume supplies failed. Now she is getting too old to do well as a professional mistress, and is having difficulty paying her rent. My friend had to give her some money to induce her to speak freely." Another pause.

"Yes, Alonzo," I said patiently, "I will reimburse it."

"I assured him you would. Well, this woman says that Mr. Hulvane did not emerge from the failure of his company with any substantial amount of money. He had to dismiss her, because he could no longer afford a mistress. According to her, it appeared at the time that he would also have to sell his expensive Caracas apartment."

"But he didn't."

"No—and she saw Hulvane a couple years later, in a chic Caracas nightclub with a new mistress, very young and very beautiful. Obviously, he was well off again. Interesting?"

98

I agreed that it was interesting. Nine years ago Hulvane had gone broke. Seven years ago his former mistress had seen him back in the bucks. Between those two came eight years ago—when five million dollars in ransom was paid to Helen Marsh's kidnappers.

"The second item of interest," Alonzo said, "comes from another friend in Caracas. He located Mr. Hulvane's *last* mistress. A lovely girl—an expensive luxury type. This girl says that in the fourteen months she was Mr. Hulvane's mistress, he never spoke of whatever his new business might be to her, or with her present. But one time, when she was nightclubbing with him, a man named Victorino Mombello came over to shake hands with Mr. Hulvane. And, she told my friend, to get a closer look at her cleavage. Which, according to my friend, is a marvel difficult to ignore."

"I have a nasty suspicion," I said, "that your friend's expense account is going to include a night of not ignoring any part of her."

"That may well be. But I think you will find what he learned from her is worth the price—and not begrudge his incorporating a little pleasure with his work. You see, Mombello was a known cocaine exporter. Specializing in shipments to Europe. As you know, Pierre-Ange, we don't grow a great deal of coca in Venezuela. But Caracas is a natural point for overseas shipments of cocaine from other nearby countries, such as Colombia."

"From what I hear," I said, "Venezuela also has some thriving cocaine refineries of its own, not far from Caracas."

"That is possible," Alonzo acknowledged. "But what is of interest for you is that the girl says she guessed from that nightclub encounter that Mr. Hulvane was somehow associated in Mombello's business. This was later confirmed, after Mr. Hulvane dropped her—and she became Mombello's mistress. Which she remained until two weeks ago—when Mombello was murdered, along with two of his associates. By some rival dope-smuggling gang, probably. It is because of his death that the girl felt able to talk freely to my friend. And it seems the late Mombello was more talkative than Mr. Hulvane. He told her that Mr. Hulvane had excellent connections for the distribution of cocaine in Europe. *Unusual* connections, according to Mombello. He didn't explain what he meant by unusual. So—that would be Mr. Hulvane's new source of funds, after his perfume enterprise collapsed.''

''You need a sizable chunk of money to start with,'' I said, ''before you can get into large-scale drug smuggling.''

''I don't have anything at all on how he would have raised that initial money. But the girl gave my friend another piece of information that may be of interest. About a week before Mombello was killed—that would be three weeks ago, now—he complained to her that Mr. Hulvane was starting to bypass him and arrange shipments from Caracas to Europe himself. *Is* this of interest to you?''

''It could turn out to be,'' I said.

Because it fitted neatly with what McKissack had said about Brent Poole's law firm representing some kingpins of the narcotics trade. Nobody goes into international dope traffic on his own, without powerful connections. It's a way to end up dead, very fast and very messily. Hulvane had to have the cooperation of a couple underworld biggies, one in South America, another in Europe.

It meant that Hulvane didn't have to know Brent Poole. Hulvane explained his problem to one of the overlords he shared his profits with. And who happened to be one of Poole's clients—a client important enough to ask for a very small favor. Like getting somebody unimportant named Peter Sawyer off the back of somebody else named Benjamin Hulvane. Easy. A short phone call to Barry Raxe in Paris. Nothing illegal said or done. Just a minor favor asked, for a minor favor owed.

''What interests me more right now,'' I told Alonzo, ''is that I've just learned that Hulvane *was* in Venezuela eight years ago. For a longish period.''

''I know. That is the last item. I was saving it for you. And he did make a trip to Europe from there. Caracas-Rome-Caracas.''

''Give me the exact dates.''

He read them out to me.

Hulvane had flown from Caracas to Rome three weeks before Helen Marsh was kidnapped. He had returned one week after the ransom was paid.

Seventy minutes later I was on an Air Inter jet flying back down to the Riviera.

❄ 16 ❄

I GOT MY CAR OUT OF THE CÔTE D'AZUR AIRPORT'S reduced-rate long-term parking lot and drove into Nice to pick up Arlette Alfani. She was supposed to be waiting for me outside the three-floor building housing her law firm's offices, but she wasn't. There was no available space for me to tuck the car into, so I double-parked. The street was one-way and too narrow for the traffic behind me to get past. One of the blocked cars honked angrily. I climbed out to yell up at Arlette's office windows. But at that moment she came striding out of the building toward me, swinging her slim briefcase and looking ravishing in a lusciously filled blue slacks suit, her huge dark eyes and ripe lips glistening in the late-morning sunlight.

One of the nice things about the French is that they don't merely accept kissing in public places. They respect it. Passing pedestrians glanced our way with smiles that shared our pleasure. The car blocked behind mine stopped honking and waited patiently.

I gave the patient driver a thank-you wave as I handed Arlette into my car. He nodded and grinned. The line of cars behind mine was a block long when I drove away.

"Fritz called half an hour ago," Arlette said, "and asked me to tell you something new that's cropped up."

The something new was that Hulvane had checked out of his hotel. By long distance. He had telephoned it in, shortly after I'd left Paris. He had spoken to an assistant manager at the Ritz, instructing him to pack everything in his suite into his bags and store them safely. He'd said he would settle his bill when he returned to pick up the bags—but couldn't be certain when that would be. Fritz's informant at the Ritz had told him the switchboard operator was certain Hulvane's call was from some country outside France.

That told me that what I guessed earlier was probably correct. If Hulvane had gone to another country and his passport was still hidden in one of the bags he'd left behind, he was traveling on false papers. That *was* what had been passed to Hulvane in the porn shop. Forged I.D. he'd arranged for the late Jacques Genoud to have made for him.

He was making it difficult to pick up his trail again. If he'd left the country, he'd done so between last evening and this morning. If he'd gone by train, bus, or car, finding out where he'd gone—without knowing what name he was using—would be close to impossible. If he'd left France by plane, that narrowed it down some. But not enough.

"Fritz said he's given the exact time of the call to a friend of yours named Sylvane Buongiorno," Arlette told me. "And she promised to try to find out where it came from as soon as she has some spare time."

Maybe picking up Hulvane's trail wasn't going to be as impossible as he'd hoped.

Arlette was looking at me curiously. "That's a lovely name, Buongiorno. She's a friend of yours I don't remember your ever mentioning to me."

"Sylvane works for the phone company in Paris," I said.

"Pretty?"

"Very."

"Bien roulée?" Nicely rolled—current French slang for lushly curved.

"Not as flagrantly *bien roulée* as you," I said. "But very pleasant."

"She told Fritz you can pay her back by taking her to an expensive dinner at a restaurant of her choice. Should I be worried?"

"Not if you continue to cater to my wishes with the submissive devotion I expect from a woman."

Arlette leaned over and took a savage bite at my earlobe.

I narrowly managed to avoid swerving into a bus that was pulling out from the curb in front of me. Arlette sat back with a pleased smile. I fingered my earlobe. No blood, but it throbbed like hell.

I drove us east out of Nice, onto the Lower Corniche. Off to our right, beyond the palms and umbrella pines and sun-drenched buildings, the Mediterranean was slashed by moving shadows of scattered clouds. Sea gulls glided in search of prey above the water a good distance from the shore, so the clouds didn't pose a threat. If a rainstorm was brewing, beyond the horizon, the gulls would be flying closer to land. When we were stopped by a red light I gave Arlette a page from my notebook. A tentative calculation of what Helen Marsh owed Fritz and me to date.

I had worked it out on the plane. Listing our basic fee, Jake McKissack's total figure, and a rough estimate of our other expenses. Including an educated guess at what the services of Alonzo and his Caracas friends were going to cost us.

Arlette took in the numbers swiftly and scowled at the total amount. "This is incredibly high for less than two days."

"It's going to get incredibly higher," I said, "if we go on with this investigation."

The light had turned green. I drove through and continued east parallel to the coastline. Arlette was waiting for me to justify the figures in the expense account. When I didn't, she nodded to herself and tucked the paper into her briefcase. She knew me well enough to understand without asking. I was saving my explanation of what was costing so much for when we got to Helen Marsh's home. I didn't feel like going through the details twice.

We reached Carnolès, just after Cap-Martin, thirty minutes after leaving Nice. I turned away from the sea and drove up the D23—a twisty little road that left any evidence of the Riviera's existence behind as it worked into the foothills of the Maritime Alps on its way to the tiny village of Gorbio.

If what Helen Marsh wanted was to hide herself away from the world, Gorbio was a good place for it.

* * *

Gorbio's tight cluster of medieval stone houses climbs a hillcrest of naked rock overlooking a deep, lush valley of cypress trees and terraced olive groves. The abandoned ruin of the *Château du Comte de Malaussene* rises like a broken crown atop the village. The D23 ends at the bottom, on one side of the small main square. Another road—even narrower, not entirely paved, and sometimes cut by rockslides—starts beyond the other side of the square and curls through the back country to Roquebrune, a village much richer and very much more frequented than Gorbio.

There wasn't a single other car using either road. The village held a lifeless silence that made me sharply aware of birds singing in the trees around its base. But it wasn't lifeless. Not quite. Three very old men sat on a weathered bench warming their stiffened joints on the sunny side of the square, beyond a nearly hollow elm tree that was planted there back in 1713.

Most of Gorbio's shrunken population was old. Younger people moved out, down to the coast or off to larger towns, drawn by attractions the village lacked. Those who hadn't left permanently were away at this time of day, doing their jobs and their shopping elsewhere. Helen Marsh was probably the only eighteen-year-old permanent resident. Any others would have migrated in search of groups their own age. There wouldn't be many people around here of Ferguson's age, either.

The three old men straightened on their shared bench and regarded the arrival of my car with interest. We were something new to look at. There'd been nothing for them to watch before that except a black and white soccer ball floating in the basin of a century-old fountain, pushed back and forth by weak gusts of hill wind.

I turned away from the base of the village and drove up a graveled path to its parking space. There were only three other cars there at that hour. One was Helen Marsh's Citröen XM.

The village cemetery was near the parking space. Some of its grave markers were of iron shaped to look like swords.

They were painted red, white, and blue, and their blades were stuck into the earth. Those were for men who had been killed in World War I, most of them in the Battle of Verdun. There were an extraordinary number of them for a village this small. The French had more than four hundred thousand casualties in that battle. Marshal Petain had been called "the hero of Verdun" for that accomplishment.

All of the swords had been freshly repainted. The entire village could have benefited from fresh paint, among other improvements, after its decades of accumulated neglect. From where Arlette and I stood when we got out of the car, Gorbio looked sad and deserted. But from that distance it also had an atmosphere most other old French villages have lost. The slightly scary romanticism of a gothic mystery.

Both impressions—of sad desertion and gothic romanticism—dissolved when we took the short walking path down toward the square and passed Gorbio's covered outdoor *lavoir*, the public clothes-washing basin. Four women were at the long, ancient stone tub, chatting cheerfully while soaping and scrubbing their morning's laundry.

There was ritual to it. The women would leave the clothing at the *lavoir* to soak during lunchtime siesta, and return in the afternoon to rinse it out with the cold mountain spring water running through the stone basin. It was a tradition still clung to by many in spite of the fact that most village houses now had their own washing machines. Because it provided what the machines could not: gossip and company, an entertaining way of employing their day.

When we entered the square, we nodded and said *"bonjour"* to the three old men. They returned the nod and greeting politely. Another tradition with a purpose, followed by country people in most lands around the Mediterranean. This one a ritual of reassurance: "Though we are strangers to each other, there is nothing to be uptight about; we recognize you as fellow human beings with minds and hearts like ours, and mean you no harm." Not unlike the old practice among American Indians, of signaling friendly intentions with a hand raised palm outward.

People in big cities would have a problem adjusting to a tradition like that. They might find themselves getting to know each other, after ten years of sharing the same apartment building elevator.

Arlette had been to Helen Marsh's place before. She took us out of the square and up the steep incline of one of the cramped passageways that are as close as Gorbio gets to having streets. Paved with knobby little cobblestones worn shiny and slippery by centuries of use. A shallow trench cut down the middle of this one, for rain runoffs. We climbed with the trench between us and crumbling walls pressing close on both sides.

Our route kept rising and shifting direction. It became short groups of steps in places. In others it tunneled under houses that spread all the way across over our heads, supported by low stone-and-timber arches.

I've always liked villages like this, the ones that have managed to avoid attracting hordes of tourists. I enjoy the sense you get inside them of the past continuing into the future. They seem to have arrested the aging process about the same time they stopped growing. Somewhere at the end of the Middle Ages. But Gorbio was suffering from its longevity.

Parts had been rebuilt in the seventeenth century, and others repaired in the nineteenth. Some houses had been restored more recently, but not many. More in evidence were houses that hadn't been inhabited for fifty years or more. Their thick walls still solid, but their roofs sagging and their unused interiors decaying behind their locked shutters and doors. Victims of vicious in-fighting between family members, which can last through generations, over shares of the inheritance.

Helen Marsh had gotten her place, almost two years ago, because Arlette had done a near-miracle job of breaking through one of those family logjams.

We turned left through a tight alley into another steep street, and there it was.

Arlette paused to look at the renovated exterior of the house with a certain amount of wry satisfaction. "There were eleven different heirs involved," she said, "and none of them would sit down with any of the others. I had to keep going back and forth between them, making a separate offer to each. I advised Helen that it was adding up to far too much for a place that needed so much work. But Helen has an obstinate streak in her. And it is her money. Anyway, we came across with enough of it to dazzle the embattled beneficiaries into finally agreeing on who got what from the sale."

The house was a modest size for someone of Helen Marsh's wealth, but large enough for four or five normal people to live in it comfortably. It was on one side of the village, halfway to the top. The main section was two stories that rose on the brink of a cliff dropping into the valley. From the street, I could see one end of a balcony that cantilevered out over the cliff from the ground floor. From the floor above that, an extension of the house stretched across the street over an archway. On top of that extension there was another story that formed a square tower.

The exterior of the house had been expensively and lovingly restored. The rough stone walls had been power-sanded clean. The roofs had been rebuilt, using orange tiles that had been aged so they blended with the other housetops of Gorbio. Woodwork had been replaced and brightly painted. There were new window shutters in dark blue, with a flower box under each window.

Ferguson had been watching for us from the topmost window, inside the tower. When we appeared, she signaled and started down to let us in. While we waited I noted that the house had only one outside door: under the archway. And that there were no ground-floor windows that could be seen from the street. There had been two, but they'd been filled in with rough stones and mortar, skillfully enough so those places almost succeeded in looking like the rest of the old wall.

It probably made the house feel more secure, for someone like Helen Marsh. Actually, all she was accomplishing by it was burrowing deeper into her hiding place. Something I was pretty sure she was never going to be able to stop doing unless she knew the people who kidnapped and mutilated her were no longer in circulation.

I was debating how much hope of that I should or shouldn't give her when Ferguson opened the only door and let us in.

◉ **17** ◉

WHEN WE WERE INSIDE, FERGUSON RELOCKED THE DOOR. Two locks. She saw me glance at the insulated wires leading from the door to a burglar alarm junction box almost concealed behind a Provençal cupboard. "All the windows are rigged, too," she told me. "The alarm bell is very loud, and the system connects to the local *gendarmerie* down the road."

The ground floor's main room spread all the way to the glass balcony doors. It was beginning to get the early afternoon sun. The furniture was pleasant but unpretentious. The kinds of nicely reconditioned pieces you can find in the better *brochantes*. But not the oriental rug. That must have cost more than everything else in the room put together.

"Mademoiselle Helen is upstairs working," Ferguson said as she led us through the main room and up a corkscrew staircase. "She has been doing as much of the interior restoration as she can herself. It is a way for her to expend excess nervous energy."

I thought of the more normal ways most good-looking girls her age let off their excess energies. On the other hand, I could think of quite a number of them who did it in ways that were much worse than Helen Marsh's.

She was up inside the square tower. It was a single large room with ceiling beams of old timber, filled with sunlight that came in through its two windows. One was the window from which Ferguson had seen Arlette and me coming up the street. The other looked across the valley to the green slopes and brownish gray cliffs on the other side, and beyond

110

that to the rugged mountain barrier along the frontier between France and Italy.

The tower room was bare of furniture except for an unpainted chair and an old kitchen table being used as a worktable. Plastic sheets protected the new flooring from the grime coming off the interior walls, which were of the same rough stones as the exterior. Helen Marsh was using a two-handed brush and a strong-smelling detergent to scrub a century's worth of encrusted soot from the walls. It was a job and a half, and she was putting all that excess energy into it. The area she was working on was almost down to the bare stone.

"There are easier and quicker ways to do that," I said as I came up off the stairway.

She paused in her work and looked at me, wiping sweat from her eyes with the back of her forearm. She was wearing thick canvas gloves. The left-hand one had the two empty fingers pinned back so they wouldn't dangle and interfere with her work. She didn't try to conceal that hand from me this time. Apparently the glove was concealment enough for her.

"I know," she told me, "but I don't want it to be quick or easy."

Her eyes were fastened on me, her body very tense, while she waited to hear what it was I'd come to tell her. I began by giving her everything that Fritz and I had turned up on Hulvane so far, taking each point in sequence. Halfway through it, she turned back to the wall and recommenced her dedicated scrubbing. She wasn't being impolite. She just couldn't continue to hold herself still while she waited for me to get to the punch line. There was only one thing about Hulvane that mattered to her. But I made her hear me out before giving it to her:

"What it adds up to is this. Hulvane is involved in some large-scale criminal activity right now. Probably narcotics smuggling. Almost certainly not connected in any way with your kidnapping. But he was in Europe at that time, and that's when he acquired a large amount of new money. That falls short, however, of being even circumstantial proof that he was one of your kidnappers.''

Helen Marsh had stopped her scrubbing. She continued to clutch the brush tightly with both hands when she turned to face me squarely.

''He *was*,'' she said, unshakably convinced of it.

''Because you remember his voice. From eight years ago. The voice with the German accent.''

''Yes.''

I didn't bother bringing up the fact that Hulvane was an American. We'd been over that the first time we'd met. She believed the German accent had been something he'd deliberately put on. And she might be right.

''Helen,'' Arlette said, ''before you make a decision, I have to make sure you know what it is costing you.'' She took my expense sheet from her briefcase. ''This is what it has already cost, in only two days.''

The girl looked at it. I didn't get the impression she was actually reading the numbers. Maybe she registered the total figure. She looked up from it and said, ''All right.'' Her tone was indifferent.

''That account is only a rough,'' I told her. ''It could go higher. You're entitled to a written explanation of each of the expenses. I'll get it to you when I have the final figures.''

''That's not necessary,'' Helen Marsh said impatiently. ''I trust you.''

''I'm pleased you trust me, but the thing to settle now is, do you want us to go on with it or drop it? Because that bill's just a starter, if you authorize us to continue the investigation. The cost may snowball drastically, and rapidly.''

''I accept that,'' she told me. ''And you *know* I want you to go on with it.''

I did know. But I had wanted it said in front of an attorney. I don't like getting stiffed. She wouldn't—but there were the trustees of her estate.

I looked at Arlette. She nodded. She would handle the trustees. Persuade them that the girl was determined to the point of desperation; and make sure they didn't start trying to renegotiate when they hit the bottom line.

I looked back to Helen Marsh. "One other thing I want to make sure you understand up front. If Hulvane was one of your kidnappers, it's extremely unlikely that we'll be able to prove it against him. If he had invested your ransom in a legitimate business there would be some hope. Maybe we could trace back the source of his investment money, and use that to pry the names of the other kidnappers out of him. But he put it into the illegal drug traffic. Those deals are strictly cash, no records. The investment, and its source, just disappears from sight."

She was looking at me steadily, and no longer impatiently. Listening to my tone as much as to what I was saying.

"Hulvane is a narcotics smuggler and probably a murderer as well," I said. "That makes him potentially vulnerable. But not for your kidnapping. I can't hold out any expectation of our being able to dredge up the evidence to nail him for that."

Helen Marsh took a long moment to analyze my words and tone. "I don't give a damn *what* those bastards are nailed *for*," she told me, with a controlled fire I hadn't heard from her before, "just so long as you do *nail* them. Hard—so they hurt and go on hurting. *I'll* know I'm the one who did it to them. Am I making myself clear enough?"

"It seems clear to me," I said, and I smiled at her.

She had read me correctly.

❈ **18** ❈

I USED THE TELEPHONE IN A ROOM THAT HAD BEEN MADE into a TV den on the floor below the tower. The window gave me a view of the cobbled street emerging from the tunnel under the house and climbing on to Gorbio's seventeenth-century church. There was a green Archimedes pump halfway up. One of mankind's simplest and oldest contraptions for getting water whenever needed from a deep source. Just spin the crank handle and its interior helix spirals it up. Invented more than two hundred years before Christ and still doing a reliable job of it in some of these backcountry communities. I admired it while waiting for Fritz to pick up his phone in Paris.

"We go on with it," I told him.

"In that case, your friend Sylvane's efforts on our behalf were not wasted. She phoned me an hour ago. Hulvane made his call this morning from Munich. The Vier Jahreszeiten."

"The best hotel in town," I said. "He's sticking to form."

"No, not this time. He made the call from the hotel bar. He paid for it, and for the bottle of wine and snacks for himself and a man he met there, with cash. According to the staff, he is not staying at the hotel. Under any name. They don't know him there; nor the man he was with. They say he spoke excellent German, for a foreigner."

"But they could spot the American accent."

"They say he does have an accent," Fritz told me. "But they are certain the accent is French."

114

"They think he's a Frenchman?" I said slowly, trying to get a grip on it.

"Yes."

Alice had problems similar to mine on the other side of the looking glass. Hulvane kept getting curiouser and curiouser.

I said, "You got all this pretty fast. Nice work."

"Munich *is* my hometown," Fritz said without pleasure. "I do still have a few contacts there. I have asked them to try to find out if there are people in Munich who remember Hulvane from his time there just after the war."

"Good thought. He might still be in touch with some of them. He might even be staying with one of them now."

"Or at any of fifty other Munich hotels and guesthouses. In which case, we can't track him down there until we find out what name he is using. Now that we've been authorized to continue the investigation, I can get to work on solving that problem."

"There won't have been many flights from Paris to Munich between last evening and this morning."

"Exactly," Fritz said. "And if Hulvane flew first-class, which he probably did, that will narrow it down even more. I'll drive out and give Hulvane's pictures to our security contacts at the Paris airports. So they can show them to the cabin crews who worked those flights, when they return."

Once a flight attendant from the plane Hulvane had taken remembered him from the photos, they should be able to work out what seat he'd been given. The seat assignment would give us the name he'd used.

Fritz said, "I'll also have the Paris airport security people fax the pictures to the Munich airport. Hulvane's cabin crew may be shifted to other flights from there."

"Or they might be on their time off. It could be two or three days before those photos get us what we want."

"No need for us to twiddle our thumbs while we wait, my boy. I had another call from Jacob McKissack half an hour ago. Hulvane's former partner in the art business, Lawrence Tuck, recently sent a picture postcard to a friend in New York. The Genoa address you have for him remains valid.

He still doesn't have a telephone, though. But from where you are, you can easily drive there in a couple hours."

"About that," I agreed. "Depends on Italy's autostrada traffic. While I'm doing that, why don't you go up to Schleswig-Holstein and find out if the police there ever turned up anything new about the kidnapping, in the eight years since."

"I've already made a reservation on the next flight to Hamburg," Fritz told me, in a voice that had gotten a hard edge to it. "On the assumption that Mademoiselle Marsh would hardly be likely to let the investigation drop at this stage."

Making the point that he was not yet so old that he needed me to tell him how to tie his shoelaces.

The West German state of Schleswig-Holstein doesn't have a commercial airport of its own. But Kiel, its capital, is only an hour's drive from Hamburg, using a rented car. Kiel would have the basic reports on the kidnapping investigation. After studying those, it wouldn't take Fritz long to drive wherever necessary to any cop who might have thoughts on the case that weren't in the dossier. No part of Schleswig-Holstein is more than an hour from Kiel.

Fritz dropped his stiff father-figure tone as he told me that, while he was away, airport security would notify Olivier Sougmanac if Hulvane's photos got identified. Olivier was our Paris dentist. We'd first gotten to know him through his younger brother, Laurent, a cop in Nice. In addition to becoming our dentist, he was now among the sharpest of Fritz's regular chess opponents. Fritz and I also agreed to use Olivier to let each other know what we were doing and where we could be reached. Starting with a call that night, and another next morning.

There was no way I could anticipate that by that night I would be in no condition to do so.

My next call was to my mother's office in Paris. I had called her apartment and her office before leaving Paris, but Babette hadn't been at either place. She had, however, grudgingly given in at last to the relentless forward march of the real world and installed an answering machine in her office. The message she'd left on it was that she would be back there in the early afternoon—but that she was working and didn't want to be disturbed unless it was *absolutely essential*.

Nothing personal. It wasn't aimed at me, in particular. If the president of the republic called, Babette would expect him to get the same message and take it seriously. My mother is not the soul of tact.

What she was working on at the moment was the final chapters of a book she'd been writing for several years. On symbolism in Romanesque art. But whatever she had worked on, during my long experience with her, she had never taken kindly to anything interrupting it. Unless it was a fellow art historian bringing her some information she'd been seeking. Which was why, when I'd been a kid, she'd sent me off to spend each school year with my father's parents in Chicago. And why, most of the time, I'd been pleased to go.

I don't want to give the impression Babette is an ogre. She's just preoccupied. There's a good heart inside that still magnificent bosom. I've seen her turn positively girlish around men who were in the Resistance with her. And I've seen the delighted way they cluster around her during their gatherings, still calling her "Baby"—her code name as a very young freedom fighter. She can be genuinely affectionate toward me; especially whenever she takes a good look and realizes I'm the spitting image of the father who died before I was born. That she loved him passionately is obvious. Maybe she still does.

I'd just learned to accept, long ago, that Babette had a relaxed—some would call it detached—view of motherhood.

You had to take Babette as you found her. And not try to take too much of her.

I had told her answering machine that I would be calling back, and that I wanted to know if she'd ever met Benjamin Hulvane or Lawrence Tuck. It was not unlikely. The professional art world is claustrophobic. Art dealers and gallery owners, big and small, spend a great deal of their time attending functions where they can meet and butter up authorities in the field. The endorsement of an old artwork as authentic, by one of Babette's prestige, is worth a lot of butter.

Her answering machine didn't pick up on the third ring, as it had before, so she was there. But she didn't pick up either. I let it go on ringing, and waited it out. Babette would be too deep inside herself, at first, to even hear it. When she did hear it, she would try to ignore it and hope the caller would get discouraged and quit. I didn't. On the eighteenth ring she picked it up.

"Yes?" A surgeon caught at the crucial stage of a delicate operation would have used the same tone.

I told her it was her beloved son and asked if she'd given any thought to my message.

"For God's sake, Pierre-Ange, I'm *busy*. What message?" She didn't sound nasty, just harried. I repeated the message to her and she broke into the middle of it: "Yes, yes—I remember now. This Benjamin Hulvane, I never heard of. I did meet Lawrence Tuck once. During a long and otherwise boring cocktail party. An unusually handsome man."

She stopped with that. I said, "Handsome is a start. What else can you tell me about him?"

"Nothing, really. He was very ingratiating. Pleasantly flattering. He had a fairly good knowledge of art, which is not that common among art dealers. That's what he was, in a small way. Ambitious to become much bigger, of course. Obviously he didn't, or I would have heard of him again. And I doubt that he is still handsome. This was years ago, and he drank far too much. Now, if you'll let me get back to work . . ."

She didn't have anything else for me. But it might be enough. If she'd found him handsome, she had probably treated him nicely. The memory of it might be a useful softening wedge in getting him to be open about Hulvane.

I thanked Babette and was preparing to hang up when she suddenly asked: "Pierre-Ange—do you love me?"

It shocked me. "What?"

"Do you love me?" she repeated, in a softer, untypically worried tone.

"Of course I love you," I told her.

"I mean, *really* love me?"

"Really," I assured her. "What's the matter with you, Babette?"

"A friend of mind died yesterday," she said. "She was two years younger than me. I suddenly realized—I'm not going to be around forever, either."

"Yes you are," I told her firmly. "Go back to work."

When I put down the phone, I found myself smiling but at the same time experiencing a touch of the regret that hits when you get a reminder of passing time—and the stretches of it that were misspent because they left no memories worth dwelling on.

I decided my drive to Genoa could wait a few hours.

Arlette and I bought the makings of a picnic meal before leaving Gorbio. Goat cheese and black olives. Hard-boiled eggs and country pâté. A loaf of fresh-baked bread and a bottle of local rosé. We drove west to have our lazy picnic in the wooded, sun-drenched hills behind Nice.

We left the car near the bottom of the Paillon river gorge and climbed high up a green slope full of wildflowers. I spread a blanket I'd brought from the car, and we settled down on it and ate while watching a shepherd and his flock of sheep work their way down another slope. There were a lot of babies among the flock, and it moved slowly. The shepherd had two dogs. One of them, a fast, smart mongrel, raced back and forth in response to whistled signals from the shepherd. The other looked like a pit bull, and it strolled around behind the flock, doing its job of guarding the rear against any of the wild dogs that sometimes attacked lagging newborns.

When the flock was lost to sight we had the gorge to ourselves. We finished off the wine lazily and took our time undressing each other, deliberately prolonging the growing urgency, and made love to each other as the urgency took control and would tolerate no further waiting. With the umbrella pines above us against a pale blue sky. With the ghost of a half-moon off in one direction and a blazing golden sun in the other. The fragrance of Arlette mingled with the scent of the wild lavender and honeysuckle, myrtle and jasmine, that were crushed underneath us.

Garden of Eden—before the serpent.

❖ 19 ❖

BY THE TIME I'D TAKEN ARLETTE BACK TO HER OFFICE AND driven across the Italian border on my way to Genoa, Fritz Donhoff's Lufthansa flight from Paris had landed him at Hamburg's airport. He rented a car there and drove north into Schleswig-Holstein, the German part of the long peninsula that separates the North Sea from the Baltic—which Germany calls the Ostsee. Fritz took the number seven autobahn most of the way to Kiel, situated halfway between Hamburg and the narrowest point of the peninsula, where it becomes Danish Jutland.

The countryside he drove through stayed lovely without ever becoming spectacular. Flat farmlands and pastures grazed by innumerable cows. Patches of woodland and a lot of water from the seas on both sides. Rivers, streams, lakes, and low-banked fjords. Small, pretty towns that were quite old but so spotlessly clean they looked like Disney replicas. None of the stores in these towns were open. Because, although it was still bright daylight, it was a little past six o'clock in the evening. By law, no more shopping would be available until next morning.

Except at gas stations. There you could buy items like cigarettes, packaged foods, magazines, and even toys and socks. The strict early-closing law made an exception for gas stations. In a country where the export of cars accounted for a sizable portion of the national income, and where people saved their money, with a determination that verged on obsession, to rise from the humbling ownership of a Volkswagen to the prestige of a Mercedes, the automobile was king, and those who served it shared in its majesty.

Government offices adhere to the regulation of the general closing hour. But Fritz's Interpol friend had arranged the appointment for him, by phone, and had made it a high-priority request. The man Fritz was to meet—Franz Regnault, an attorney who'd been a high official with the Schleswig-Holstein police for over a decade—had agreed to wait for him after hours, in front of his ministry. With the dossier on the Helen Marsh kidnapping case.

But when Fritz arrived at the closed ministry, there was no one in sight who looked like an attorney serving in an important government position. Germans do tend to match their dress and manner to their rank. Fritz went up the steps to a uniformed policeman on guard outside the entrance. The cop was young, with a big, strong build and intelligent, observant eyes. It struck Fritz that he himself had looked much like that when he'd been a young cop. He experienced a twinge of nostalgia as he explained about his appointment there.

"Herr Doktor Regnault instructed me to sincerely apologize to you for him," the cop said, stiffening to attention. Anyone rating a sincere apology from Herr Doktor Regnault was clearly someone to be treated with respect. "His son became ill. He had to pick up his wife and hurry off to his son's home."

He gave Fritz a slip of paper with an address on it. "Herr Doktor Regnault regrets the inconvenience, but he asks if it is possible for you to meet him there. It is not far."

Fritz thanked him and returned to his car. He drove northwest over the cross-peninsula Kiel Canal to the small city of Schleswig, believed to be the oldest in this part of Germany. Vikings from the Baltic Sea established settlements there while hauling their boats across the peninsula to the North Sea for their raids on the British and French coasts.

Fritz had been there before, long ago. The town's old center hadn't changed much and wasn't big enough to get lost in. He parked behind St. Peter's Cathedral and walked through the Altstadt quarter. It was virtually deserted. Good citizens were inside their homes finishing their dinners and fastening themselves to their television sets. Fritz turned into the brick-paved Süderholmstrasse, a relic of the past that showed none of the ravages of age. There was no litter. Its gray bricks were damp from its daily scrubbing.

Süderholmstrasse brought him to a small square that had been turned into an immaculate cemetery. Brightly shined tombstones, neatly trimmed hedges, profusions of colorful flowering plants. The address of Franz Regnault's son was one of the tidy little houses surrounding the cemetery square. They'd once been fishermen's cottages. Time and money had been spent on their pristine condition. Every facade was fastidiously painted. Not a single tile was out of place on any of their gabled roofs.

It was Regnault who responded to Fritz's knock on the polished door. A trim, good-looking man in his mid-fifties. He was still dressed for the office. A sober, well-cut blue suit, of a lightweight material that held its press. A conservative necktie with a discreet stripe. His eyes, though, revealed a sharp sense of humor that, Fritz guessed, must require constant repression in the man's role as a no-nonsense functionary. It was in Regnault's voice, too: "I am truly sorry you had to make this extra drive, Herr Donhoff. My son's young wife has a tendency to exaggerate small problems. And my own wife, though no longer so young, is easily alarmed."

Instead of inviting Fritz in, he stepped outside with him, carrying a heavy briefcase. "It will be easier to concentrate on the dossier elsewhere. The house is very small and full of nervous women. My wife, my son's wife, her mother and sister."

"I hope your son's condition is not serious," Fritz said as they strolled away from the house.

"Not serious enough to justify all the fuss that was made, prematurely. It proved to be a simple case of appendicitis. And not an emergency. The doctor is arranging for his appendix to be removed tomorrow morning."

Regnault turned them in to a grassy lane, with a wide expanse of water in sight beyond its far end. "Do you mind my asking,'' he said casually, ''what your job is at Interpol?''

What he was after, Fritz knew, was their relative positions on the social ladder. It was automatic when two Germans met for the first time: learning which one outranked the other.

''We're not part of Interpol,'' Fritz told him, deliberately vague. ''We do work with them at times.'' He didn't explain the ''we''—allowing Regnault, if he wished, to guess he was part of an intelligence service or some other branch of French government.

Regnault gave him a sidelong smile, surprisingly impish. ''I see,'' he said. Realizing that Fritz was avoiding giving him a clear answer, but not minding too much. ''I was told you have been a French citizen since the war, but you still have a strong Bavarian accent.''

''And you,'' Fritz countered, ''are German, but you have a French name.''

''My ancestors were probably among the Huguenots who fled to Germany in the seventeenth century, to escape the murderous prejudice against the Protestants in France. And almost exactly three hundred years later, I assume, you had to escape in the opposite direction, for much the same reason.''

Regnault hadn't *entirely* given up fishing for what Fritz Donhoff was.

''Not quite,'' Fritz said. ''I am not a Jew, so I can't claim to have been the victim of prejudice. It was a simpler matter. I hated the Nazis, and they hated my attitude.''

''It must take a great deal of courage to give up one's native land for one's personal morality.''

''Not great courage, Herr Regnault. Great disgust.''

Regnault looked at him thoughtfully. ''I was only a boy at that time. Too young, thank God, to either take part in the Nazi insanity or to test my own personal courage and disgust against it. Yet, oddly, it is my generation that feels the most responsible for those gruesome horrors that were committed with such Germanic efficiency and attention to detail.''

Fritz nodded. ''The generation before yours—my generation—pretends it was not aware of what was being done around them." It took an effort for him to speak that frankly. Being back inside Germany always made him feel emotionally constipated. There were so few Germans with whom he could let his guard down. Too often he became grouchy under the self-imposed restraint.

"And among the generations after mine," Regnault was saying, "so many pretend to believe the horrors committed in Hitler's name never happened. Revisionist history, they call it. Sometimes I am not sure who bears the most guilt. The sadistic creatures who carried out the inhuman crimes, or those who failed to oppose them, or those who now ignore what it taught us about how deep a cultured people can sink into the slime."

He waited for a response from Fritz, but Fritz said nothing. Though he found himself liking Franz Regnault, habit prevented him from opening himself to him.

Regnault looked at him again, curious. "You have never regreted quitting your Fatherland—becoming its enemy?"

"Never."

They reached the edge of the water. Where the Schlei, a long, inland arm of the Baltic, spread out and reached its end. There was a café-restaurant called Der Alte Wiking facing the Schlei. It had an outside terrace, a wooden deck extending partly over the water. Franz Regnault led the way up five wooden steps to it.

The deck was painted a dark green. The tables and chairs were white. The tables were empty except for one where two fat men sat over large steins of beer and stared at each other in sleepy silence. Four steins they'd already emptied were arranged together like a miniature fortress in the precise center of their table. The ones the men had in front of them were covered with coasters, to keep out wasps that were trying to get at the beer inside. As Fritz glanced their way, both men removed the coasters and drank deeply. As soon as they set their steins down, they put the coasters back on top.

"Damn wasps," Regnault said. "The whole region has been infested with them this summer. Also an incredible number of ladybugs. In some parts of the countryside, they are so many it is impossible to walk without crushing them underfoot. But the wasps and ladybugs are not the worst. Come and look.'' He walked to the deck's edge and pointed at the water.

Fritz, coming up beside him, didn't see what he meant at first. Then he did. Just below the surface floated shiny, semi-transparent discs. Thousands of them. So close together in places that they seemed parts of a single marine entity.

"Medusas," Regnault said. "Jellyfish. I went by ferry-boat across the Ostsee for an official meeting two weeks ago. All the water, from the German coast to Denmark, is filled with them. Pollution is killing off everything else in the sea, but these things thrive on it.''

"Perhaps," Fritz said, "they are destined to inherit the world.''

"If they do, we will deserve it. Come, let us go inside. No wasps in there.''

"If you are needed at your son's house," Fritz said, "I can read the dossier alone here, and phone you there when I have finished it.''

"I'm not *needed*. My wife would like me to stand around there acting as anxious as she and the other women. To prove my concern. I don't care to be pushed into an attitude I don't feel.'' Regnault sighed, and then laughed softly. "Women. You are married, Herr Donhoff?''

"I was," Fritz said.

The way he said it made it evident to someone as percep-tive as Regnault that the marriage hadn't ended in divorce. "Your wife died?''

"Yes.''

"I am very sorry," Regnault said; and his sympathy sounded genuine.

He probably assumed from Fritz's look and tone that the death was recent. But the girl Fritz had married in Paris during the war had been killed in 1944. Beaten to death by Gestapo agents trying to wring the location of Fritz's hideout from her. I was one of the very few who knew about her. Even between us, the subject was never discussed. Nor did I ever ask him why, in spite of his great fondness for women, he had never married again.

There were dozens of wasps clinging to the café's screen door. Regnault opened it swiftly, and shut it just as swiftly after they were inside. The Old Viking's interior was a pleasant haven. Glossy woodwork, old-fashioned lamps, deep padded booths. As they settled into a booth the proprietor came hurrying over to greet them, brushing past a stout waitress.

"Herr Doktor! I am honored. How may I serve you?" His German had a Greek accent.

"Have you had your dinner?" Regnault asked Fritz.

"No."

"If you wait until the French hour for dining, you will find most of the restaurants in this region closed. I suggest you eat while you go through the dossier. The food here is good."

The proprietor beamed. Fritz opened the menu and ordered a *Lebernudelsuppe* to start with. The proprietor recommended that he follow that with salmon grilled in butter and chives: "You will find the taste delicious."

"I *don't* recommend it," Regnault told Fritz. "It is Ostsee salmon. Contaminated."

The Greek proprietor looked unhappy, but did not contradict Regnault. Fritz ordered *Schweinbraten* for his main course. Knowing the meat would be a large portion, accompanied by heaping amounts of applesauce, roast potatoes, and baked bananas. A heavy meal. But there were some things German that he did sometimes miss in France.

"I will only have some wine," Regnault told the proprietor, and looked to Fritz. Fritz nodded, and Regnault ordered a bottle of The Old Viking's best *Rotwein*. Then he opened the briefcase he'd put down beside him, and brought out the thick police dossier on the Helen Marsh kidnapping.

Fritz took it from him and asked, "Were you personally involved in this case, Herr Regnault?"

"I was put in charge of the investigation after the girl was found. I can answer any questions you have about what is in the dossier. Although after eight years, I admit I had to glance through it myself to refresh my memory."

Their wine arrived. Regnault tasted and nodded. Fritz sipped and approved. When the proprietor went away, Regnault said, "If you in France have turned up some new development in the case, I would appreciate being informed of it."

"So far it is too nebulous," Fritz told him. "And will probably prove to be nothing at all connected to the kidnapping. If it should harden into a real possibility, I will notify you." He got out his monocle, opened the dossier, and began flipping through its pages from the start.

The dossier's bulk didn't faze him. Fritz was used to police reports, knew what to ignore and what to pause over. Most of the pages he skimmed through in a couple seconds. Now and then he came across information that was news to him. But none of it bore on our own investigation. Like the fact that the German Federal Interior Ministry had quietly lent the Schleswig-Hostein police a team from its counterterrorist unit, the GSG 9, well before Helen Marsh was found. In case her kidnapping turned into a hostage situation. When that didn't happen, the GSG 9 team had been withdrawn with the same lack of publicity that had covered its being sent.

Fritz's soup came. He positioned the dossier behind it, propped against a folded napkin, and continued to flip and skim while he ate. Regnault sipped his wine, smoked menthol-flavored low-nicotine cigarettes, and watched him with no betrayal of impatience.

Fritz had gone through half of the dossier by the time he finished his hefty main course. His belt was beginning to dig into his stomach, but he couldn't resist ordering something more that was unavailable in France: a *Rote Grütze* for dessert. He was savoring the delicious fruit compote and its fresh cream when he came across what was to prove the only item of real interest to him in the entire dossier.

It concerned two men who had been found dead, eleven days after the kidnapped Helen Marsh had been recovered, under a sand dune on a long stretch of Schleswig-Holstein beach between Laboe and Todendorf. A storm wind from the Baltic had shifted the dune's base, uncovering their bodies. Each of the men had been shot twice. Once in the chest, once in the head.

Their fingerprints and a detailed report on their dental work had been forwarded to both the German Federal police and to Interpol. It was Interpol that had eventually come through with the identities of the two men. Both were Italian and wanted by the police in Italy.

Fritz took out his notebook and carefully copied down their names. There was nothing else on them in the police report. Only a reference, at the bottom, to another numbered dossier. Fritz asked Regnault about this.

"That is in this dossier," Regnault explained after crushing his cigarette in the ashtray, "only because these two murdered men were Italian. And because Helen Marsh told us—when she recovered enough to speak coherently, quite some time after those bodies were found—that her three kidnappers spoke Italian among themselves. It seemed possible these had been two of them. Killed by the third one so he wouldn't have to share the ransom with them. But we never turned up even the slightest confirmation that they were connected to the kidnapping. So finally everything relating to their murder—a case which remains unsolved—was left in a separate dossier. A very thin one. I can show it to you tomorrow, if you wish. But I am sure I remember the few pertinent facts in it."

"Please tell me."

"The two murdered Italians were middle-aged men who had belonged, since their youth, to various neo-Fascist groups." Regnault shrugged. "It is not only among us Germans that there are some with a nostalgia for the days when sadists were officially encouraged to brutalize the helpless."

Fritz nodded. "In France a few nights ago, some of them entered a Carpentras cemetery, dug up the corpse of an eighty-year-old Jew who had died two weeks before, impaled his body with a beach umbrella, and left on his chest a Star of David torn from his coffin."

"I read about that," Regnault said with a grimace of contempt. "I also noticed that Le Pen, the chief of your shameless Front National party, made a point of disclaiming any responsibility for it. He was meeting, at the time, with one of our own more flagrant neo-Nazi politicians. Franz Shoenhuber—an arrogant former member of the Waffen-SS that killed babies with the same enthusiasm that it devoted to the torture and murder of helpless adults consigned to their concentration camps.''

Regnault sighed and leaned back, looking at Fritz with a crooked smile. ''Obviously, I am trusting that you will not repeat my inflammatory opinions to others.'' He thought about that, and then shook his head. ''No, perhaps I am secretly hoping that you will. I have been a government official for so very long. I am good at it, but I have never been able to shake off a belief that I was born to be an impoverished artist. Ignored in my own time, like Van Gogh, but adulated by future generations.''

Fritz eased him back to the subject: ''What did the Italian police want the two dead men for?''

''They were charged with taking part in a number of terrorist killings in and around Genoa.''

Fritz repeated the city's name quietly: *''Genoa . . .''*

''Yes. That is where they were from.''

Fritz got out of the booth and asked the proprietor if he could use Der Alte Wiking's telephone for a call to France. ''I'll have the operator call back with the charges so I can pay you immediately.''

Franz Regnault countermanded the offer: ''I'll pay for the call. And charge it to the ministry. We like to exchange favors with Interpol. And even with men like yourself, Herr Donhoff, who prefer to remain vague about what you are, but have Interpol's cooperation.''

Fritz called Olivier Sougmanac, our mutual contact in Paris. Olivier told him he still hadn't heard anything on Hulvane from airport security. And that I hadn't called him yet from Genoa. Fritz told Olivier about the two Italians from Genoa who'd been found dead under the dune not far from where Helen Marsh had been kidnapped.

''Pass this on to Pierre-Ange when he calls,'' Fritz said. ''And tell him to be *extremely* careful down there.''

I wondered later if it would have made any difference in what happened to me in Genoa if I had gotten that message in time.

But I decided it wouldn't have changed any of it.

❖ 20 ❖

OF ALL THE EUROPEAN CITIES I'VE KNOWN, GENOA IS ONE of the easiest for a driver to get lost in. Especially around the Porto Vecchio's tangle of railroad tracks, freight sheds, waterfront bars, pizza parlors, strip joints, and construction cranes. My having been there before, and the city map I'd bought from an autostrada service station, were not all that much help. Night and the scarcity of street signs compounded the complexity as I drove uphill from the dock area, on my third try at finding my way to the part of the medieval quarter where Lawrence Tuck lived.

This time I got it right. I was only a few short blocks from his address when the crooked streets became too narrow for a car to go any farther. I left my car against the side of a slum tenement, walked around a collection of overflowing garbage cans in front of the timeworn palazzo next to it, and joined the moving crowd. In the evenings, Italians take to their streets. Strolling and talking. Sitting outside cafés and talking. Standing in clusters and talking. Their voices reverberated between the closely spaced walls.

Genoa was having a hot night. I took off my jacket and held it close in front of me. In Italian cities the most cherubic-looking kids can turn out to be accomplished pickpockets. I reached a tiny piazza where three alleylike streets met. According to my map, the widest one was the one I wanted, but I couldn't find its name sign.

There were two open stands on the piazza. One selling secondhand magazines and paperbacks, the other dispensing

131

espressos and ice cream cones. I showed the address on my slip of paper to a young man who'd just bought a double-decker vanilla cone, and asked for his help. My command of Italian was rudimentary and my pronunciation slipshod, but the Italians are a kindly people who will make the mental effort necessary to understand a fumbling foreigner. Unlike most of the French in big cities. He pointed into the street I'd thought was it, and told me it would be the third house on my right. He held up three fingers to make sure I understood, and gestured to the right with his ice cream cone. I thanked him and we smiled and nodded on parting.

Beside the doorway of the third house on my right, a middle-aged man and woman sat against a scabby wall with shredding political party posters exhorting citizens to vote for them in an election that had been held a year ago. The woman was knitting and the man was drinking wine from a chipped cup with a broken-off handle. Slowly and carefully, I told them I was looking for an American named Lawrence Tuck.

They looked at me with suspicion—and what seemed like distaste. The woman said, "Lorenzo is not here. He is working."

"When will he come home from work?" I asked.

"In the morning," she told me. Definitely not friendly.

"He works all night?"

"All night. Yes."

"Where?"

"If you do not know that," she demanded, "what do you want with him?"

The man spoke for the first time, in halting English: "You are American, too?" When I said I was, he said, "You know Lorenzo from there—America?"

"My mother knows him," I said. "She knew I was coming to Genoa, and she asked me to say hello to him for her."

"Ah!" the man said, and dropped his suspicious scowl. He translated what I'd said to the woman, and she, too, exchanged the scowl for a warm smile.

In a country where even the Church is regarded with a growing cynicism, "Mother" is still a sacred word. An

American bearing a message from his mother could not be a threat.

It relaxed the woman, but something still worried her. She spoke to the man in rapid Italian. By concentrating hard, I made out the gist of what she said: that it would embarrass "Lorenzo"—Lawrence Tuck—if the son of an old friend found him at his work.

The man nodded and rose politely to his feet as he spoke to me again in English. "Lorenzo is our cousin," he said. "He lives with us. Come back tomorrow. He will be here. Not early. Lorenzo sleeps late."

"I won't be here tomorrow," I told him. "I'm just passing through Genoa. By morning I'll be gone." He continued to look reticent, but I took the city map out of my jacket and said, "Please tell where I can find him now. *Per favore.* My mother will be very unhappy if I have to say I was here and didn't say hello to your cousin for her."

He sighed, and reluctantly studied my map. "You have a car?"

"Near here."

He pointed out the place where we were, and then trailed his finger across the map while he explained the best way to drive to where Lawrence Tuck was. The woman watched with frowning disapproval. They were arguing in heated, rapid-fire Italian when I walked away, back in the direction of my car.

The place where I'd been told I could find Lawrence Tuck was in one of the streets off Via XX Settembre's stretch of department stores and skyscrapers. High above the medieval quarter, both physically and financially. I found a parking space directly across from a neon-lit commercial arcade that bore the name I was looking for.

It was almost as hot up there on the hill as it had been down below. I slung my jacket over my shoulder, holding on to its collar with one hand, and started to cross the street. A sporty red and black Yamaha motorcycle came roaring along the street in my direction. Its driver and the guy riding behind him wore bubble-style crash helmets that concealed their heads and faces. The rider reached out and grabbed my jacket as the Yamaha whipped past me. But by then I had tightened my own grip on it.

The snatcher's pull jerked my arm out full length. The jacket didn't have much stretch to it. I didn't let go, and neither did he. I was almost yanked off my feet. He was yanked off the motorcycle and hit the street awkwardly on his back and side, with a heavy thump and a shrill squeal of agony. I heard the crunch of bones breaking, but the helmet saved him from getting his head cracked open.

"Son of a bitch!" I yelled, more at my own carelessness than at him.

The Yamaha sped away and disappeared around the next corner. The snatcher lurched to his feet and staggered after it, his right arm dangling uselessly. I let him go. Our account was settled. I had my jacket and he had a smashed shoulder.

From just inside the arcade an American voice called out, "Beautiful! That's mighty fast reflexes you've got there, friend."

I carried my jacket into the arcade and looked at him. A tallish, very skinny guy somewhere in his sixties. Impossible to judge if that was low, high, or middle sixties. Too much of the degeneration was the result of dissipation, not age. He wore a flowery sport shirt hanging over newly pressed blue denim trousers. His brown saddle shoes had a good shine. He had thick, dull-white hair, carefully combed. His face must once have reminded people of a young Cary Grant, but it had become emaciated and blurred, furrowed like a badly plowed field.

He sat at an arcade table outside a place called the Honolulu Bar, toying with a tall, dark drink, his scrawny neck stretched by the tilt of his head as he looked up at me with eyes that had an unnatural brightness. The yellow and blue neon from the bar splashed across him and the two young women sharing his table, combining with the arcade shadows to give them a dreamlike unreality.

One of the women was a slinky blonde. The crimson outfit she wore looked like silk pajamas. The shiny silk clung to her pointy breasts. She gave me a tempting smile, and held it as though she were waiting to have her picture taken.

The one on the other side of him wore a halter and hot pants that advertised her much fuller figure. In five years she might be getting fat, but right now the only word for her body was voluptuous. There was a pantherish strength in the way she sat there, one heel hooked on the seat of her chair, the other leg stretched out on another chair. The panther was in her expression, too. Her hair and eyes were as black as Arlette's. She had a strong nose and a wide, sullen mouth, her plump lips parting slightly to reveal the gleam of her teeth. She wasn't a smiler. Her look smouldered, with as much threat of destruction as promise of paradise in it.

I had to clamp down on an instant reaction to her. The itch in the palms and tingle in the groin. She was a woman a man could get hooked on very quickly, and as badly as on heroin.

It helped to look away from her, back to the man. I said, "You Lawrence Tuck?"

"That's me, friend. You can call me Larry, being a fellow American and all." His voice was harsh, as if he'd burned out much of his throat. He gestured at an empty chair across from him. "Sit down, relax."

I managed to avoid looking at the panther again as I settled into the chair.

Tuck grinned at me. "You're starting off my business evening earlier than usual. Not that I mind, and I guess you don't either." He waved a bony hand at the two women. "Take your pick. Or both. You're in luck. These are my very best."

That was why his cousins had been embarrassed to send me where he worked. They didn't want me—and my mother—to find out he'd become a pimp.

"Or I can introduce you to some others," Tuck said, "if you need to see all the merchandise before making up your mind. But the price goes up the more I got to work at it. And while we're talking price, who sent you to me? I got to split with whoever steered you."

"I'm not whore-hunting," I told him. "I'm a private detective. I want to talk to you about a man you used to work with. Benjamin Hulvane.''

"If you're not business," he snapped, "get lost. I got no time for nonsense. I have a living to earn here. Fuck off.''

"Be more careful with that mouth," I snapped back. "I'm not all that tolerant with bankrupt art dealers that wind up as drunken flesh peddlers.''

Tuck let out a laugh that sounded more like a cough. "Wrong on one count, friend." He raised his tall glass. "Just Coca-Cola. I'm not a drunk anymore. Now I gobble down pills instead. In great quantity. Nobody seems to mind that as much as alcohol, and I guess it won't kill me any quicker.''

I eased my own tone: "My mother asked me to give you her regards.''

Tuck stared at me blankly. "Your mother?''

"Babette Onimus." Though she'd given me my father's family name, Babette had kept her own.

His eyes almost closed. He put down his glass. "Madame Onimus is your mother?''

"Yep. I spoke to her on the phone today. Told her I might be seeing you. She remembers you well. She told me you were a very charming and handsome man.''

"Charming and handsome," he repeated softly, and with some pain. "Yes, perhaps I was. . . . '' His speech had suddenly become that of a cultured man, with the jovial tough-guy veneer peeled away. "My God—that was long ago. I remember I was so proud to meet her—the woman who'd written such distinguished works on art. How is she?''

"Fine. Working on a new book. Romanesque symbolism.''

"With a mother like that, how in the world did you end up in such a seamy profession? A private eye—good Lord.''

"Against her will," I said. "But she's finally accepted me for what I am. A reprobate son.''

"Aren't we all. . . . '' Tuck motioned for his two hookers to go inside the bar and leave us alone. They obeyed lazily, without a word.

An old Jamal tape had begun playing in there. Its music drifted out to join the other echoes in the arcade. The footsteps of people passing through. And the listless chatter of six teenagers gathered around two tables they'd pulled together. Three boys and three girls. With beautiful, bored faces, badly scuffed leather jackets, and dungarees that were ripped and frayed. Rich kids into the fashion for paying a lot to dress like the poor, in a way that let everyone know they weren't. The poor repair their old clothes, as inconspicuously as possible.

Tuck sipped from his glass and asked what I wanted to drink. I said I could use an espresso. He called in for it and took a longer drag at his Coca-Cola. The physical act of drinking seemed to soothe him almost as much as hard liquor once had. Or maybe he'd laced the drink with some of his pills.

"Your mother," he reminisced, "was a remarkably handsome woman when I met her."

"Still is," I told him. "Babette has that strong bone structure, the kind that holds the face and figure pretty much the same over the years. And she's lucky enough to have good basic health."

"Which she doesn't abuse," Tuck murmured, and fingered his own withered cheek.

My espresso arrived. I dropped in sugar, stirred, and sipped. It was very strong, jolting me out of the lassitude of a long day. "Tell me about Hulvane," I said.

✵ 21 ✵

Tuck swallowed more of his drink. "Ben Hulvane," he said slowly and with distaste. "That was long ago. Several lifetimes. What is the bastard up to now?"

"That's what I'm trying to find out," I said.

"Well, I'll predict one thing. When you find out what he is doing, it will be something nasty, done without any scruples and without giving a damn how much he hurts other people dumb enough to trust him. Ben Hulvane is a conniving rat, without a trace of conscience."

"But you became his partner."

"I didn't know what he was really like, until he did me in." Tuck finished off his Coca-Cola and called into the bar for another. I watched him take three small envelopes from the pocket of his sport shirt. He extracted one pill from each. A yellow, a white, and a blue. But he didn't crush them into his drink when it arrived. He popped the pills in his mouth and swallowed them with the aid of his first swig.

"How'd you meet Hulvane?" I asked him.

"That happened right here, in Genoa. Almost two years after the end of World War Two. I had just opened a little art gallery in New York, with money inherited from my parents. They died young, an automobile accident."

It made me speculate whether that had given Hulvane the idea for the way his own parents were killed later, in California.

"I came over to Europe looking for art for my gallery," Tuck said. "There was a lot of it on the loose in Europe at that time. Some of it available at rock-bottom prices, from people in one sort of trouble or another. I used Genoa as my base because my mother had made sure I knew Italian, and she had family here. Uncles, aunts, cousins . . .''

''I met two of your cousins,'' I said. ''The ones you live with.''

''They were just kids, the first time I came over. I didn't pay much attention to them. Thank God they have more family feeling than I had. When I came back here, a couple of years ago, in bad shape, they took me in without hesitation. I couldn't even pay them any rent at first. I do now, of course. They don't like how I earn it. But they can't afford to refuse it.''

A well-dressed middle-aged man with a sad face had strolled into the arcade and taken up a stance against the arcade wall across from us, his hands in his pockets. Tuck looked over at him, and the man nodded without altering his sad expression.

Tuck stood up. ''This will only take a minute,'' he told me, and crossed the arcade. The man took one hand out of his pocket. There was money in it. Tuck took it from him, counted it, and folded it into his own pocket. After a few words between them, Tuck came back across the arcade and went into the Honolulu Bar. When he came out the hookers were with him.

As they walked toward the waiting man, another man wandered into the arcade and stopped, glancing around. A lean man wearing a flight jacket, tight jeans, and combat boots. He had short-cropped gray hair and a small, pointy nose. I gave him a little attention because his glance took in Tuck and the two women without pausing, even briefly. Not even on the panther.

Then he turned around and wandered back out, the way he'd come in. His glance around hadn't continued on to me and the teenagers. But I didn't give that any more thought, at the time. I just figured he was looking for what Tuck sold, but had become too shy to make the approach.

Tuck delivered the hookers to the sad-faced man. They went off with him toward the other end of the arcade. He kept his hands in his pockets, even when they linked their arms through his and led him out into the night.

Tuck returned to the table and sat down. "Poor guy," he said, with real sympathy. "He's a well-off local businessman whose wife ran off with a lover. She took his balls with her. My girls are trying to give him a new pair. It's heavy work, but he's willing to pay for heavy."

"Are they really your girls?" I asked him.

"Of course not. Do I look rich? It's just a figure of speech. They're part of a stable that belongs to a . . . well, let's just say a local organization. I'm only a baby-sitter for their girls. Supposed to watch over them, deliver them to clients, collect for them, pick them up afterwards when necessary. For a small percentage."

He drank from his glass. My cup was already empty. There hadn't been much in it to start with. Typical Italian espresso: the big punch in a little package. "Hulvane," I said.

Tuck nodded and frowned, thinking back. "I met him about a month after I'd come here that first time, after the war. There weren't many Americans in Genoa at the time. There were a couple places we'd gravitate to at night. Hulvane and I met in one of those."

"What was he doing in Genoa?"

"He'd been in the occupation army in Germany, mustered out there, and came down here to learn Italian. He was a whiz at languages. Already had total command of both German and French, and by the time I got to know him, his Italian was better than mine. But he wanted to perfect it. Wouldn't speak anything but Italian, to me or anyone else. By the time he came back to America, he had loused up his ability to speak English normally. It took him over a month to get rid of that mélange of foreign accents and sound like a real American again."

That gave me an interesting notion. But I didn't pursue it right away. I thought I would be able to get back to it later, after Tuck finished sketching out the basic information.

"Hulvane was interested in art," he told me. "And in the fact that I was starting a gallery in New York. He said he had quite a number of good works of art, and let me look at some of them. They were more than good. Two paintings by Salvator Rosa, I remember. A crayon sketch by Delacroix and several drawings by Renoir. A fifteenth-century German Bible. And each accompanied by a perfectly valid provenance, with its recent sales witnessed by attorneys. I was very impressed. And Hulvane told me he had more, elsewhere. Which proved to be true.''

"How did he get hold of all of that?''

"I assumed at first that he obtained them in the way many members of the U.S. occupation army did after the war. From impoverished Germans forced to sell their valuables cheaply. Jewels, silverware, artworks. Or from Germans guilty of war crimes, using the valuables as bribes to escape discovery and prosecution. But the provenances showed that Hulvane had bought every item in France. During the war. Though all from a man with a German name—who had purchased them from various different sources, again in France—somewhere in the Southwest. . . . ''

Tuck fell silent, concentrating deeply. I waited. Finally he said, "The man Hulvane bought everything from was named Clemens von *Something*. I'm sorry, but I can't remember the last name. Alcoholism sometimes burns out sections of the memory. Along with much else of one's life.''

"I can find out the man's last name from people you sold the works to,'' I said, "since they'll have gotten the provenances with what they bought. I'm assuming the two of you did finally sell them off, as partners.''

"Yes. Our partnership was based on Hulvane contributing those works, and my contributing the gallery and works I had purchased myself.''

"I'll want the names of people you sold Hulvane's stuff to,'' I said.

He nodded abstractedly. "If I can remember any of them.'' He drank more Coca-Cola, brooding over old grievances. "Our partnership didn't last long. Just long enough for me to teach him the field and introduce him to potential buyers. Once he knew enough of them, he broke our deal. Unbeknownst to me, Hulvane withheld most of his artworks from the partnership agreement. He sold it all on his own. Pocketed the money and went off to do the Devil knows what with it. Leaving me with a business that went down the drain. I tried to get it started again a number of times over the following years, but I never managed it.''

I liked him for not offering that as his excuse for becoming a drunk. I placed the two photos of Hulvane on the table in front of him. ''These were taken recently. Do you recognize them as the Hulvane you knew—taking all the years between into consideration?''

Tuck studied the pictures. ''I think so.''

''You're not sure?''

''He had a beard when I knew him. A bushy black beard . . .'' Tuck put a thumb on the full-face passport photo, covering the lower part of Hulvane's face. He squinted at it. ''Oh yes, that's the bastard. Same nose and forehead. Same look to the eyes—that hard, blank stare that shrivels the recipient because there's no compunction or human sympathy behind it. He would have made a perfect FBI man. Old J. Edgar would have loved him.''

Tuck removed his thumb and studied Hulvane's face again. ''If that's what he looks like, the years have treated him better than they have me. A lot better than he deserves.''

A man came out of the bar and told Tuck that he was wanted on the phone. Tuck excused himself and hurried inside. When he came out, he said, ''I have to pick up three of my girls and drive them down to Portofino. Some men on a yacht there want to have a party. I'll have to wait on the quay until the girls return from the boat, so I can bring them back to Genoa. Why don't you come down with me? We can talk more down there, while I wait for them.''

I said that would be okay, and we left the arcade together. His car, a Fiat Uno, was parked across the street only a few spaces from mine. As Tuck got into his, I said, ''Wait until I pull out to follow you.''

''Why bother?'' Tuck motioned for me to get in beside him. ''I'll drive you down and bring you back.''

I shook my head. ''I'd rather follow in my own car. That way we're both free to go off on our own from Portofino, after we've finished talking.''

Tuck shrugged and shut his door. I was striding toward my car when I heard him start the Fiat's motor behind me.

Followed by a tremendous explosion that was felt, rather than heard.

The force of the blast hurled me off my feet and spun me around in the air. I got a dazed glimpse of the shattered car, and of the flaming torch inside it that had been Lawrence Tuck.

Then my shoulders and head slammed against a stone wall. I must have fallen away from it to the pavement, but I have no recollection of doing so, nor of anything else for quite some time afterwards.

❄ **22** ❄

WHEN I SURFACED I WAS LOOKING UP AT A NUN. SHE SAW my eyes open and smiled down at me, putting a finger to her lips, although I wasn't aware of trying to speak. Her other hand was a long way off, taking my pulse.

I was numb from the neck down. There was a creaking noise in my head when I turned it, but it didn't hurt. The painkillers they'd pumped into me were doing their job but keeping me from breaking out of my stupor. I was in a small, single-bed hospital room with a window to my left. It was still night outside. A sleepy uniformed cop sat in a chair placed against the wall beside the door.

The nun was still smiling when my eyes got back to her. I wanted to ask her something. I wasn't sure what it was, though, so I had to think about it for a while. I had an impression I'd finally worked out the question, but by then I was asleep again.

When I woke a second time my spine felt knotted to my left shoulder and my neck seemed to be a rivet that had rusted in place, fastening my head immovably to my body. Bursts of pain accompanied by flashes of livid color exploded inside my skull and ran down to my right foot when I rolled my head on the pillow. But I persisted, forcing the turn. To the left, then to the right.

There was bleak morning light outside the window. The nun was gone. So was the uniformed cop, but his chair was still there beside the door. A second chair had been pulled over close to the right side of my bed. A hard-faced guy in an ill-fitting suit sat in it, scowling at me.

He told me, in accented English, that he was a police detective. I didn't need to be told. Everything about him said *cop*.

"You misjudged the timing, eh?" he said unpleasantly. "Too bad for you. What group were you working for?"

I tried to speak, but no sound came out.

"You were seen," he told me. "When Lawrence Tuck got into his automobile. He tried to persuade you to get in with him. But you refused, of course. Because you knew what was going to happen. You walked away. Very fast, but not fast enough. He started the car quicker than you expected. But you were lucky. There is nothing wrong with you except some bruises, a twisted back, and a little concussion. We will be able to move you out of here by tonight. To a prison cell."

I tried again. This time I made some noises, but they weren't comprehensible as words.

"We examined your papers and know you were imported from France. We also examined your car, very carefully. And we found the hidden pistol you brought into Italy illegally. It will go easier for you if you tell me who paid you to arrange the killing of Lawrence Tuck—and why."

"Contact Major Bandini," I croaked. "The *carabinieri* in Rome."

The detective leaned closer. "What?"

"Rome," I repeated. "Major Diego Bandini." I shut my eyes and pretended to pass out.

After a time I heard his footsteps cross the room. I gave it another minute and then opened my eyes just a little. He was gone. The uniformed cop was back in his chair.

The news that there was nothing drastically wrong with me made me feel better in spite of the pain. I was starting to notice I was hungry when my eyes closed of their own accord and I did pass out.

When I came to, afternoon sunlight slanted in through the window and my watchdog and his chair were gone. A familiar face regarded me with a slight frown. An old friend.

Handsome Diego Bandini in his resplendent *carabinieri* major's uniform. He was winding up the head of my bed, bringing me to a partially seated position. The movement hurt my head, but not more than I could tolerate. They must have shot more sedative into me. A milder dose than previous ones, because I wasn't too groggy this time. Just very listless.

Diego sat down on the edge of my bed next to my legs, and took a ballpoint pen and a small spiral notebook from the briefcase he set down between us. "Now, Pierre-Ange, tell me about the bomb murder of Lawrence Tuck." He spoke in French, which was better than his English, and I answered in the same language:

"You tell me, Diego."

"No," he insisted, "you tell me. There are several local gangs presently competing for control of prostitution in Genoa. The police here assume one of those put the explosives in the car as a warning to the gang Lawrence Tuck worked for. They also assumed that you were brought here to arrange the killing. I have persuaded them that they are probably wrong about your taking part in such an act. I also persuaded them that you would tell me anything you know that might help them with this case. And that you should be allowed to go free, with the understanding that we will be able to contact each other in the future, if I have further questions or you have new information."

"Thanks, Diego. I'd appreciate it if you could also manage to get my gun and papers returned to me."

"I have taken care of that." Diego nodded toward the room's closet. "Your papers are back in your jacket. Your pistol is back in its hiding place in your car, and all mention of its existence has been erased from the police report."

The Italians are even better than the French at bending their way around inconvenient regulations.

Diego, with his pen poised over the pad on his thigh, was regarding me sternly and waiting for me to tell him what I knew and thought about Tuck's killing. I didn't know anything. What I thought was that Hulvane had engineered the murder, like he had the one of Jacques Genoud in Paris. He was wiping out people who knew uncomfortable things about his past. But there was no evidence to support that suspicion. Without it, the police could only annoy Hulvane briefly. That would be counterproductive for Fritz and me. Hulvane would cover up more tightly. He might temporarily suspend whatever criminal activity he was now engaged in. We'd lose a chance to grab hold of something we could use to claw him down to us.

"I think," I told Diego, "I may have seen the person who planted the bomb." I described the lean man who'd wandered into the arcade, glanced at Tuck, and wandered out. The short gray hair, pointy little nose, and what he'd been wearing.

Diego wrote it down in his own swift shorthand. "You are probably right. The police are already searching the city for a man of that description. Witnesses outside the arcade saw him get into Lawrence Tuck's car, and get out again after a short time. They assumed he intended to steal the car but couldn't get it started. These are not the sort of witnesses who would bother summoning the police for something as common as car theft."

He raised his pen an inch from the notepad, looking at me and waiting.

I said, "Fritz and I have a client who is searching for a man whom she believes may be her father. I found out Tuck used to know this man, long ago. So I came down here to talk to him."

"What is the name of this client and this man who may be her father?"

I made up two names. Diego wrote them down, but looked at me skeptically. "And was Tuck able to help you?"

"Not much. Tuck used to be an alcoholic. He got weaned off alcohol with pills. To which he became addicted. He couldn't remember everything in his past." It was a relief to be able to say something that was entirely true. "He told me the man I'm interested in was several lifetimes ago, for him. And he didn't know where the man is now."

Diego didn't stop looking skeptical. "And you are not being helpful to me. Deliberately, I think."

"Look, Diego, have I ever gone back on a promise to you?"

He thought about it, and then said, "No."

"I promise you this. If I come across any real proof of who had Lawrence Tuck killed, I'll inform you before anyone else."

"That means you have nothing further to tell me now."

"Not right now, no."

He put the notepad and pen back in his briefcase. "I expect you to honor that promise, Pierre-Ange."

"I will," I told him. "Can you get them to put a phone in here? I want to call Fritz. He'll be worrying about me by now."

"I have already phoned and informed him," Diego said.

"He's back in Paris?"

"No, but his answering machine gave me the number of a man in Paris to call. I did, and was told where I could contact Fritz. In Munich." Diego gave me one of his official calling cards as he stood up. On the back of it, he had printed a Munich phone number and address. "He expects you to meet him there tomorrow. I told him the doctors here say you will be well enough to leave the hospital tonight."

"I'm well enough right now," I said. "Hold on while I get dressed, and you can drive me down to Rome with you. I can get a plane to Munich from there."

I climbed out of bed. My brain spun and my legs buckled as my bare feet touched the cold floor tiles. I crawled back onto the bed, slowly, and grimaced at Diego. "I think it's mainly hunger," I said weakly. "I need a meal. A big one."

"I'll have one sent in to you. The food they serve in here is like all hospital food. I will also arrange to have your car kept safe until you return to pick it up."

After he'd left, I leaned back and fought against letting my eyes close again.

The meal Diego sent in was as large and nourishing as I'd wished. A lot of rare steak and plenty of pasta. And it did help.

So did a session with the hospital's physical therapist, who straightened out my back and unlocked my neck.

By six that evening I could walk upright, with care. I made my way out of the hospital—shaky and sore and still a little dizzy—and climbed into the chauffeured car I'd ordered. Three hours later I was at the airport outside Rome, carrying my bruised body and throbbing head aboard the last flight of the night to Munich.

❖ 23 ❖

THE BRUISES STILL HURT AND THERE WAS AN ODD ECHO inside my skull when I sat down to my late breakfast in the little hotel off Burgstrasse. But three aspirins with my second cup of coffee had me functional when Fritz phoned and told me where to meet him. I walked to Marienplatz steadily enough, lengthening my steps as I eased into it.

The sun was strong and the air was heavy. The body heat of the throngs in the vast pedestrian square at the heart of Munich pressed against me as I maneuvered among them. The customary mob of well-heeled shoppers had been joined by a crowd that had come to watch the glockenspiel on the Neues Rathaus tower do its thing. Big mechanical knights and dancers were making their jerky transit up there to the chiming of the clock, informing Munich that it was precisely eleven in the morning.

I went down into the subway and boarded a train on the S-2 line. It continued underground until it was beyond the city center and then rose to the surface and sped through the countryside.

Twenty minutes from Marienplatz, I got off at Dachau.

A handsome town older than Munich; but with its history blighted by Himmler's decision to build the first of the Nazi concentration camps there.

Fritz was waiting for me outside the station in a rented four-door Audi. We had spoken by phone while I was still in the Genoa hospital and he'd explained why he was in Munich. He had gotten the fake name Hulvane had used on his flight there from Paris: Heinz Graff. A Munich police officer—one of the European network of contacts Fritz had built up over his decades as a private investigator—was checking registrations at local hotels and guesthouses for that name.

When I'd arrived at his Munich hotel late the previous night Fritz hadn't been there, but he'd left a message for me. His police contact hadn't so far come across "Heinz Graff" among the guest registration lists. But another contact—an elderly man who'd fled Germany when Fritz had, but who'd gone back after the war—had given Fritz the name of a woman who had known Hulvane when he'd been a U.S. Army officer in Munich.

She had been Hulvane's mistress back then. Her name was Zenta Bremme. She was believed to be living now somewhere in Dachau, though she wasn't listed in its telephone book or in the town's register of citizens. Fritz had gone out there looking for her. I'd settled in for a long, healing sleep in the double-bedded room he'd rented for us, and hadn't heard from him until after my late breakfast.

"Have you spoken to her?" I asked as I slid onto the car seat next to him.

"Not yet," Fritz said, and studied me with some concern. "You do not look well, my boy. Not well at all. Perhaps I should not have dragged you here."

"There's nothing wrong with me now that aspirins can't keep under control," I told him. "Why haven't you talked with her? I thought you found out where she lived."

"Zenta Bremme has been living here with a niece and the niece's husband. But she went into Munich last evening before I learned about the niece. To meet a friend and see a film. I waited at her niece's house until almost one A.M., but she didn't return. I took a room here and asked the niece to call me immediately when she came home or they heard from her."

Fritz started the Audi and drove us out of the town center. "But she didn't come home. She phoned this morning to apologize to her niece for making her and her husband worry. She said she got drunk with her friend, and spent the night at the friend's apartment in Munich."

"Considering what happened to Jacques Genoud and Lawrence Tuck," I said, "that may have been the safest thing she could have done."

Fritz agreed. "He is cutting out witnesses to his back history. We will have to persuade Zenta Bremme to move for a time to someplace where anyone Hulvane might send would not be likely to find her."

We were into a new fringe of the town. It looked like the close-in suburbs of most American cities. Large houses on small, mowed lawns. "Where are we going?" I asked.

"To the place where Zenta Bremme works." Fritz turned left at the outskirts of Dachau, drove past a big, prosperous-looking Mercedes-Benz plant, and pulled into a parking space in front of a roofed roadside snack stand that also displayed Bavarian postcards and souvenirs. I got out of the car and looked across the road at the entrance to the Dachau concentration camp.

It was an official memorial site now, as clean and orderly as everything else in western Germany. Fritz came to a halt beside me. His jaws clenched as his gaze traveled slowly along the barbed wire atop the concentration camp walls.

"You have not been here before," he said, in a strained voice I had heard only once before. The single time he had spoken to me about the death of his wife.

"I've never visited any concentration camp," I said. "I didn't figure I needed more proof of humanity's inhumanity."

"I have been here," Fritz told me. "And to eleven other Nazi concentration camps. A pilgrimage I felt compelled to make. My obligation, as a German, to pay homage to those millions of innocent, terrified men, women, and children who were beaten, starved, and gassed to death in them. To assure them—and myself—that their obscene suffering is not forgotten."

He started across the road so suddenly, I had to take a fast stride and grab his arm to keep him from being hit by a speeding truck. I held on to his arm until the road was clear of traffic. Then we crossed the road together.

* * *

We entered the camp between two guard towers flanking a gateway, crossed a ditch between the wall and a wide strip of grass.

"Any prisoner who put a foot on this grass," Fritz said as we followed a path across it, "was instantly machine-gunned by the SS guards in the towers. Some prisoners chose to deliberately walk onto it."

Beyond the grass strip I stopped and looked around. I had known a redneck career sergeant, long ago, who had been one of the American troopers who'd liberated this camp. He'd dropped to his knees and vomited after less than a minute inside here. Other battle-hardened GIs fainted.

Nothing of what he'd described to me was left. The barracks into which the prisoners had been crammed stretched away in ordered rows between manicured gravel paths. Spotless, empty, silent. Lobotomized ghosts. The blood, the dead and dying, the stench of decaying people and excrement and the crematorium at the far end—all gone. What was absent made my skin crawl.

Fritz might have been reading my thoughts. "If you listen," he said in that voice I didn't like, "you can still hear them crying."

I couldn't; and I didn't want to.

We went into the *Wirtschaftsgebäude*, a large building that was now the memorial museum. It had once contained, Fritz informed me, the communal shower rooms in which people were whipped and hung up by their wrists in such a way as to slowly dislocate their shoulders. They were showered first because their stink was offensive to the SS torturers.

A man at the reception table told Fritz that Zenta Bremme was guiding a group through the interior of the museum but should be finished soon. We strolled through the vestibule and into the exhibition halls, in the direction she would have taken, allowing time for her to complete her tour. There weren't many other visitors. A few Scandinavians. An African in a tribal chieftain's regalia. A Japanese group with a young German guide who spoke their language effortlessly. They moved slowly from one exhibit to the next.

Many of the displays were blowups of photographs taken

by the concentration camp staff. The Nazis had been meticulous about recording everything. Like obsessed stamp collectors.

There was a photo series of a prisoner being subjected to a scientific experiment in which he was repeatedly frozen, then thawed out, then refrozen. Another series of an agonized prisoner slowly dying under an air-pressure experiment. Prisoners being flogged with wire whips by SS soldiers who took pride in their work. A prisoner who'd escaped all this by hanging himself from the top rung of a ladder too short for a drop to break his neck. He's simply forced himself to continue to hang there until he strangled to death.

Other displays were enlargements of the camp's SS documents, with translations next to the German originals.

One was a Himmler directive: "A principle which must be strictly adhered to by every SS man is to be honest, decent, loyal and helpful to everyone of our own blood but to no one else."

Another was a directive to camp commanders from a Waffen-SS *Generalmajor*:

> The hair of concentration camp prisoners is to be put to use . . . in the manufacture of hair-yarn-socks for U-boat crews and hair-felt footwear for the Reichs-railway. It is therefore ordered that hair of female prisoners be disinfected and stored. Men's hair can only be put to use if it is longer than 20 mm. SS Obergruppenfüher Pohl therefore agrees to the growing of prisoners' hair to a length of 20 mm before it is cut. It is planned to set up a hair processing workshop. Further details as to the delivery of the accumulated hair will follow. The total monthly amount of male and female hair is to be reported to this office on the 5th of every month.

Fritz touched my elbow and nodded ahead toward a small tour group approaching the exit. It was an all British group. Their guide—a plump, red-cheeked woman in her early sixties—spoke to them in an English that was distinctly American, with just a bit of German intonation coming through.

"Zenta Bremme," Fritz said quietly. We stopped and waited while she stood by the exit accepting tips from her group as it filed out. I looked at enlargements of two letters on display.

One was from the Reichsführer SS, concerning increasingly ruthless experiments by a Dachau doctor named Rascher: "There exists absolutely no objection to the experiments proposed . . . to be carried out in the Rascher department in the Dachau concentration camp. Where possible, Jews or quarantine prisoners should be used. Heil Hitler!"

The other had been written by Dr. Rascher's wife:

Highly esteemed, dear Reichsführer!

You have given us great pleasure once again! So many good things! The children's evening porridge will be enriched now for quite a while. Heinrich Peter always fidgets with excitement when a parcel arrives. He guessed who sent it and was of course given some chocolate immediately.

I thank you from the bottom of my heart for the presents and . . . for the letter you enclosed! My husband is very pleased at the interest which you have shown in his experiments. At Easter he conducted the experiments for which Dr. Romberg would have shown too much restraint and compassion. Always gratefully yours, Nina Rascher.

The last of Zenta Bremme's group had been ushered out. She put her tips into a little red change purse, stuck it inside her black shoulder bag, and started back through the museum in our direction. Her stride was brisk, and her plump figure had a solid look to it. She had honey brown hair, cut short and neat, with very little gray in it. She was still pretty.

We moved to intercept her. "Excuse me," I said in English, "are you Zenta Bremme?"

"Yes I am," she said, her manner friendly, her tone perky. "Someone has recommended me? That often happens—I am the best guide here."

"We will gladly pay for your time with us, Frau Bremme," Fritz told her, keeping to English for my benefit. "But not for a tour. We would like to talk to you about a man you used to know. Benjamin Hulvane.''

She stared at him in astonishment. *''Benny Hulvane?''*

''You do remember him.''

''Well of course.'' She gave a soft laugh and shook her head in wonder. ''But my goodness that was a very long time ago. I was only seventeen—and something of a beauty then.''

Her clear green eyes switched back from Fritz to me. ''You are American.''

''That's right.''

''So was Benny.'' She smiled gently, remembering. ''The nicest type of American. Such a sweet, kind young man.''

✦ 24 ✦

"YOU SOUND TO ME LIKE A BAVARIAN, HERR DONHOFF," she said as she led us away from the museum, towards the prisoner barracks. "Which part?"

"Like you, Frau Bremme. Munich."

"Ah! I would like to ask you, then," she said challengingly, "if you had *any* idea of what the SS did to the people who were imprisoned in this camp."

"I was a police officer," Fritz told her. "I knew more than most."

"And what did you do about what you knew?" she demanded quietly, the challenge still there.

Fritz told her what he had done.

She looked at him in a new way, the challenge gone. "You have my respect. A policeman who actually turned against the Nazi government! I was under the impression that the German resistance to Hitler was a myth."

"There was no resistance, Frau Remme, because the secret police very early found and killed anyone who had said a word against government policies. Except for those, like me, who ran away."

"I apologize for the tone of my question, Herr Donhoff. I have grown nasty on that subject. Because I have lived in the town of Dachau now for almost two years, since my husband's death, and I have not met a single person, who was an adult Dachau citizen during the Nazi time, who admits to knowing what was being done to people inside this place."

We were strolling now between the barracks, with Zenta

157

Bremme between us carrying her lunch in a string bag. Two thick wrapped sandwiches and a plastic container of orange juice. We had offered to take her to a restaurant or beer garden for lunch, but she had said no. The sandwiches she'd prepared wouldn't be good tomorrow, and she'd known too much hunger as a young teenager to waste food.

"What makes it difficult to believe them," she continued, "is that *we* knew—off in Munich. *I* knew, and I was only a kid. Once—I must have been about fourteen—I saw the SS soldiers dragging a group of Jews out of a cellar where they'd been hiding. They were herded into two separate trucks. One for those who were young enough and strong enough to join the prisoner labor force in the camp—until they became too weak from malnutrition and mistreatment. Those who were too old or too young or too ill were sent directly to the gas chambers installed in Hartheim Castle. The SS always made the selection immediately.

"Some people passed by quickly, trying not to look at this. Fear and shame, maybe. But some of us stayed there and watched it. I saw two children, both less than five, torn from their mother and shoved into the death truck. The SS clubbed the mother to the ground with their rifle butts and threw her into the labor-force truck. One of the teenagers watching with me yelled at the prisoners, 'Don't worry, you'll come back to us—*as soap*!' Oh yes, we knew."

Zenta Bremme made a wide gesture at the concentration camp around us. "Maybe this is my penance—working here as a guide."

"No," Fritz told her heavily, "the guilt belongs to the guilty. You were too young to be responsible for what was done here."

"Yes, that is my excuse." She shook her head and forced a tight laugh, one hand patting her shoulder bag. "But it also pays well enough—when I add my tips to my widow's pension. It's hard to find a decent job. Germany still doesn't believe in women working. Especially in Bavaria. Jobs are for the men."

The silent emptiness of the prisoner barracks on either side of us continued to give me the creeps. But Zenta Bremme automatically fell back into her guide's role at times, gesturing at one barracks building or another:

"This one was the *Totenkammer*—the prisoners' morgue. It was always packed to overflowing with bodies. Because the crematorium incinerators couldn't burn up the corpses fast enough."

"This one was called the *Priesterblock*. It was the barrack for clergymen—Catholic priests and Protestant ministers—who'd been arrested for saying things the Nazis didn't approve of. The clergymen and the Jews were always the first chosen for the terminal experiments of Dr. Rascher and Professor Schilling. The ones they intended to carry out until the patient died."

I didn't need any more of this. I said, "I apologize if what I'm about to say is offensive, but we've been told you were once Benjamin Hulvane's mistress."

"Yes, I was," she responded with no sign of embarrassment. "For almost a year. When I was seventeen, at the end of the war, when the American army occupied Bavaria. I was very lucky to become the mistress of an American officer. You look at Munich today, all rebuilt so nicely, and you get no idea of what it was like at the end of the war. So much of it smashed to rubble by Allied bombers. Most of us had lost our homes. Our only clothing was what we had on our backs. The food supplies were cornered by the black market, and there were few people left in Munich who had money to buy there. Most of us had lost at least part of our families. We were living in cellars under the Munich ruins. . . . "

She paused a bit, thinking back to that time. "Nowadays, young people ask how the Allied bombers could have had the heart to do such a terrible thing to such a civilized city. If you tell them maybe it was retribution for what we did first, they don't know what you're talking about. The schools don't teach them what our bombers did at the start of the war to Rotterdam, Warsaw, Coventry."

Fritz said, "Was it Hulvane who told you about those?"

"Yes. And about so much else. I was too young to know much, and Benny loved to teach. Is that what he became, a teacher?"

"No," I said, and didn't elaborate on it. I wanted her story first.

"He was so generous with me, in every way," she said. "Generous and gentle. No more hunger for me. Good, warm clothes. Living in the nice house Benny requisitioned for himself. That was standard procedure—the military taking over places that hadn't been destroyed. Benny's was on the edge of the city and belonged to a cultured couple who moved into its basement and became his servants. Benny never stopped being embarrassed about that, although they kept assuring him they were grateful for his being there. And they were. He was as generous with them as he was with me. . . . No, I've never let myself forget how lucky I was that he chose me for his mistress."

I was finding it difficult to reconcile what she was saying with what I knew about Benjamin Hulvane; even considering the changes age might have wrought.

"Of course," she added, "I was *very* pretty, at seventeen."

"And you still are," Fritz told her, with that sincere gallantry most women stirred in him.

Zenta Bremme stopped for a second and looked at him, her red cheeks becoming a darker red. "Oh, you flatterer. You must have charmed all the girls when you were young."

Fritz smiled. "I sometimes delude myself that I still do."

"If you aren't married," she told him, "I just might be interested."

He laughed. "Now you are the flatterer."

Zenta Bremme laughed with him, and led us on. Away from the barracks. In the direction of the crematorium.

I was sure its interior had been scrubbed as clean of its history as everything else. But I very much hoped that she wasn't intending to have her lunch in there.

She stopped when she reached the Memorial to the Unknown Prisoner. A statue of a gaunt man in a threadbare overcoat and wooden clogs, his eyes hollow and the flesh of his face shrunk against the skull beneath, but the mouth still clamped in an expression of defiant contempt. Zenta Bremme gazed up at that face for a moment, and then sat down on a nearby bench placed against a line of red and white flower beds backed by a wall of green bushes.

Fritz and I settled down on either side of her. She reached into her string bag for a sandwich, but I said, "Wait a minute, please, Frau Bremme. I'd like to make sure we're talking about the same Benjamin Hulvane." I got out the pictures of Hulvane. "Is this him?"

She took the photographs from me, one in each hand, and looked at them for some seconds. "This is an elderly man," she said. "Benny was in his twenties. It is hard to be sure."

"Did he have a beard when you knew him?"

"Benny? No, he shaved every morning. Before breakfast. Sometimes he liked to have *me* shave him." She gave the pictures of Hulvane more attention. "This could be Benny—forty-five years later—I suppose. But it could also be *Clemens*. They looked a lot like each other, basically. Although their characters were so different."

Inside my head I heard Lawrence Tuck, back in that Genoa arcade, telling me that all of Hulvane's artworks came from a "Clemens von Somebody."

"Do you remember the full name of this Clemens?" I asked her.

"Sure. Clemens von Langsdorf. But the name doesn't mean he was really German, although he spoke the language rather well. Clemens was from France. Still had the French accent."

Once again, I got that Alice in Wonderland sensation. I was silent, taking a hard look at this confusion of identities, while Fritz took over for a while:

"Please tell us more, Frau Bremme, about this Clemens von Langsdorf—who was actually French."

She looked again at the pictures in her hands. "Clemens knew Munich very well. He first came there from France before the war. To learn German. Because, he said, he was in love with our culture. So much that he even had his name legally changed to a German one, that first time he was here."

She put the two photos together and gave them back to me, not looking at me or at Fritz, but at the statue of the Unknown

Prisoner. "Clemens admitted he was seduced, for a short time, by the Nazi's propaganda. But when the war came, he said, he managed to get back to France to help it fight—and then help it through the long German occupation. Personally, I never believed that. *I* think he went back to help the Nazis—against France. But I could be entirely wrong about that. The fact is, I just never liked Clemens."

"What was his French name?" Fritz asked.

"I don't know. I don't think he ever even mentioned it to Benny—though he and Benny became very close."

"How did they get to know each other?"

"Clemens came back to Munich immediately after the war. He admitted it was because he knew the black market there would provide opportunities for a clever man like him to get rich. He *was* clever enough, and unscrupulous enough. And he attached himself to Benny. That was important for any black market operator—a good connection with someone in the United States military. The GIs had everything the rest of us needed. Food and clothing. Gasoline for cars. Liquor and cigarettes that were worth more than gold. They exchanged those for what *they* wanted. Jewelry, silverware, and other precious heirlooms. Luxurious furniture for the rooms they requisitioned for themselves. And women, of course. Clemens began acting as Benny's liaison with the Munich black market, buying and selling for him."

Zenta Bremme paused uncomfortably, and then shrugged. "Benny was a nice man—but he wasn't a saint, after all. Anyway, that's what brought the two of them together, at the start. But soon he was doing all sorts of other things for Benny. Clemens is the one who found the house we moved into. He began acting as Benny's off-duty chauffeur. He also began to introduce Benny to other women. Trying to push me out. Because Benny chose me before he met Clemens, and Clemens had no control over me. Sometimes one of the women—or even two—would spend the night with Benny, and I would have to sleep in another room." Zenta Bremme looked embarrassed for the first time. "Well, I did say Benny wasn't a saint."

"It doesn't seem," I said, "to have lessened your liking for him. You didn't mind?"

"Not very much, really. He was a man, after all. A young and vigorous man. What right had I to be upset about him enjoying himself? As long as he didn't kick me out and replace me with one of those others. To be honest with you, I wasn't really that interested in . . . the sexual act. Not when I was that young. Though I pretended, naturally."

"So Clemens was basically Ben Hulvane's pimp and black market fixer."

"He also helped him with his work, unofficially. Benny's job for the army was to find and interrogate suspected war criminals. Clemens did some investigating on his own, and gave him tips on former Nazi officials hiding behind false names." Zenta Bremme's lips tightened. "I always thought of Clemens as a zig-zag man. You understand? His life zigged and zagged—but always with the wind, never against it. He left his native France when it was weak and in trouble, and came to Germany when it was becoming the strongest country in Europe. He attached himself to—or at least flirted with—the Nazis because they were in power. He came back to Germany because it was broken and beaten—easy pickings for a clever and corrupt man like him. He attached himself to the American army because it was victorious, and betrayed Nazis because they had lost. A zig-zag man."

Fritz asked her about when she'd last seen or heard of both of them. Benjamin Hulvane and Clemens von Langsdorf.

"Clemens went away first. One evening Benny came back from his headquarters looking troubled. He told Clemens a French investigator cooperating with his unit had seen Clemens driving Benny, and thought he looked very much like a photograph of a Frenchman wanted by his own country. For what they called 'crimes against humanity.' Clemens got angry and said the French investigator was wrong and should take a better look at that photograph. But the next day he'd disappeared. We never saw him again."

"How did Hulvane take that?"

"He had to assume it meant the French investigator was right, and he didn't like that at all. You can imagine his feelings. His job was uncovering war criminals, and if all that time he'd been harboring one—well, Benny didn't enjoy being made a fool of like that. And he didn't want to discuss it. He didn't have to very long, officially, because his term with the army was finished less than two weeks later.''

''Is that the last you saw of him?''

''He stayed in Munich a *little* longer. But pretty soon he told me he wanted to get back to California—that's where he was from—and see his parents again. And he wanted to see a little more of Europe before he went. But he was very generous even at the end. He gave the couple that owned the house a case of whiskey and cartons of cigarettes to sell on the black market. He gave me the rest of his whiskey and cigarettes. And money. American dollars—at the unofficial exchange rate, it was enough to keep me going until conditions in Munich began to improve. I cried like a child when I saw Benny off on that train.''

''The train to where?''

''To Paris. He wanted to see Paris before he went home. It was a long trip in those days. The trains made so many local stops along the way.''

''Did you hear from him again?''

''He promised to write to me, from California. But he never did. I wasn't offended. I was in one life, he went back into another.'' Zenta Bremme leaned against the back of our bench and looked from Fritz to me, and then back to Fritz. ''Now I think I have suffered enough from my curiosity. Tell me what this is all about. Your interest in Benny.''

''There is a young American woman,'' Fritz told her, ''who believes he is one of several men who kidnapped her. And chopped off some of her fingers to make her father pay the ransom.''

Zenta Bremme's look was incredulous. *''Benny Hulvane?''* She shook her head fiercely. *''Never.''*

''Suppose,'' I said, ''we told you the same thing about this Clemens von Langsdorf?''

She thought about that. ''There—it would be possible. Shocking, but not unbelievable.''

I was still holding the photographs. She took them back

from me and studied them again with a hard frown. "This is how old they would both be now. Benny and Clemens. They *are* still alive?"

"I doubt very much," I said, "that both of them are."

FRITZ AND I CROSSED THE ROAD TO HIS RENTED AUDI. WHAT we had worked out with Zenta Bremme was that we would return in time to pick her up when she left work at the concentration camp. We'd told her just enough of the truth to make her agree to being taken where no one would look for her. Until it was safe for her to come out of hiding. She had accepted the necessity only after we had promised to make it up to her for whatever she estimated she would lose in tips during that period. We'd also said we would buy her some new clothes and other necessities, so she wouldn't have to stop off at her niece's house first before going where Fritz intended to stash her.

We got in the car and drove to Dachau's main post office to make some vital phone calls. On the way we had no trouble agreeing on the most important fact:

It was not Benjamin Hulvane we were investigating. It was a Frenchman who'd renamed himself Clemens von Langsdorf.

"He knew Hulvane was due to muster out soon," I said. "He hung around after he disappeared. In the shadows, but keeping an eye on Hulvane. Or having others do it for him. He slipped aboard the same train Hulvane took to Paris."

"And in some way persuaded or forced him to get off with him at one of the local stops. Followed by a walk out into the countryside."

"Where he killed and buried him. And took over Hulvane's identity. To shake off the people hunting him for war crimes.''

Fritz said softly: ''The zig-zag man.''

It explained a lot.

He'd gone to Genoa because he wasn't likely to meet anyone there who knew the real Hulvane; and he'd grown the beard just in case he ran into one by mischance. He must have boned up on his English there, getting lessons from some unknown American. Refusing to speak English to anyone else and not returning to the States until he had the accent right. And he'd probably kept the beard for years, until age could explain the changes in ''Hulvane's'' face.

Guessing from what we knew of this Clemens von Langsdorf—formerly thought to be Hulvane—he had probably killed his American language instructor after he was finished needing him. For the same reason he'd had Hulvane's parents killed. To insure against anyone breaking his new identity.

The two new murders—of Genoud and Tuck—were to cover his more recent past. Fritz and I didn't dwell on the fact that it was almost certainly my shadowing of von Langsdorf that had worried him enough to start this latest round of killings. And we agreed that the first hunch of the German police about the two dead Italians found under the dune was probably correct. Von Langsdorf had killed them to keep for himself all of the ransom paid by Helen Marsh's father after her second finger had been chopped off.

''Langsdorf'' was how we referred to him between ourselves. Temporarily—knowing it was as unreal as his ''Benjamin Hulvane'' name had been. There was a third identity lurking behind it. One we didn't know yet. What we did know was that everything we'd attributed to Hulvane had been done by a slippery monster whom we could, for the moment, call ''Langsdorf.'' And that the death toll in his wake was mounting.

With that in mind, I would have felt better if we were armed. But the kind of people Fritz knew in Munich these days were either too innocent or too official to supply us with illegal weapons.

All we had was the additional fountain pen that Fritz had clipped next to his usual one in the breast pocket of his jacket. It was thicker than the other one, but nobody else was likely to take notice of that.

At the Dachau post office, Fritz made two phone calls. One local, the other long-distance. The long-distance call was to his man at Interpol. Asking him to look for the name Clemens von Langsdorf among Interpol's normal criminal files—and also in the old dossiers on war criminals who had never been caught.

His local call was to his Munich police connection. Who told him that Heinz Graff—the fake name used by Langsdorf on his Paris-Munich flight—still hadn't turned up in the registrations at Munich hotels and guesthouses. Fritz asked him to check the registrations again, for Clemens von Langsdorf—and to institute a search for the same name in the files of both the Bavarian state police and the police of Federal Germany.

Both of my calls were long-distance, to Paris. The first was to Babette. I had phoned her yesterday, from the Genoa hospital. Enough of that rare motherly sentiment had clung to her at the time for Babette to agree to make some overseas calls and use her prestige to nudge New York art world professionals into delving into the records for the information I needed.

When I got her on the phone this time, her brief flare of sentimentality had burned out in a renewed surge of work fever. But she did have what I was after. Enough of it so I didn't need more.

In 1959 the Philadelphia Art Museum had purchased two works from a Benjamin Hulvane—although the real Hulvane must have been dead by then. A Delacroix self-portrait and a drawing by Pannini of a Roman palace in ruins.

According to their provenance papers, both had been sold to "Hulvane" by a man named Clemens von Langsdorf. In Munich, on November 7, 1945, with the sale witnessed by a German attorney. Langsdorf had bought the works from two different people, a month apart in early 1944, in the French city of Dijon. Both sales were witnessed by a French attorney.

I jotted all of this down in my notebook, with the names of the people who'd sold the pictures to Langsdorf and of the French and German attorneys, and thanked Babette fervently. She seemed less interested in my reassurance that I loved her than in my promise to not interrupt her work again.

My second Paris call was to Captain Thierry Gallion of the DGSE—France's secret service, roughly equivalent to the CIA.

We had known each other since we were boys. His family used to spend every August near my mother's house, the one I lived in now. Thierry's father had been an admiral, and he'd followed him into the navy. But a sub he'd commanded had sunk to the bottom because of a technical failure, and by the time they repaired the problem and returned to the surface, the pressure had given him the heart and hearing trouble that got him shifted from active duty to the DGSE desk job.

I asked him to find out if there was anything on record about a Clemens von Langsdorf—a native Frenchman under some other name—who might have committed war crimes in France, perhaps in or around Dijon.

"War criminals," he told me, "are not my department, Pierre-Ange. You know that."

"I know you can reach into the right department more easily than I can, Thierry. And if you're instrumental in capturing a war criminal nobody else has been able to track down in all this time, it won't do your position at that spook factory any harm."

He agreed to give it a try. I gave him all the information I'd gotten from Babette, to help him in his try.

Fritz and I left the post office experiencing hunger pangs. It is hard to get a real meal in Bavaria after normal lunch hours. But the *Gasthaus* where Fritz had taken a room for his night in Dachau had a little beer garden where they were willing to serve us an assortment of hot sausages. Fritz was not devoted to sausages and beer with salted rolls. Perhaps a hangover from his rejection of Bavaria during the Nazi supremacy. He lunched on the combination out of necessity and without joy. Personally, I enjoyed every bit of it.

Afterwards we stayed in the garden mulling over what Babette's information meant. What it came down to was that Langsdorf had sold all those artworks to himself, back in 1945. The odds were that the real Benjamin Hulvane hadn't even known about the sale, before Langsdorf killed him and took over his identity. I was also willing to give odds that we would learn that the Munich attorney who'd witnessed the transaction had died about the same time as Hulvane.

There was an hour to go before Zenta Bremme would be leaving her job at the camp when Fritz and I returned to the post office.

I phoned Thierry Gallion. He told me he'd passed on my information and request to the right people, and hadn't gotten a response as yet.

Fritz called his same two contacts again. The one at Interpol told him there was nothing in its computer files on a Clemens von Langsdorf. The one with the Munich police said Langsdorf wasn't in the files of the Bavarian or Federal police, either. And that the name hadn't turned up as yet among local guest registrations.

I put on my sunglasses when we emerged from the post office into the bright daylight, and took over the driving back to the Dachau concentration camp. We still had half an hour to spare when I slowed and began turning the Audi in to the snack stand's parking space.

There was a black BMW among the other cars parked there. A man sat behind its steering wheel, gazing across the road at the concentration camp's entrance and the nearby bus stop. I averted my face and swung past the BMW, parking as far from it as I could.

Even in that brief glimpse of the man inside it, I couldn't be mistaken about that combination of short gray hair, lean face, and pointy little nose.

It was the man who'd come into the arcade in Genoa, glanced at Lawrence Tuck, and gone back out. Minutes before Tuck had been blown up in his car.

❂ 26 ❂

I TOLD FRITZ ABOUT THE MAN IN THE BMW. I DIDN'T THINK he'd paid any attention to me when I drove past him, and it was unlikely he'd recognize me if he got a clearer look. In the Genoa arcade his brief attention had been on Tuck. If he'd noticed me at all down there, my face would have been blurred by the night shadows and the arcade's neon. I was dressed differently now and my sunglasses formed a partial mask.

But there was no sense in taking the chance.

Fritz climbed out of the Audi and went to the snack stand's souvenir rack behind the BMW. He returned with a tourist version of a Tyrolean hat. I put it on. Nice and loose. Tugging it low on my forehead shaded much of my face. Fritz stayed between me and the BMW when we walked across the road and into the camp.

Fritz used the public phone booth in the museum to call his Munich police connection and give him the BMW's license number. Then we stayed close to the booth and waited. His contact called back twelve minutes later. Computers do have their uses.

The BMW's owner was Max Höss. His profession was listed as chauffeur. His description matched the pointy-nosed man waiting on the other side of the road.

Fritz's contact had programmed the name and address of Max Höss into the computerized files on local criminals. What had come out was interesting. Höss had served sixteen months in prison, five years ago, for the savage beating of a

171

Turkish immigrant in a racist attack by himself and four Munich skinheads. He'd later been suspected of bombing a Greek restaurant, but there hadn't been enough evidence against him to convict.

Where he lived was even more interesting. It was on the estate of the man he worked for: Rudolf Gottfried Aumeier. An aging industrialist whose use of slave labor during the Nazi era—coupled with the number of those slaves who had died while working in his factories—had gotten him sentenced to twenty years imprisonment. But Aumeier had been released after serving less than two years—"in the interests of reviving German industry."

Aumeier was known to currently have associations with extreme-right leaders throughout Europe. They were often guests at his estate, singly or in groups, presumably for strategy meetings. Under the law, such meetings were not a criminal act; though the secret plans hatched at them might be.

He was also believed to be financing the German distribution of literature extolling the Nazis. Publishing such literature in Germany *was* a crime. But these books and pamphlets, though in German, were imported from the United States, where they were published by American racist groups. *Distributing* the imports was not illegal.

With a background like that, Rudolf Gottfried Aumeier was a likely European contact for our Clemens von Langsdorf. It meshed with what we knew of Langsdorf's distant past from Zenta Bremme—and of his more recent association, in Paris, with the late pro-Fascist Jacques Genoud.

That Max Höss—the man who'd killed Lawrence Tuck for Langsdorf—worked for Aumeier and lived on his estate, cinched it.

I walked back across the road to the snack stand with my sunglasses in place and the hat tilted rakishly to shadow my face. Max Höss was still there behind the wheel of his BMW, watching the camp entrance and the bus stop. I got into the Audi and started the motor. Preparing to ram the BMW if Höss made his try at Zenta Bremme here.

That wasn't likely, though. Not using his own car. There

were two woman behind the snack stand's counter; and already five people waiting at the bus stop on the other side. At least one of them might memorize his license number before he sped away from the murder scene.

Fritz appeared, coming out through the camp's entrance and halting there. Looking first at his watch and then up at a few small clouds. His timing was perfect. The bus to the town's center was due within the next minute. In Germany you can depend on the schedules.

Zenta Bremme came out behind him. She must have said something, because Fritz began walking toward the bus stop at the same time she did. Without appearing to be with her, he managed it so his large figure was always between her and the road.

I saw Höss start the BMW. But then he stayed where he was, waiting. He continued to wait when the bus came along and pulled over to its stop. Fritz stood aside politely to allow the waiting female passengers, including Zenta Bremme, to board it first. The BMW still didn't move out. Fritz got on the bus last. It pulled away.

Höss drove after it, taking his time. All he had to do was to follow the bus and see where Zenta Bremme got off. Then continue to tail her, by car or on foot, as long as it took. Through the evening and into the night, if necessary. Until he found an opportunity for a safe kill.

Fritz and I had two different jobs to handle now.

One was to give Zenta Bremme a chance to shake off the tail. That was Fritz's job.

The other focused on finding Langsdorf. There was a good possibility that the reason he wasn't registered at a local hotel or guesthouse—under any of the names known to us—was that he was a guest of Rudolf Aumeier. And we knew where Aumeier's estate was. But if Langsdorf wasn't there, our next best bet would be to follow Höss and hope he led us to Langsdorf.

Both possibilities centered on the Aumeier estate. If Langsdorf wasn't there, we had the certainty that Höss was bound to return there sooner or later. Because that's where he lived.

The thing now was to insure that he went back there sooner rather than later. Before going off to do a number of other things, which might include a meeting with Langsdorf.

That was my job.

I got out of the Audi and went to the snack stand. There were a number of plastic squirt containers of mustard and ketchup on the counter. I hefted a mustard one. It felt half-full. I told one of the women behind the counter that I would like to buy it. She thought I was crazy. But she didn't feel the amount of cash I put down on the counter for her was so crazy. She even put the mustard container in a nice little paper bag for me.

I took it back to the Audi and drove toward the center of town. I passed the BMW and the bus along the way. Reaching the S-Bahn station well ahead of both. Pulling into the parking area, I stayed in the car and waited.

The bus came into the station, its last stop. Höss parked three cars away from me, jumped out of his BMW, and stood beside it watching the passengers come out of the bus. He was dressed differently than he'd been in Genoa. A brown Bavarian jacket and dark green trousers. Conservative shoes instead of boots.

Zenta Bremme got off the bus and hurried toward the station entrance, along with most of the other passengers. Fritz came off behind her and headed in the same direction, putting on his weary-old-man walk.

Höss strode away from the BMW, angling to follow Zenta Bremme into the station. She was going in when he came abreast of Fritz. Fritz stumbled and fell against him, clutching at Höss to keep from going all the way down. Höss tried to push him away but Fritz hung on, breathing hard and gasping apologies. By the time Höss got loose Zenta Bremme had disappeared among the crowd inside the station.

He hurried in to look for her. In the same moment I was out of the Audi. With my paper bag. I did a fast turn behind the other cars to the BMW, reached through its open front window, and squirted mustard on the seat and lower backrest on the driver's side. I made it back to the Audi just as fast, dropping the bag-wrapped mustard container in a trash can on the way.

Pulling out of my parking spot, I swung around the far side of the station. Zenta Bremme had slipped out through a door there and was waiting for me. She was lying flat down on the Audi's rear seat an instant later. I backed the Audi into another parking spot with a view along the front of the station.

Höss came out a few minutes later, looking around with frowning concentration. Not spotting her outside, either, he walked slowly back to his BMW. He was still looking around for her when he opened its door and slid into the driver's seat.

He was out of the car a second later, looking at the mustard smeared on his right hand and jacket sleeve, his mouth moving in what had to be a string of curses. His head jerked up and he scanned the parking area again, this time in fury. But he didn't spot anyone who looked like the sort of drunken lout who would find such a nasty practical joke amusing.

His anger gave way to disgust as he gave up the search. Very carefully, he used his left hand to take out a handkerchief and used it to clean the mustard off his right hand. He looked at the mustard on his sleeve, and then back over his shoulder, seeing a lot more of it on the lower back of his jacket and the seat and legs of his trousers. With a sick expression, he dropped the handkerchief to the ground, opened the BMW's back door, and got out a roll of paper towels.

He was wiping the BMW's seat as clean as he could when a couple of teenage girls coming from the station walked by and saw the mustard all over the back of his clothing. One of them began to giggle. Höss straightened and twisted around. Even at that distance, I could see his face reddening with rage and embarrassment. His glare scared the girls into hurrying away.

I watched Höss use up the rest of his paper towels on his jacket and trousers. Getting off most of the wet mustard, but spreading its stain in the process. He gave it up finally. A lot of passengers from a just-arrived train were coming out of the station, some of them angling into the parking area. Höss got into his BMW, hiding his shame, and slammed the door. A minute later he was driving away from the station.

Where he'd go next was obvious. To the house where Zenta Bremme boarded with her niece. If Höss knew where she worked, he also had to know where she lived. She was lucky that Fritz had better local informants than Clemens von Langsdorf—or Höss would have gotten to her before we did.

He would stake out the house where she lived watching for her to come back there. From his car. He wouldn't be doing much walking around. Not with his clothes in that condition.

But when it got dark, and she still hadn't showed up, he would use some public phone to call the niece's house. Giving a false identity and a good reason for having to locate Zenta Bremme as soon as possible.

By then she would have phoned her niece. Saying she was going off to visit some friends in Austria—not specifying who or exactly where—and wouldn't be back for several days.

When Höss got that information, he would quit his surveillance for the time being. There was little question of where he'd go after that, before doing anything else. Back home. To change his clothes.

Seconds after the BMW went off, Fritz emerged from the station. I eased the Audi over to him. He got in front beside me, warning Zenta Bremme to stay down in back until we were out of town. With Fritz directing, I drove us away from Dachau and back into Munich. To the place where he had arranged to stash Zenta Bremme for a while.

It was in the Schwabing section of the city—Munich's version of the Paris Left Bank. Full of inexpensive restaurants, bars with sidewalk tables, discos, jazz joints, movie houses, and secondhand bookshops. It was a neighborhood that drew a lot of Munich's youth, but Fritz's friend there—one of the few left from before the war—was an elderly widower. His apartment had a spare bedroom, and he'd told Fritz he'd be pleased to have a nice woman move in with him.

The apartment was in a newish building near the top end of the *Englischer Garten*, facing across the park toward the

Isar River. I stopped in front and waited with the car while Fritz took Zenta Bremme inside. It was fifteen minutes before he came out, carrying a brown paper bag. His friend and Zenta Bremme had liked each other immediately, he told me as he got into the car. The bag contained a picnic dinner they prepared for us together. There wasn't much likelihood of our finding spare time for a restaurant meal that evening.

Zenta Bremme had made her call to her niece from the apartment, Fritz said. And he had phoned his cop contact and gotten exact directions to Rudolph Aumeier's estate—plus a fairly detailed description of its layout. It was southeast of Munich, close to the Alps along the Austrian border. One of a number of big country estates on the Chiemsee, Bavaria's largest lake. Aumeier's property was heavily wooded and protected by prowling guards armed with weighted clubs. At least two of them also had shotguns, which Aumeier claimed were for shooting ducks in the lakeside marsh along one edge of his land.

Fritz's cop contact knew about this and the layout of the estate because the police had pulled a surprise search of the estate a little more than a year ago. Acting on a tip that terrorist weapons and explosives were stored there. The searchers hadn't been able to find where the arms cache was hidden, and the superior officer who'd ordered the raid had been severely reprimanded. Aumeier still had political clout—even in a Germany whose government was more sensitive than most to any resurgence of Nazi fanatics.

We went to a nearby sporting goods shop that Fritz knew. The owner was locking the front door for the night. But the amount we were prepared to spend convinced him to reopen long enough to sell what we needed. For Fritz it was a pair of binoculars with night lenses. For me it was a small inflatable rowboat, with a compressed-air container for it and a pair of oars.

After getting that into the back of the Audi, our next stop was a car rental agency. I stayed with the Audi while Fritz went in. He came out driving a Honda two-door hatchback.

The sky was darkening as I followed him out of the city and across an increasingly hilly countryside. An hour from

Munich we crossed the Inn River at Rosenheim and angled due east. Toward the Chiemsee and the estate of Rudolph Gottfried Aumeier.

❄ 27 ❄

DENSE MIST ROSE FROM THE SURFACE OF THE VAST LAKE AND spread into the land around it under the last of the evening light. The air was muggy, with almost no movement to it. The mist drifted of its own volition, directionless, slowly unveiling individual trees and houses and then just as slowly blotting them out again.

The narrow unlit country road we took cut past the end of a Chiemsee inlet and behind Aumeier's lakeside property. It wasn't a road for fast driving, which suited us fine. We were taking it easy when my Audi trailed Fritz's Honda past the estate's drive-in gateway. It was open, and the big lamps atop the gateposts on either side were on, casting strong light on the young, burly guard there.

He wore a quasi uniform. Brown shirt and trousers. Black boots, wide black belt, black necktie. The apprentice storm trooper impression was completed by the military-short hair and the club hanging from his belt. The smug hands-on-hips stance and the stupid face he turned to watch our cars go by. I watched him in my rearview mirror until we went around a tight bend in the road and he was out of sight behind us. He hadn't seen anything about our passing that warranted using the small radio transceiver strapped to his left shoulder.

Just beyond the bend Fritz pulled off the road, across from Aumeier's property, and stopped his Honda behind a concealing patch of wild brush. I tucked the Audi in beside it, with thornbushes scratching my paintwork on one side as I came to a halt. Fritz was unwrapping our picnic dinner when

I climbed into the Honda beside him. We ate while we waited for night's full darkness.

The sandwiches were substantial. We divided them evenly and finished every crumb. When we shared the last of the coffee from the thermos, it was dark enough.

Fritz climbed out of the Honda with the night binoculars and walked back along the edge of the road, keeping to the bushes, looking for a hiding place across from the estate's gateway. Somebody had to watch it for the return of Höss, ready to get back to his own car and tail Höss if he drove out again. Or—better still—to follow Clemens von Langsdorf, if he was here and left first.

Someone else had to slip into the estate and see what he could find out in there. And that had to be me. Fritz didn't like it but he was a realist. He remained a strong man, but his legs were no longer up to moving fast for more than ten seconds. And the one who went into the estate might have to get out very fast.

I got back into the Audi, got it out of the bushes, and turned left onto the road—going in the opposite direction from the one Fritz had taken on foot. After the end of Aumeier's property, there was a stretch of much smaller lakefront estates. Between the last of those and the beginning of another extensive estate, I turned in to a twisty dirt track that led down through pine woods to the water. It brought me to an unpaved parking area, empty now, behind a small public boating dock.

I drove through the parking area to the land end of the dock, and turned the Audi around to face back toward the access track. Ready for a swift getaway. The thick ground mist blanketed the car and hid the far end of the dock from me. But when I climbed out of the car I saw that above the height of my shoulders the mist was in a gradual process of shredding apart. Far out in the middle of the Chiemsee, spectral moonlight shafting through a gap in the upper mist illuminated an onion-domed white tower: Frauenwörth, an island abbey dating back to Charlemagne's time.

I walked out along the boat dock. It was a long one, stretching over the marshy shore to reach clear water. When

I got to the end I looked off to my right. Aumeier's place was in that direction, but I couldn't see it from the dock. Just varying degrees of darkness over there; and some tiny lights, higher up, that seemed to wink on and off as mists shifted past them.

Going back to the car, I pulled out the deflated rowboat and the bottle of compressed air, and carried them out to the dock end. When the boat was inflated I went back to get the oars from the Audi. Along with the car's tire iron. That wasn't going to be much use if I came up against a shotgun; but its hard weight in my fist comforted my nerves. Something like a baby's pacifier.

Inserting the oars in the boat's rowlocks and lowering the boat into the water, I climbed in, put the tire iron down beside me, and began rowing. Following the shoreline, but not too close in. Trusting to the night and the mist to screen my approach. Using the oars with care so their sound wouldn't be heard by anyone ashore.

About six minutes of rowing brought me to the near end of Aumeier's property. According to the layout Fritz's police contact had described, this was the point farthest from the buildings. I turned in toward the dark shore. Dipping the oars with the delicacy of a seamstress threading a needle. Taking long, slow pulls. Waiting a moment each time before raising the oar blades very gently out of the water. As silent an approach as I could manage.

The swamp smell grew stronger as I got closer in. The gassy odor of stagnant bogs and decomposing vegetation. The pointy bow of my rubber boat nosed in between tall stands of coarse grass growing straight up out of the lake water. They grew taller and more numerous as the shore got nearer.

Finally the growths were so dense I couldn't row any farther through them. The smell of wet decay was very strong now. I drew in the oars and used one to measure the depth of the water there. Gripping the blade to keep the oar vertical as I forced the other end down. Not too deep. The water would barely come up to my knees.

I took off my jacket and put it in the bottom of the boat. I picked up the comforting tire iron and stuck it in my belt. I took off my shoes, tied their laces together with a slipknot, and hung them around the back of my neck. Took off my socks and put them inside the shoes. Rolled up my denim slacks, forcing them above my knees.

Then I didn't do anything for some thirty seconds. Just sat there in my boat and listened. I couldn't hear anything but the croaking of frogs. A chorus loud enough to cover the slight splash when I went over the side and lowered my legs into the water.

It came up to above my knees—because the bottom was mushy-soft and my bare feet sank into the ooze almost to my ankles before they got to firmer mud. It slowed progress considerably. I trudged toward the blur of the shore, dragging the little boat after me by its bow ring through the forest of swamp grass higher than my head.

I angled between two large clumps of marsh shrubs. And came to a dead end. There was another shrub tangle ahead of me, and not enough room to get the boat through. I didn't want to take it in any further, anyway. This was a good place to leave it, fairly well hidden by the shrubs.

I turned it until its bow was pointed out toward the open water. For the same reason that I'd turned the car around. In case getting back out became urgent. I snagged one of the boat's safety lines around a stout, crooked branch to hold it in place, and eased myself past the shrubs.

The swamp water shallowed as I continued through a quagmire in what I hoped was the shortest direction to a solid shore. But the soft mud kept sucking at my bare feet, trying to cement them to the bottom. My legs and lungs are pretty good from all the swimming I do in the sea below my house. But I was having to fight to keep my panting from getting too noisy by the time I reached drier ground inside the fringe of a pine thicket.

I leaned against a pine trunk, listening again while I brought my breathing back to normal. The frogs nearest to my position had stopped croaking. As they always do when they sense a large animal getting too close. But the rest of the frogs kept up enough of a din to cover that giveaway to my presence. I didn't hear anything else.

Using the ground's deep carpet of pine needles and bark fragments to rub mud off my feet, I got back into my socks and shoes and rolled down my slacks. Enough of the mud remained dry-glued to my skin to make that uncomfortable. I didn't linger to do a better job.

Moving quietly, I followed a gradual rise in the land. Feeling my way with outstretched fingers. Testing the ground underfoot for dry twigs and avoiding them. The last of the ground mist was dissolving and some stars were beginning to show in the night sky. But in among the trees, the dark held, with only occasional lighter patches. The pines got bigger. Here and there an oak hogged all the space for itself.

I came to a stretch of bushes that seemed to line one side of a path. I eased partway through the bushes to make sure. It was definitely a man-made path. I stepped back in the bushes and considered. There was no question of my using any path. The question was whether to parallel its course on this side or to cross over. Before I could decide, I heard bushes moving on the other side.

There wasn't enough wind to move any bushes. I drew the tire iron out of my belt and took another backward step, plastering myself against a tree trunk with the low branches of a smaller tree partially screening me. The beam of a powerful flashlight showed through the bushes on the other side, moving toward the path. It reached the path, with two men coming out of the bushes behind it.

There was enough backshine from the flash for me to see they were both wearing those storm trooper outfits. And both had those little walkie-talkies strapped to their shoulders. The one in the lead carried the flashlight in one hand and dangled a club from his other. The second one had a compact submachine gun cradled in both hands.

Part of that hidden weapons cache the police search had failed to locate.

The one with the flashlight shined it in my general direction. My fist tightened around the tire iron, but otherwise I didn't move a muscle. The beam of the flash swept back and forth across my position. But it was a cursory sweep. They weren't expecting to find any problem. It was just part of a routine patrol of the grounds.

And it is difficult to distinguish a motionless man from his cover, even in better light.

They moved on, going left along the path. When they were gone I crossed the path and entered the bushes, taking the direction from which they'd come. The untamed woods gave way to ordered rows of trees, with no underbrush between them. Instead of wild bushes there were trimmed hedges and geometric arrangements of flower beds and grass plots. I reached a tall line of hedge and looked through it. Beyond was a large clearing with a field of grass and stables, surrounded by a low split-rail fence. Beyond that were a number of buildings, some with light showing through their windows. The largest was a Bavarian schloss, built when Italian baroque was the rage; old but well preserved.

I circled around the clearing toward it, sticking to the shadows all the way. Continuing to do so when I approached the buildings.

The first I reached was a spacious, open garage. There were three cars inside it—and six more out on the gravel space in front of it. Three of those six had license plates from different parts of West Germany. One of the other three was from Austria. Another from Holland. A third from Italy.

A man in a chauffeur's uniform leaned against one of the West German cars, a Mercedes sedan, smoking a cigar. His manner was that of someone accustomed to long, patient waiting.

Sticking to the darkest routes under trees and along hedges, I moved past one end of the garage toward the baroque schloss. I stopped against the back of a cottage near it, not liking the clear area that would have to be crossed to get any closer. It was much too well lighted. I didn't like the storm trooper guarding its entrance, either. Nor the other one, patrolling around the big building with a pump-action shotgun in the crook of his left arm.

Behind me, I heard the noise of a car crunching along the gravel drive toward the parking area. I worked my way back there. Another car was now outside the garage. The BMW belonging to Max Höss.

Looking around swiftly, I spotted him entering a small, one-story house near the far end of the garage. Lights went on inside it. The only way I could get there, without being seen by the smoking chauffeur, was by detouring away through two of the estate's tree groves and then curving back toward the rear of the little house. It took time. When I was finally nearing the house, Höss came out of it.

He had shed his mustard-stained clothes. Now he was dressed as he'd been in Genoa. Flight jacket, jeans, and combat boots. He went back to the parking area and spoke briefly to the chauffeur, whose reply was just as brief. Höss hurried from the parking area, away from the buildings, taking a path that led toward the lake—but a different part of it than I'd come in from.

If Clemens von Langsdorf was anywhere on this estate, Höss would be going to report to him about the slight delay in finding and killing Zenta Bremme.

I went after him, keeping away from the path but angling in the same direction.

❈ 28 ❈

I WAS DOWN TO WHERE THE TANGLED PINE THICKET MERGED into the swampy stretch along the lakefront when I saw where Höss was going. The path he had taken became a raised boardwalk that arched over the marsh to a boat dock I hadn't seen before.

There was an outboard motorboat moored to one side of the dock. On the other side was a luxury cabin cruiser. A twin-engined sixty-footer. Constructed for the sea, not for a lake. But as lakes go, the Chiemsee is a big one; and the wind from the Bavarian Alps can sometimes churn its surface into sizable waves. Aumeier wouldn't be the only rich man around the Chiemsee indulging his fancy with a seagoing yacht.

There was a lot of light coming through the long, opened windows of its main cabin. A storm trooper, with another of those compact submachine guns slung from one shoulder, stood guard where the dock met the boardwalk. Höss reached him and said something. The guard motioned for him to stay put, and went along the dock to the yacht. He squatted down until his face was level with one of the cabin windows, and spoke to someone inside. Then he straightened and walked back to the boardwalk, motioning for Höss to go past him to the yacht.

By then I had my shoes and socks off again, and my slacks rolled up, and was wading through the marsh toward the dock. Keeping to the tall weeds that hid me; advancing cautiously through them without disturbing any enough to advertise my presence.

The lean, harsh-faced man I'd originally thought of as Hulvane—and now as Langsdorf—came out of the cabin to the yacht's cockpit. He stepped up onto the gunwale, and from there, onto the dock. As I'd noticed that first morning in Paris, age hadn't sapped his legs much.

Höss reached him and spoke quickly, looking slightly apologetic. Langsdorf's face remained coldly impassive when he replied. I wasn't near enough to hear what they were saying to each other. In the light from the yacht's cabin Höss showed some relief from tension when he spoke again. Langsdorf nodded shortly, climbed back down to the yacht's cockpit and returned to its cabin. Höss strode back along the dock, past the armed guard and onto the boardwalk, heading for the path he'd come from.

The water was up to my knees when I stopped and balanced my shoes, with the socks inside them, on top of a tangle of shrubs. I removed the rest of my clothes and left them there as well before wading farther. All I took with me was the tire iron. If I had to make the fast escape bare-assed, I would just have to handle the embarrassment as best I could.

The water got deeper and the tall weeds got thinner as I angled out of the marsh toward the docked motorboat. That was on my side of the dock. The yacht was moored to the other side. I never took my eyes off the armed guard.

He was a restless devil. Strolling from the dock onto the boardwalk and back again. Whenever he was turned in my direction, I froze in position.

When the water was up to my chest I put the tire iron between my teeth and began swimming. Using a slow, silent breaststroke, keeping my arms and legs well below the surface. And I kept watching the guard while I swam. Each time he looked my way I stopped and floated, pretending I was part of the dark water. Each time he looked away I stroked forward again—but with infinite care. Anyone who has ever watched a gecko advance toward a stationary, unwary insect will have a notion of *how* carefully I did it. You don't see the gecko's webbed feet move. Yet whenever you look away for twenty seconds, and then look back, it is that much closer to its target.

When I finally had the motorboat's low hull between me and the guard, it became easier. I swam under the dock. When I reached the hull of the yacht I submerged, went under its keel, and surfaced on the other side.

The yacht's high bulk did a complete job of screening me from the dock guard. Treading water, I reached high with both hands and hooked my fingers over the side gunwale between the cabin and the stern. I hung there and listened once again. There were men's voices but they were indistinct, coming from inside the cabin. There were no footsteps close enough to hear. With the tire iron still between my teeth, I took a silent drag of air and chinned myself. Just high enough to peek over the gunwale.

The big cockpit was empty. There was no one in sight anywhere on the yacht. Its cabin kept me hidden from the dock guard and the long cabin windows were comfortably above the level of my head. I kept the rest of me down at that level when I hauled myself across the gunwale and went flat on the cockpit deck.

I was dripping wet but the night air was warm enough to keep me from shivering. What did bother me was all the light coming from the cabin and the fact that there was no cover at all for me on that outside deck. If anybody came out they were going to see me. Being naked didn't help to make me feel less vulerable. I had to struggle against a strong urge to go back into the water.

Taking the tire iron from my teeth with my right hand, I began inching forward along the deck toward my side of the cabin. Staying flat and using just my elbows and toes. The voices from the cabin became more distinct. All male voices. Speaking German. When I was under the first open window I lay still and listened.

I can understand a good deal of German—if it's spoken slowly and clearly. But most of these men inside weren't enunciating carefully enough for me. What I got out of it was that some of them were telling "Herr von Langsdorf" they were looking forward to delivery of his merchandise.

I raised myself cautiously to look in over a lower corner of the window. Nobody was looking in my direction, and I hoped I'd be quick enough to duck back down before any of them did.

There were six formidable-looking men sitting stiffly on two adjacent L-shaped settees, facing a seventh man seated in a deck chair. Langsdorf was the oldest of the men on the settees, but the man in the deck chair was older. Close to eighty, and almost entirely bald. He had a lumpy, sagging body that his tailored Tyrolean suit could do nothing to improve. A bulbous, broken-veined nose. Eyes that were slits between swollen lids, barely visible behind the thick lenses of his rimless glasses.

He was clearly the most important man at this meeting. The deferential way the others looked at him said it. So did his own expression of almost contemptuous authority. He was just finishing a short speech I didn't get.

Langsdorf nodded and rose to his feet. "You may be certain of it, Herr Aumeier."

The other five men got off their settees one at a time, to give Langsdorf a businesslike handshake before sitting down again. Aumeier didn't budge from his deck chair. Langsdorf turned back to him and said, "You must allow four days, Herr Aumeier. Or even five. Transporting it this distance, by car and van, presents certain difficulties."

"Naturally," Aumeier said. "That is why I send Max along. To minimize some of those difficulties."

Langsdorf gave him an ingratiating smile that was as put on as everything about him seemed to be. "And I wish to say again how greatly I appreciate your lending me Max Höss to help solve those other two little problems of mine."

Aumeier's answering smile had no humor in it at all. "He will take care of that second one when he returns. Be sure of that. My Max is a dependable worker."

Langsdorf was thanking him again when I went over the side and back into the water.

I got back to the shore the way I'd come. I waited until I reached dry ground inside the pine thicket before getting dressed. My clothes absorbed the wetness of my body almost immediately. But wearing clothes again—even wet clothes— gave me that irrational little extra sense of security.

The shortest route to where I'd hidden my little rubber rowboat cut straight across the estate past the main buildings and parking area. I was under the shadowy protection of a maple grove, within sight of the parking area, when I saw Max Höss coming out of his little house.

He was carrying a bucket and some cloths. Taking them to his BMW, he opened the front door on the driver's side and dipped a cloth into the bucket. The uniformed chauffeur leaning against the Mercedes with the Munich plates lit a new cigar and watched, curiously, as Höss began swabbing at the mustard stains on his upholstery.

I looked toward the little house, tempted. There just might be something of interest in there. And what Höss was doing wasn't a task he'd be able to complete in a hurry.

I glanced back at the parking area. The chauffeur suddenly straightened and dropped the cigar to the gravel, crushing it out under his heel. Langsdorf was striding to the parking area from the Aumeier schloss, followed by a storm trooper carrying a suitcase.

The chauffeur opened a rear door of the Mercedes and touched a hand to the peak of his uniform cap as Langsdorf approached. Höss straightened from his BMW and called out to Langsdorf.

I didn't understand all of it—but part of it had to do with his seeing Langsdorf again tomorrow.

Langsdorf nodded and got into the rear seat of the Mercedes. The chauffeur closed the door, took the suitcase from the storm trooper, and stowed it in the Mercedes trunk. Then he got in front behind the wheel. A second after the Mercedes' motor came to life its rear windows slid all the way open. Apparently Langsdorf liked plenty of fresh air. That was nice. The open windows made it certain that Fritz would spot him through his night glasses.

Automatically I memorized the license number of the Mercedes as it pulled away—though Fritz was bound to do the same. I just hoped he'd be able to get to his Honda quickly enough to catch up with the Mercedes—and to stick with it until he saw where it took Langsdorf. A single-car tail through open country at night is a chancy business.

When the Mercedes was gone, I looked at Höss. He was back to work on the BMW's upholstery. Getting out mustard stains is a time-consuming bitch. I looked again toward his little house. What he'd called to Langsdorf, in conjunction with what I'd overheard on the yacht, made the temptation stronger.

The lights in his little house were still on, and he'd opened the front windows. But I couldn't get to the front of the house without being seen from the parking area. I backed off through the maple grove and took a long circuit that brought me to the rear of the house.

One of its rear corners touched against the back of a large, dark greenhouse. Creating a *cul-de-sac* there. I didn't like that. But I did like seeing that Höss had left the back windows of his house open, too. I climbed in through one of them.

There wasn't much to the interior, although it was nicely furnished. A living room with a dining alcove. A bedroom and bathroom. Ample closets. I did find something interesting— and less than four minutes after I'd begun to search.

It was on top of a large chest of drawers in his bedroom. An airline ticket, made out to Max Höss. For a flight to Paris. Leaving Munich tomorrow at a few minutes after one P.M.

I put it back on the chest exactly the way I'd found it. The rest of my search was swift, netting no more discoveries. Time was pressing, hard. Warning me I had already been inside the Aumeier estate much too long. The urge to get out was becoming imperative.

I left the house the way I'd gotten in. Through the rear window. And my luck ran out, there and then. While I was turning to get out of the *cul-de-sac* formed where the house cornered against the greenhouse.

Three storm troopers were strolling by the open end. They saw me at the same time I saw them. And they stopped dead, frowning at me.

They didn't know me. There was enough light pouring out of the house's back windows to show them that. And if they didn't know me, I wasn't one of the people who had a right to be in the estate. It didn't require smarts to realize they'd cornered a trespasser.

They got their clubs in hand quickly and spread out just enough to block my exit. They had mean faces, and their brown shirts bulged with pumped-up beef. Wall-to-wall muscle. They closed in on me, looking eager but deliberately taking their time. Storm troopers get their orgasms from watching the fear build in a victim's face.

Luckily, these three weren't armed with anything but the clubs they hefted as they advanced. I yanked the tire iron from my belt and let my own mean streak take over.

It gave them pause.

Fascist paramilitary organizations make a big thing of teaching their stronger members how to fight when they don't have any loaded guns handy. But that training tends to concentrate on how five of their boys can manage the beating up of a solitary old man if they really stick together.

I feinted at the one to my left and took out the one to the right with a tire-iron chop to his kidney. He went down with a shuddering cry and the middle man instinctively threw up an arm to protect himself when the tire iron lashed back at him. It shattered his elbow and spun him against the guy to the left.

I went through the gap and took off like a jackrabbit.

❂ **29** ❂

A LOUD WHISTLE BLEW BEHIND ME AS I LEFT THE BUILDINGS
behind and sprinted toward the fenced-off field of grass. The
whistle blower had to be the one I hadn't tire-ironed. His two
buddies would be too involved with their pain.

I jumped the low fence and streaked across the field. The
whistle blower would be using his radio transceiver now—
alerting the estate's other guards. The ones who would come
after me from around the buildings weren't my only problem.
There were the others somewhere ahead of me, patrolling
the woods near the lake. In communication with each other
via their own walkie-talkies. They would move to block off
my escape route as soon as they were given its direction.

But the direction I was taking didn't lead to where I intended to go as soon as I got out of sight.

I cleared the next low fence and rammed through a high
hedge. Went through an orderly grove of trees and into the
wild pine thicket. When I was deep enough inside the thicket
I shifted direction. Making a sharp left turn and heading for
the place where I'd left my rowboat.

I'd taken about fifteen steps along that route when a whistle
blew inside the thicket somewhere ahead. That stopped me.
A second whistle blew—off to my left. It was answered by a
third—off to my right.

I stood still, trying to judge the exact location of each of
those whistles. All of the frogs were silent now.

The whistles sounded again. First the one ahead, then the
ones to my left and right. Closer this time.

But there was no answering whistle from *behind* me.

I turned around to head in that direction. And stopped myself after two steps. I felt a tight smile stretch my lips against my teeth, though I wasn't feeling funny about anything at that moment.

They didn't need the whistles to communicate with each other. They had their little radio transceivers for that. And those could do the job a lot more quietly; without alerting me.

They were *herding* me. Coming in noisily from three sides to drive me toward the fourth—where the strongest section of their mantrap would be waiting.

I turned around again, and once more headed toward my hidden rowboat. But at an angle I hoped would take me midway between the whistler ahead and the one to the right.

The whistles blew again. The one that had been to the left was farther away from me now. But the center one was closer. And the third was much closer.

I stopped and braced my back against a wide tree trunk. Its upper half had been broken off, probably by lightning, and lay moldering on the ground. But the thick stump that was left was higher than my head. I waited and gripped the tire iron tightly but didn't feel much security from it this time. These hunters would all have guns. I wanted them to pass by without noticing me.

When the center whistle sounded again, it had passed the line of my position. The second whistle was even farther past me.

The blast of the third whistle, directly behind me, was so close and loud it almost jarred me loose from my tree trunk.

My heart lurched, but I managed to stop the rest of me from lurching with it. I also stopped breathing. He was on the other side of the trunk. I hadn't heard his approach.

But I heard him now. His slow breathing. And, after a long moment, the faint crack of a dry twig under his boot as he moved on.

I turned my head in that direction, very slightly and slowly. I saw the indistinct blur of a single figure moving away from me through the thicket shadows—and the glint of a weapon barrel attached to the blur. Then the blur and the glint were swallowed by the general darkness.

I waited there for two full minutes. Then I detached myself from the tree trunk and continued along the route to my rowboat, going down through the thicket and along the land end of the lake's marsh. Several times I heard movement through the bushes around me. But never too close. And each time I stopped and waited, the sound dwindled away.

When I waded out into the marsh this time I didn't waste any precious moments taking off my shoes and rolling up my slacks first. The thick slush of the bottom tried to pull my shoes off for me, but I didn't let the mud have them. I was almost to the rowboat when I saw the shadowed figure standing there, knee-deep in the water beside it.

He was holding a pump-action shotgun up against one shoulder. In his other hand he held his radio transceiver, and he was speaking into it. I couldn't understand what he was saying, but I didn't need to hear the words to know he was informing the other hunters that he'd discovered the exit point I'd be coming to.

I had gone into a crouch the instant I spotted him. He was looking toward the shore, but angled away from my direction. I kept to the crouch, using swamp shrubs and tall clumps of grass to cover my approach as I waded toward him. One slow, long step at a time. Taking infinite care with each step.

I was very near when his walkie-talkie squawked something short and he hung it back on his shoulder and turned toward me. I closed the last of the distance between us with a lunge that splashed muddy water over both of us. His reaction was quick. The shotgun was off his shoulder and leveled by the time I reached him. His finger was feeling for the trigger when I rammed the end of the tire iron into him below his breastbone.

He folded forward like a wet rag. The top of his head thumped against my chest. I let the tire iron drop into the water so I could catch the shotgun spilling out of his hands. He sagged away from me and settled down with his back propped against a dense bush, his head hanging with chin against his chest, and his nose a scant inch from the water.

His eyes were shut but his mouth was open and he was doing as much breathing through it as through his nose. If he slid down that extra inch, though, he was going to be breathing water and drown. That was his problem. I had my own and it was urgent.

I did a swift scan of the murky shore and an equally fast check on whether the shotgun had a shell in its firing chamber. It did. Holding the shotgun ready in one hand with my finger touching the trigger, I used my other hand to unsnag the little rowboat from its shrub. I began backing toward clearer water, pulling the boat along with me by its bow ring. I didn't stop scanning the shore.

A storm trooper stepped out between two swamp bushes with one of those submachine guns. I flung myself into the boat, as flat down as I could get. The first sweeping burst lashed over my head like a whip and tore up a lot of weeds and water. He lowered his aim for a second burst but by then I had a bead on him. I squeezed the trigger. The harsh thud of the shotgun and the jolt of its stock against my shoulder seemed to come at the same instant its blast hit the machine-gunner's chest and kicked him off his feet.

He disappeared. But I could hear him. The nasty squelch of his body dropping into a bog of weedy ooze.

I worked the shotgun's pump, jacking another shell into the chamber while I surveyed the shore. No more storm troopers yet. But they'd be coming. I sat up, put the shotgun across my thighs, and grabbed the oars. I rowed away from the shore. Forcing the boat through the high grass. It parted reluctantly and then closed again across the boat's wake, hiding the shore from me. And me from the shore.

I turned to parallel the shoreline before reaching clear water. I didn't want to be all the way out in the open. Sticking with the edge of the high grass, I cut toward the dock where I'd parked the Audi.

It was in sight when I heard a sound that chilled me. A motorboat. I looked toward the sound and saw it appear from around a jut in the lakefront. The one with the outboard, from Aumeier's dock. With three men in it. I couldn't see weapons, but they wouldn't be coming after me without them.

I've never rowed harder. Fast, back-straining work that helped blunt the corkscrew twist of panic in my liver. The motorboat closed the distance between us with disconcerting speed.

I turned in to the shore before reaching my boat dock. Grabbed the shotgun with one hand and jumped out of the boat where the water was still halfway up my shins. Slogged through the stretch of marsh and up onto the dry ground of the public parking lot. Had the ignition key out of my pocket while I ran to the car.

The motorboat sped past me and the Audi and the dock. Doing a churning turn-in beyond the dock. Nosing into the marshy shore near the dirt track that was my way out of the parking lot.

I swung myself into the Audi, dropped my ass onto the driver's seat and the shotgun down beside me, and jabbed the key into the ignition lock. I had the car in motion when I saw the three men from the motorboat running toward my exit track. And now I saw their weapons. Two shotguns and a submachine gun.

The guy toting that last item was a hell of a sprinter, way ahead of the other two. I gunned the Audi across the lot. The machine-gunner halted short of the track and got set to rake the car when I went past. I swerved away from the track with the accelerator floored and drove straight at him.

He dived away, hit the ground awkwardly, and somersaulted into a jumble of wild brush. I swerved back toward the track and heard and felt the crunch of my right fender against a stump I hadn't seen on time. The damage wasn't bad enough to slow the car. I had it racing up the track when I heard the thump of a shotgun somewhere behind me. Far enough back for the scattered shot to spiderweb the rear window without breaking through it. The next instant I had the car around a sharp bend, with trees screening me from the shooters.

Seconds later I was out of the top end of the track, making a skidding turn onto the paved road. Away from the direction of Aumeier's place.

❄ **30** ❄

I WASN'T GOING ANYWHERE IN PARTICULAR. JUST AWAY. BE-
fore they came after me in cars. The Audi was a pretty fast
car, but Aumeier's watchdogs would have some that were
faster.

I took a left into the first crossroad I came to. A couple
miles farther I took a right into another crossroad.

Fifteen minutes later I was lost in a maze of meandering
farm roads with no sign of pursuit behind me. I turned in to
a dirt tractor path and came to a stop between a neat line of
trees and a wheat field. I cut the motor and lights and then
sat there and waited. Wishing I had something hard to drink.
My nerves were still jangling and my blood pressure was
causing a windy sound between my ears.

I slowed my breathing while I waited, and speculated on
what would be going on back at the estate. It was doubtful
that they'd be making any connection between me and
Langsdorf's back history. Probably nobody there knew much
about that history except Aumeier—and his knowledge would
be limited to what Langsdorf wanted him to know.

Aumeier's thoughts about the unknown man who'd slipped
into his estate would follow a more immediate and obvious
line. Connecting me to that unsuccessful police search of his
estate. The police were smarting from that failure to uncover
anything incriminating. The presence of a trespasser could
mean a more careful attempt—perhaps by some lone informant acting on the promise of a reward—to find out something the law could use against Aumeier.

It wasn't likely he'd think I'd found out much. I'd been discovered too far from the yacht where that meeting was being held. His worst worry would be that I'd report about all those weapons his storm troopers were carrying. Those were probably being returned to hiding now, just in case.

I didn't have to do much brain work to put what I'd over-heard at that meeting together with Langsdorf's current business. Langsdorf was expecting a shipment of South American cocaine—probably arriving by ship from Venezuela in the next couple days at some point along Europe's Atlantic coast-line. The other men at the meeting were waiting for him to sell it to them.

His "unique" connections for distributing narcotics in Europe were its growing number of neo-Nazi organizations. He was using his contacts with old Nazis like Aumeier to make his arrangements with the newer ones. They all needed money to finance their activities. With the European prices for retail sales of illegal drugs skyrocketing, they could pay heavy amounts for Langsdorf's shipments and still net a large profit from their local distributors.

I didn't believe Langsdorf had any devotion to the politics of these organizations, though he might pretend he did. As Zenta Bremme had said, he shifted with the wind, never against it. The new Nazis were growing in number, but they hadn't yet achieved any real power. His allegiance now was to something that was becoming more powerful than most governments. The narcotics trade.

I waited beside that wheat field for a full half hour. Not a single car went past me in either direction. There were no headlights moving through the night-shrouded farmlands anywhere within my circle of vision.

Switching on the Audi's interior light, I opened the road map supplied by the rental agency. It took a while to figure out exactly where I was. And then to figure how to get out of there without going back anywhere near Aumeier's estate.

I only got lost twice before I found the road I wanted that would take me to a crossing of the Inn River. When I reached the river, I turned away from the near end of the bridge and drove along the bank. Until I found a secluded spot where I could toss the shotgun into the water. Then I swung back to the bridge, crossed over the river, and drove on to Munich.

Fritz and I had agreed to leave any messages for each other at the lobby desk of our Munich hotel. There was no message for me. Fritz was up in our room, finishing a phone call that wasn't making him happy.

He hung up when I stepped inside and closed the door. There was an opened bottle of brandy on the table between our beds. Fritz poured a generous amount into the glass, drank some, and sighed wearily.

I took the glass from him and finished what was left in it. "You lost Langsdorf."

Fritz looked angry and embarrassed, about half and half. "He came out of the estate in a chauffeur-driven Mercedes. I had no difficulty in keeping it in sight—until it got onto the autobahn going in the direction of Munich. There we came into a great deal of traffic, and the Mercedes put on considerable speed weaving through it. I *thought* I'd managed to stick with it through that traffic. But when I followed the Mercedes taillights off the autobahn, I discovered it wasn't the one carrying Langsdorf."

Fritz took the empty glass back with a rueful grimace. He poured more brandy into it, took a small sip, and told me the rest of it. He'd driven straight to the apartment of his Munich police contact and given him the license number of Langsdorf's Mercedes. A phone check revealed that it belonged to a limousine-hire agency. The agency was closed for the night, and its manager wasn't at his home. It took four more phone calls to locate him. And more time for him to go to his agency office and check its records.

Langsdorf had hired the Mercedes and its chauffeur using his fake "Heinz Graff" I.D.—paying the full amount in advance. In cash.

More time went into finding the chauffeur—who was also not at home. He reported that he'd driven Langsdorf straight from the Aumeier estate to the Munich airport. Langsdorf had been in a hurry. He had a reservation on the last night plane to Paris. They made it with only fifteen minutes to spare.

That flight was scheduled to land at Paris's Charles de Gaulle Airport. Fritz had phoned there. And had been told the plane from Munich had already landed and its passengers were gone.

He gestured at our room phone. "I have just learned that wherever our man has gone, it was not back to the Hotel Ritz. We are going to have a very difficult time trying to locate him again."

"Not necessarily." I told Fritz about Max Höss expecting to meet with Langsdorf tomorrow—and about his ticket for an early afternoon flight to Paris.

Fritz began to perk up. "So—we get on the same plane. And follow him when he gets off."

"Our problem is going to be sticking to Höss until he meets Langsdorf. There's no guarantee they're meeting in Paris. Or even close to it. The further we have to tag after him, the more chance we'll lose him along the way."

Fritz took a reflective taste of his brandy. "We don't have any alternative."

"No," I agreed. I took the glass from him again and had more than a taste.

Neither of us knew it yet, but we were slated to get some extra help. From an unexpected source. The French secret service.

We had each had more brandy and were preparing to go to bed when our room phone rang. It was for me, from Paris. Thierry Gallion—navy captain and DGSE desk jockey.

"We have to meet and have a talk," Thierry told me. "I'm coming to Munich on the first morning plane."

We decided to meet at the Devil's footprint.

❄ **31** ❄

THE REDBRICK TOWERS OF THE *FRAUENKIRCHE* DOMINATED the skyline of central Munich even more in the fifteenth century, when the cathedral was built, than it does today. Shortly after it was finished, the Devil decided to see what the interior looked like. The step he took inside remains implanted in the marble of the entrance floor. Just that one step—because the Devil was so frightened by the cathedral's candlelit holiness that he immediately turned and rushed out. He left so fast he stirred up a wind that continues to blow through that part of the *Frauenkirche*.

I was measuring my own foot against that footprint when Thierry Gallion arrived. "Apparently," he commented, "the Devil is a bigger man than you are."

"I've long suspected that," I told him. "Do you want to walk while we talk?"

"Yes."

I'd known he would. He'd been trapped inside that malfunctioning submarine on the ocean bottom too long. In addition to damaging his heart and hearing, it had left Thierry with a slight but permanent case of claustrophobia. Being surrounded by office walls much of the time aggravated that condition. He liked to get out in the open whenever he could.

Leaving the *Frauenkirche*, I remembered our last two business meetings, in Paris. One had been conducted during a stroll through the Tuileries, the other in the Luxembourg Gardens. Whenever he spent a summer week at my Riviera house with his wife and kids, he stayed outdoors most of the time. Even sometimes taking his night's sleep out on my patio.

"I had an awful breakfast at the airport before my plane took off," Thierry said. "Let's go to the *Viktualienmarkt* and get something tasty."

We turned in that direction at the same time. Thierry's job brought him to Munich—long an East-West espionage center—often enough for him to know his way around it. I walked on his left side, because that was the ear with his hearing aid. We walked slowly, because though mild physical activity was good for his heart, exerting himself was not.

He inquired politely about Fritz's health. I told him that he was in fine form. Fritz had gone to secure us seats on the plane Max Höss would be taking. And then to accompany Zenta Bremme on a shopping tour for clothes and other necessities. After which she was not to leave his friend's apartment again, until hearing from him that the danger was past.

"You have stirred up considerable excitement in the Swimming Pool," Thierry told me. The DGSE had acquired that popular nickname from the public swimming pool across the street from the fort containing its headquarters. "We think you've stumbled on a French war criminal who has been at the top of a priority wanted list for forty-five years."

"You told me war criminals aren't the DGSE's department," I reminded Thierry.

"That is true," he said with a dry humor, "and we certainly intend to turn him over to the proper governmental department—after *we* catch him."

"The DGSE needs some good publicity."

"We do indeed. My superiors would dearly love to let both the government and the public know we are good for something besides making boo-boos."

In recent years the DGSE—*Direction Général de la Sécurité Extérieure*—had become involved in almost as many errors and indiscretions as the CIA. The French government was just more successful than Washington at preventing excess press coverage of the fumbles.

"It is almost a certainty," Thierry said, "that this war criminal is the man you referred to as Clemens von Langsdorf. Though no one ever discovered he was using that alias, until you mentioned him to me. His real name is Clement Laforge. Same initials.''

I very much hoped that was going to be the end of the names I'd have to know him by. It was getting annoying, trying to keep track. Hulvane to Langsdorf to Laforge. I decided to keep him straight in my mind by thinking of him as a double-barreled name: Langsdorf-Laforge.

''My superior officers,'' Thierry went on, ''feel that catching him would be a greater sensation than the capture and trial of Klaus Barbie, the Nazi Butcher of Lyon. Because Laforge is French.''

''He's not here anymore,'' I told Thierry.

He came to a dismayed halt. ''*Merde . . .*''

''But I think we can find him again.''

Thierry drew a relieved breath. ''That's better. Don't do that to me again. I don't need to add an ulcer to my other complaints.''

''I think he's back in France.''

''*Much* better,'' Thierry said, and we resumed our stroll. ''That makes it so much easier for us to take and hold him.''

Taking and holding a wanted criminal, inside France, was supposed to be a privilege confined to the French police—or in some cases to the DST, the French equivalent of the FBI. The DGSE was only supposed to act outside the country. But Thierry's bosses obviously figured the glory of this capture would excuse infraction of departmental regulations.

Thierry was nodding to himself. ''I was right when I told my superiors that I was the best one to send here. That because we're old friends, you would be entirely open and co-operative with me. I warned them against sending someone with more authority and, ah—threatening power. I explained that you have an extremely hard obstinate streak that makes you as difficult to push around as General de Gaulle.''

''You just wanted to take a trip, Thierry. You're getting better at lying than you used to be.''

He grinned. ''Since that is a talent much prized in my current profession, I do try my best to cultivate it.''

We turned in to an alley that brought us out to the

Viktualienmarkt. A large, open area full of food-produce vendors and statues of Bavaria's old music hall favorites, trees and flowers, restaurants and snack pavilions. We joined a line at one of the pavilions and bought coffee and apple strudels. The coffee was thin, but the strudels were fresh and yummy. Thierry licked the last crumbs from his fingertips— somehow managing to make it look elegant—while we walked away from the food market.

"Those artworks you told me about," he said, "belonged to prominent Dijon people who died in German concentration camps. Some weeks before being sent to Germany, they sold the paintings to Clement Laforge. The same man who then denounced them to the Gestapo as Resistance sympathizers."

"According to their papers, those paintings were sold to him under the German name he adopted. Clemens von Langsdorf."

"Nobody in France ever heard of that name or saw those papers. Nobody still alive, that is. The attorney who witnessed the signing of the sales document was shot by the SS, shortly before the Germans pulled out of Dijon near the war's end."

"Denounced by Langsdorf-Laforge, I assume."

"Probably. Perhaps I had better give you some of his background first."

"I wish you would," I said.

"Clement Laforge was born in Reims and grew up there. At a young age he joined Doriot's *Parti Populaire Française.*" Thierry glanced at me to see if I needed a history lesson.

I didn't. Jacques Doriot had been a charismic anti-Semite who switched from the Communist Party to the extreme right and became leader of the strongest Fascist party in prewar France.

"A year after joining Doriot," Thierry resumed, "young Clement Laforge became a member of *La Cagoule*—the extreme right's terrorist group."

"The one that got some of its weapons from Mussolini,

in exchange for murdering anti-Fascist Italians who'd fled to France.''

"That's right. But according to those who knew Laforge then, he was much more enamored of Hitler than of Mussolini. And in 1937 he went off to Nazi Germany—'to become part of the future,' he said. As far as anyone knows, he never returned to Reims.

"At the end of 1941 he turned up in Dijon. Using his French name and claiming to be on the run from the German occupation authorities and their servants, the French *Milice* and the Vichy police. In that way he got to know many of the people in Dijon who had real reason to fear both the Germans and Vichy. Then what he really was became known. He was working for the Gestapo. As a sort of liaison-adviser—assisting in the finding and arrest of 'undesirables.' Members of the Resistance or those he claimed were sympathetic to it. Jews and Gypsies and Germans who'd fled from the Nazi regime. Also those critical of Pétain or any of the policies of his Vichy government. And some people that Laforge simply wanted to rob of whatever they had of value.''

"Including all those artworks he acquired,'' I said.

"Yes. The amounts stated in the papers that accompanied those are false. The truth was that people just *gave* him what he wanted. Under his threat to denounce them to the Gestapo. And on his promise not to, if they were cooperative. The Gestapo must have known what he was doing. Perhaps he shared his loot with them. At any rate, once these people were milked of everything he wanted, they were arrested and shipped to Germany. Very few ever returned.

"Among those he subjected to extortion were nine Dijon families who were hiding Jewish children whose parents had been rounded up. *None* of those survived the concentration camps. Not the families, and not the children.''

Thierry suddenly raised his hands and looked at them. They had clenched into fists. He stuffed them into his pockets, shaking his head as we walked on. "You know, there are people who are against continuing to prosecute war criminals like Barbie and this Laforge. They say, 'What's the point? All those old war criminals are going to die off soon, anyway.' You try to explain—it's not just to punish them for what they did. It's also so people of younger generations will *learn* what those men did. Because they don't know. Look at all the kids and so-called adults playing games with what little they understand of that period. Wearing swastikas and collecting Nazi souvenirs . . .''

"What's the last you know of him?" I cut in. "Under the Laforge name or any other."

"Just Laforge," Thierry said. "None of the Dijon survivors knew him as anything else. He left when the Germans pulled out. When the Allied armies were coming close."

"Taking his loot with him."

"Apparently. There is a report on file from someone who thought he saw him in Munich, shortly after the war. But if it *was* Laforge, he wasn't spotted again. And no one I know of connected that Langsdorf name to him, until now."

We had turned into Maximilianstrasse, going toward the river. Thierry took his hands out of his pockets and pointed ahead. "I have a friend who has his apartment and office on this street. Claus Froschmeier. A distinguished attorney, with excellent government connections. I phoned him yesterday, and he instituted a search through the old files for me. There is no record of a Frenchman having his name legally changed from Clement Laforge to Clemens von Langsdorf."

"A lot of the files were wiped out by bombs and fire near the end of the war," I said.

"That's true. And a great many more were destroyed to get rid of incriminating documents about various Nazis." Thierry stopped walking and turned to face me. "All right, Pierre-Ange—now tell me what *you* know about him. This Laforge who took the name Langsdorf."

I told him enough of what I knew about the man. And then I told him about Max Höss—and about his ticket on a plane leaving for Paris in just a few hours.

❄ **32** ❄

ALLIED BOMBERS HIT FRANCE'S ATLANTIC PORT OF SAINT-
Nazaire so hard and so often, when it was under German
control in World War II, that its harbor and shipbuilding
facilities were wrecked and the town itself was reduced to
rubble. But the primary target—the massive U-boat base inside the harbor—survived every attack. Its protective shell of
reinforced concrete was too thick and strong for any bomb
of the time to penetrate.

The residential section we were driving through was entirely new, built after the war. So was the town's main shopping area, grouped around a blocks-long commercial
building everyone called "The Ship" because it had the con-
figuration of an ocean liner. Only the German U-boat base,
looming ahead of us as we neared the rebuilt harbor, remained from the past. It had proved as difficult to remove in
peacetime, at a practical cost, as it had been to destroy in the
war.

There were three tail cars on Max Höss. One ahead of him
and two behind. Fritz and I were in a fourth car, bringing up
the rear. I was driving it the way Thierry Gallion had instructed me to. Staying as far behind as I could without losing sight of the last tail car.

"I can't afford to have questions asked about why I had
two civilians involved in this part," he'd said, "when I
couldn't manage to notify the police before making the capture."

The only reason Thierry had let us tag along at all on this leg of the trip was because I'd blackmailed him into it.

That hadn't become necessary until we were back on French soil. In Munich, Thierry had gotten one of his opposite numbers in German Intelligence to obtain seats for the three of us in the front section of the plane for Paris. After making sure that Max Höss was seated back in the rear passenger section. We'd waited until Höss was in his seat before boarding. And Thierry had gone just ahead of Fritz and me, standing in the aisle to screen us from Höss until we were seated with our backs to him.

Höss was still unlikely to recognize me. But he would remember Fritz. The old man who'd stumbled into him outside the Dachau S-Bahn station, accidentally preventing him from catching up to Zenta Bremme. If he spotted Fritz again, on the same plane, he'd know it was no accident.

But he didn't spot him, and when we landed in Paris we were off the plane well before Höss. Thierry got us through passport control before any of the other passengers had lined up there. Two men were waiting for us on the other side. A couple DGSE agents that Thierry had arranged for by phone from Munich.

One was a burly, middle-aged guy with a sleepy face and small dark eyes that were very awake. The other was a blonde in his early twenties. Handsome enough to have been a stand-in for young Robert Redford; looking athletic enough to do the actor's stunt work for him as well. I remembered him from a couple years back, when I'd spotted him inconspicuously bodyguarding a group of lunching DGSE officers. Thierry had later told me his name was Fabrice Pradel.

Back then young Pradel had been wearing a sport shirt and jeans, with his hair almost hippie-long. Now he had a trim haircut and wore a nice linen suit that hid some of the strength of his body. And he'd obviously gone up in rank. Because it was to Pradel that Thierry slipped a picture of Max Höss. Which meant he was the leader of this two-man team.

They stayed put, waiting for Höss to come through passport control, while Fritz and I followed Thierry through the terminal building. Near its exit he gave another photo of Höss to a second two-man team he'd arranged to have posted near the exit. Thierry had a pocket full of those pictures. Copies of one that had been taken of Höss the last time he'd been arrested. Fritz had gotten them from his Munich police connection.

In addition to the two secret service teams, Thierry had arranged for cars to be waiting outside the terminal, for tailing Höss away from the airport. But Höss didn't leave the terminal. Shadowed by Fabrice Pradel and his partner, and carrying the weekender bag he'd taken on the plane with him, Höss went straight to an Air Inter counter and picked up another airline ticket waiting for him there.

When he strolled away with his ticket, Fabrice Pradel had a short talk with the woman behind the counter. Then he reported to Thierry. The ticket was for a flight to Nantes, leaving in forty minutes.

Max Höss had settled down to wait on a bench near the flight's departure gate. Fritz and I disappeared into a dark corner of the terminal bar, while Thierry hurried off to make new arrangements. I was well into a half bottle of rosé and Fritz was having his second cup of tea when Thierry joined us, looking more tense than usual.

"All fixed," he said as he dropped into a chair facing us. "I have seats on the same plane, and I phoned ahead to have two of our men in Nantes that I can trust waiting at the airport there. With cars ready to follow Höss wherever he goes from the Nantes airport. Now I want you two to go home and not say anything about any of this until—"

I didn't let him finish that: "While you were calling ahead, Thierry, did you get around to calling for some police help out there?"

"No." His smile was nervous. "There wasn't enough time for that. The plane's leaving in fifteen minutes."

"I have a feeling you didn't notify your bosses at the Swimming Pool, either."

"Again, not enough time. I'd have to go through channels and all that red tape. Explaining everything in detail all along the line. It would take too long."

"And you want to hog some of the glory of this capture for yourself."

"I've manned a desk as a captain long enough," he said defensively. "When you are not fit for active duty any longer, opportunities to do something that will earn you a higher rank are very hard to come by."

Fritz stirred his tea, looked sympathetic, and kept silent. Thierry was *my* friend.

I sympathized with his motives, too. But my sympathy had some reservations and a time limit. "How many are you taking with you on the plane?"

"Fabrice Pradel and his partner, Joel Legoff."

"With you, that makes three. And the two waiting in Nantes makes it five altogether. You're seriously under-manned, Thierry. Our Langsdorf-Laforge is waiting for a shipment of dope worth millions. He won't be picking that up with just Max Höss for protection. He'll have others with him, and at least some of them will be armed."

"We will be, too," Thierry told me stiffly. "My men in Nantes are going to have weapons waiting there. But that's *my* problem. Not yours. I told you, I want both of you to go—"

"I just made a call to Rome," I interrupted again, and I pointed toward the phone booths outside the bar. "To Major Bandini, of the *carabinieri*. The Italian police are hunting Max Höss for the murder of Lawrence Tuck. I notified Major Bandini that Höss is about to be arrested here in France."

Thierry had gone pale.

I gave him the rest of it: "Major Bandini is preparing to apply for the extradition of Höss from France to Italy. A strong official request, government to government. But for that, he needs to know where Höss is being held—and by whom. I told him I'll call him again—very soon—and let him know."

"You can't do that," Thierry said, furious but keeping it under control. "Not until I've taken Laforge."

"Sorry, Thierry. I have an obligation to Bandini."

"On the other hand," Fritz chimed in blandly, "If you take us along with you, Pierre-Ange won't be able to make that second call for quite some time. Long enough for your purposes.''

From Nantes to Saint-Nazaire is an hour's drive. Max Höss did it in a VW Transporter van that was waiting for him, along with its driver, at the Nantes airport. The three tail cars, each very different from the others, were well spread out. One ahead of the van, another behind it, the third farther back. They kept in touch with each other via their two-way radios, and exchanged positions often enough so Höss and his driver wouldn't start wondering about seeing the same car ahead or behind too long. The heavy highway traffic from Nantes to Saint-Nazaire helped. Most of the time the two tail cars nearest the van had at least one car between them and it.

Thierry Gallion and Fabrice Pradel shared one car. One of the local agents had the second car to himself. Pradel's partner, Legoff, was in the one driven by the other local man. I kept the fourth car too far back to see the van. But Fritz and I could hear what the other three cars were saying to each other, over the radio in our own.

What we didn't have were guns. Thierry wouldn't let us have any from the weapons his local pair had waiting, and his refusal was final. ''It is bad enough I've let you come along. If I let you take an active part, and one of you gets killed, I'll never be able to explain it.''

''Arlette would understand and forgive,'' I told him. ''My mother would, too.''

''My superior officers wouldn't.''

It was after eight in the evening when we crossed the long new bridge over the mouth of the Loire and entered Saint-Nazaire. But the daylight hadn't faded much yet. It would be another hour before the street lamps went on. Thierry's car dropped back from first place to last, letting the local men bracket the van. They knew the street layout here intimately, and he didn't.

We went deep inside the town, getting very close to the harbor. So close that though none of the buildings around us were high, they hid the harbor from us. The voice of the local driver in the lead suddenly came crackling over the radio: "The van just turned off to the right behind me into Rue Gautier. . . ."

"I saw it," responded the second local driver. "I'm turning after it." Seconds later: "There it is, almost two blocks ahead of me. Continuing on Rue Gautier."

The lead driver: "I'm circling fast. I'll try to cut in ahead of it again."

Thierry Gallion: "Not too close, either of you. We don't want them getting familiar with us."

Second driver: "Continuing on Gautier . . . Still Rue Gautier."

The lead driver came in again: "I'm back in front of him on Gautier. A full block ahead. I'm lengthening that distance a little. . . . I—*Merde!* I can't see the van back there anymore. . . ."

Second driver: "He turned left a block behind you. That's a dead-end street, Captain Gallion. The van can't get out the other end. . . ."

Thierry Gallion: "*Don't* turn in after it. Drive on after the lead car and park somewhere past that street."

I saw Thierry's car pull over to the curb well before the street the van had turned in to. At the same time his voice came through again: "*Pierre-Ange*—stop back where you are and stay there."

The second driver: "I'm cruising past that dead-end street now. The van is parked. Near the other end, almost to the fence. I can't see if anybody is still in it. Now I can't see it anymore. . . ."

I turned left in to a narrow street before the one the van had taken. It dead-ended, too, against a high wire fence. Through which I could see the harbor again. The houses on both sides of the narrow street had been built after the war. But they'd deteriorated fast and were already abandoned, their upper windows smashed and the lower ones partially boarded up. Just waiting for the wreckers to make way for new construction.

I parked at the street's end facing the wire fence. On the other side of it, the vast above-ground bulk of the U-boat base spread out like an enormous prehistoric mammoth that had settled down to die there. Its gray, windowless walls were pockmarked by all the bombs that had struck it and bounced off, failing to kill it or the lethal submarines in its belly. But it *was* dead now. Dead and indisposable and unusable. Attempts had been made to utilize it for industry. But its cavernous interior, largely floored with water, didn't lend itself to manageable conversion.

"Go see what's happening," Fritz said gruffly. He didn't like having to stay put in the car. But he couldn't get around the facts. He was the one Max Höss would recognize immediately, if they came on each other unexpectedly. We couldn't chance having Höss scuttle off before leading us to Laforge.

I walked back from the car to the open end of the street. Between that corner and the street the van had gone into, Thierry and Fabrice Pradel were waiting beside their car. The two local men stood half a block beyond the next corner, also waiting. Legoff had left them and was sauntering in Thierry's direction, taking his time.

I walked up behind Thierry. Pradel was half-turned from him, scanning the block, and saw me. Thierry didn't. His attention was on Legoff. I didn't see Legoff turn his head to look into that other dead-end street as he crossed its open end. But when he reached Thierry, he said, "The van looks empty now, Captain. And neither of them is in sight anywhere around it. They must have gone into one of the buildings. But there's no sign of life in any of them. They all look abandoned."

I said quietly, "The same on the street back, where I parked."

Thierry twisted toward me, startled. He was wound up much too tight for that heart condition, and the strain was showing. I knew guys in the military who'd pushed all their careers just to reach the rank of sergeant. And here was Thierry, pushing harder than his health warranted because he wasn't satisfied with being a captain. But his father had been an admiral. I guessed that was behind the push.

Fabrice Pradel said, "Maybe they went through a hole in the fence at the other end."

"I didn't see any hole," his partner said. "But there could be one I wasn't close enough to see."

Thierry turned to Pradel. "Take a look down that street."

Pradel took off his suit jacket and tossed it into the car. He threw his necktie in after it, undid half the buttons of his shirt, pulled it out of his trousers, crumpled it and let it hang. Then he slouched away, head hanging, placing each step with exaggerated care in a not too successful effort to keep from staggering. He stumbled and almost fell when he turned into the street where the van was parked. A far-gone drunk, wandering aimlessly through the early dusk.

"I'll have a look along the street where I parked," I said. "The condition of the houses in this block, anybody could easily get through the backs of them. From a house on one street to one on the other street."

"I told you to stay in your car," Thierry growled. His voice had a worrying rasp to it.

"Take it easy, Thierry. You need all the help you can get. I warned you that you were undermanned."

He glared at me. That came easier than having to admit I'd been right. But his anger couldn't hold against his anxiety. "All right," he said finally. "Report back quickly on whatever you find—or don't find."

I patted his shoulder and went back into the street where I'd left Fritz waiting in the car.

The car was still there.

But Fritz wasn't.

❂ 33 ❂

TWO POSSIBILITIES:

One: Fritz had detected something of such immediate interest that it had overruled prudence and he'd gone to investigate it.

Two: Max Höss had spotted Fritz from inside one of the abandoned houses, and Fritz had been forced into it.

The fact that the houses across from the car backed onto houses facing the street where the van was parked inclined me to the latter. I became sure of it when the door of one of those houses opened and I saw what came out.

He was large and young, about twenty. His black T-shirt bulged with muscle and fat. His leather jeans and motorcycle boots were black, too. He had a shaved skull with a word I couldn't make out tattooed on it. More tattoos on both thick arms, starting at the knuckles and continuing up inside his short sleeves. "RAPE THE WORLD" was printed in yellow across the T-shirt's front. A swastika dangled from his left earlobe. He wore a heavy chain in place of a belt, and there were steel caps on the toes and heels of his boots.

Without shutting the door behind him, the skinhead stepped out onto the cracked sidewalk to do a scan of the street. The scan stopped when he saw me. He fixed me with a menacing scowl that must have taken him months in front of a mirror to get just right. His left hand went into his pocket as I crossed over to him briskly, my smile friendly and inquiring.

"Pardon me, monsieur," I said, "I'm supposed to meet

someone at the side gate to the harbor, but I can't seem to find it.''

"Well, it's not here." His voice had a hard edge with as much practice behind it as his scowl. "This street's private. Get lost."

His hand came out of the pocket wearing brass knuckles.

I eyed that nervously. "Excuse me, I didn't mean to bother you. . . .''

"Go away."

I nodded hastily and turned to go. I spun back very fast and rammed my elbow into his throat. His eyes bulged and his mouth snapped open so wide I could hear his jaw hinges pop. The sound that fought its way through his strangling throat was a little louder than that, but not loud enough to carry into the house behind him. He sank to his knees. I kicked him in the temple. As hard as I could. He folded over on his side and stayed that way. Breathing, but not well.

I dragged the inert skinhead through the open door and onto the buckling tiles of the entry floor. I hunched down beside him and listened. There was no sound at all inside the house. I patted him down, looking for a weapon. No gun, no knife. Cursing silently, I stood up and stripped off my jacket. There was no time to go back and get help. Every second now could be the one in which Fritz died.

I dropped my jacket outside the door on the pavement and put my wallet on top of it, opened to my I.D. Hoping Thierry and his men would find it before anyone else did. And that they'd understand what it meant.

Leaving the door open as a final indication, I returned to the unconscious skinhead and hunkered down beside him again. The word tattooed on his shaved head was "DEATH." I grabbed his ears, raised his head, and slammed it back down against the tile floor. Twice. Insurance that he would not be coming to in the near future and sounding an alarm.

I stripped him of the brass knuckles and the belt chain. With the knuckles on my left fist and the chain dangling from my right, I did a swift reconnoiter of the house.

There was no one else in it, downstairs or up. Nothing but congealing dust and crunchy chunks of plaster, peeling wallpaper and worn-down linoleum. The only part of the flooring that wasn't thickly layered with dust and plaster was down in the cellar. On and around a closed trapdoor.

I lifted it open. It made no noise. The hinges had been oiled. Recently. Bright light came up at me from the bottom of a deep shaft with a steel ladder. An electric lantern, resting on the floor down there. Nobody around it as far as I could see—which was limited by the sides of the shaft.

My gut tightened as I descended the ladder. I didn't like going into that bright light. A perfectly outlined target, if anyone was watching down there. But Fritz was in here somewhere.

I reached the bottom of the shaft. No one shouted or shot me. There was a long, straight tunnel, going away from the shaft and its light toward a total blackness in the distance. Like the shaft, the tunnel looked older than the house above, and better-made. Probably a wartime passage between the U-boat base and some of its outworks. Germany's Todt organization, using a lot of forced labor in constructing the fortifications, had made sure its troops were as solidly protected against air raids as its submarines.

When I turned out the lantern, all of the tunnel got as black as the far end. I went in through the blackness, guiding myself with one hand against the tunnel's cold stone wall. About halfway through my eyes adjusted enough to make out a lightening of the dark at the other end. Not artificial light. Daylight. It was dim, but it was there. Enough to show me where I was when I emerged from the tunnel.

I was inside the U-boat base's main fortification. At the back of it. Under a boardwalk that stretched along the closed ends of the submarine pens. I was standing on a ledge of reinforced concrete, just above the oily-smelling, scum-covered water in one of the pens. The fading daylight was at the other end of the long pens, coming in through the submarine exits that led out into the harbor's Saint-Nazaire Basin.

Very little of that light reached as far inside the high-roofed base as the murky area where I was. It took a while before I located the wooden steps that took me up onto the boardwalk.

It was just as difficult to see anything up there. I heard voices but had trouble locating their direction. There was too much echo within the lofty cavern of the base. I started off to the left. The boardwalk was backed by deep, dark bays. Probably they'd once contained the U-boat repair shops and living quarters for the crews and maintenance workers. I moved ahead cautiously, testing my way. The boardwalk planking sagged in places, with some planks missing.

An indistinct figure materialized ahead, coming toward me through the shadowed gloom. He saw my equally murky figure at the same time and said, "Ramon?"

I said, "Yes"—and took a long stride to meet him. Knowing he might be carrying a weapon but unable to see it in that murk. The stride brought me close enough to lash the heavy chain at him. Aiming at where I judged his neck would be. But it must have gotten him in the face, because there was nothing strangled about his scream. He stumbled and grabbed the chain to keep from going down. I let go of it and he fell and I landed on top of him and punched him in the head with the brass knuckles. Whatever part of the head it hit, it was enough to put him out.

I felt around for the chain but couldn't find it soon enough. There was no time for a longer search. Bootsteps were pounding toward me along the boardwalk. Coming from the left—to investigate that scream.

I headed back the other way. But not far. More boots sounded from that direction. I couldn't see the men the boots belonged to yet—but that meant they didn't see me, either. I sat down on the edge of the boardwalk and lowered myself from it, my feet reaching for the concrete ledge below.

There wasn't any ledge. It didn't extend this far. Probably just a short section, for access to the tunnel. I lowered myself to the full length of my arms and went into the water as quietly as I could, trusting to the noise the boots were making to cover the minimal splash.

The thick, oily scum on the surface was unpleasant. Clamping my mouth shut and trying not to breathe deeply, I used a silent sidestroke to get in underneath the boardwalk. Boots hammered across the planking above me, and kept going. I kicked off my shoes and swam away, staying under the boardwalk and sticking with the sidestroke.

By now they would be finding the guy who'd screamed. It wasn't likely he'd be in any condition to explain what had happened for some time. But it was obvious *someone* had knocked him out. If luck was with me, they would search first through the deep, dark bays behind the boardwalk.

When I came to the long side dock of the U-boat pen, I eased out from under the boardwalk for a quick look back. Flashlights were moving inside the dark bays. One turned to aim out at the water in the pen, swinging back and forth across its surface.

There was a gap in the side dock and wall. I swam through it into the next pen. Treaded water and listened. There was no sound from anyone in that pen. But I thought I heard the muffled murmur of voices some distance ahead of me. Swimming across, I went through a similar gap on the other side. Into a third U-boat pen.

The voices were much stronger there. And one of them sounded like Fritz, though I wasn't close enough to make out the words. I looked in that direction. Halfway out along this pen's side dock was a small group of men, sharply outlined by the dimming daylight coming in through the pen's water exit.

I swam toward them, hugging the side dock, hidden inside its darker shadow. I stopped when their voices were directly above my head, and quite clear.

I reached up, hooked my fingers on the top edge of the dock, and very slowly pulled myself up. Just until my eyes were level with the soles of their shoes, and I could look up and see the men wearing the shoes.

◈ 34 ◈

THERE WERE FIVE OF THEM.

One was Max Höss. He was holding a revolver pointed at the second man: Fritz Donhoff.

Two others had shaved skulls and were dressed like the skinhead I'd left on the floor of the house. But there the resemblance—to him or to each other—ended. One of this pair was small and plump and delicate-featured. He had a switchblade knife open in his right fist and looked eager to use it. The other skinhead didn't have a weapon. He didn't need one. His size and strength were weapon enough. He was at least three inches taller than me, and jumbo-wide. The big belly pushing against his belt chain looked as solid as the rest of him.

Laforge—the man we'd first known as Hulvane, and then as Langsdorf—stood facing Fritz with his fists on his hips and his lean figure held stiffly erect. His stance and expression had the same cold arrogance I'd seen in those pictures of SS officers in the Dachau concentration camp.

Fritz was practically cowering before him, his hands spread in pleading. "... and I swear it, you are making a mistake. I told you ... I have never been to Dachau in my life. ..."

"You are a liar!" Höss snarled, his French distorted by his anger and the heavy Germanic accent. "You *are* the old man who interfered with me there! I am not wrong!"

Fritz didn't look at him. Didn't take his eyes off Laforge. "I don't even know who you are, so how can I be working

221

on a case involving you? I am not working on *any* case right now, I told you, I'm only here taking a vacation from work. . . . "

He was speaking so fast the words tumbled over each other. Almost babbling in his display of abject terror. Stalling for time. Knowing I'd be coming in after him. Hoping I'd be bringing some troops with me.

"Stop this nonsense!" Laforge barked. "No one believes you. You didn't just *happen* to be in that car across the street when Höss entered the house and saw you through the window. You will tell me how you knew about that house."

"I didn't know *anything*," Fritz pleaded. "I was waiting for a prostitute. . . . She promised to meet me there and I—"

"Stop it!" Laforge repeated impatiently. "You will also tell me where your partner is and—"

"In Paris, I think . . ."

"*And* you will tell me who hired you to spy on me—and why."

"I can't tell you what I don't know!" Fritz shouted. "Please let me go! I can't understand what you want with me. . . . " He went on like that, not expecting to be believed, just trying to keep the words going and delay the hurting as long as he could.

But Laforge wasn't even listening to him anymore. He looked at the little skinhead: "Use your knife on him. Remove one of his eyes. We'll see if he prefers telling the truth to losing the other eye."

The skinhead grinned and brought his switchblade up as he took a step forward. Laforge gestured to the jumbo-size skinhead: "Hold him still for it."

Jumbo reached for Fritz. But Fritz backed away from him, fast. Two steps back—then he was against the side wall. Höss gestured with his gun, warning him not to move again.

"Wait!" Fritz blurted. "I have a great deal of money! I'll give it to you! All of it!"

I raised up and braced my left forearm and right hand on the dock, ready to move. The four of them—Laforge, Höss, Jumbo, and the short one with the knife—were forming a semicircle around Fritz, their backs to me. Fritz, his back to the wall, was facing in the opposite direction. But if he saw me, there was no sign of it.

He was concentrating on them and his babbling: "More than two hundred thousand francs! In the bank! I'll make out a check for you!" He was fumbling at the two fountain pens sticking out of his breast pocket, taking the fatter one. "Just let me get out my checkbook and tell me what name you—"

Fritz had the cap off the fountain pen at that point. He shot Höss with it.

A fountain pen firing device has certain built-in limitations. It only carries one bullet. A little .22, without much punch behind it. It's no good at all at any distance. Even for close work, if you're in a hurry to do real damage, you have to aim at some soft and sensitive part of the body.

Fritz shot him in the stomach. The little bullet disappeared like a hot needle going into a tub of butter. Höss screeched and did a stumbling turn. The revolver flew out of his hand, bounced off the dock, and fell into the water. Too far for me to grab before it sank.

For a long moment the other three were too stunned to do anything but stare at their gut-shot killer clutching his stomach and making a shrill whining noise through his clenched teeth as his knees buckled under him. Fritz used that moment—launching himself away from the wall and throwing a punch at Laforge's face. Laforge slipped the punch and grabbed Fritz by the throat, and Fritz hit him across the back of the neck. They went down together, two old men locked in battle. An ancient battle, though they had never met before.

I used the moment, too. Hauling myself most of the way onto the dock. The little skinhead was the nearest to me. He was turning to go to Laforge's aid, his knife held ready. I grabbed his ankle and yanked him off his feet, at the same time using my hold on the ankle to drag the rest of me onto the dock.

He landed hard, on his face. Blood spurted to one side from his smashed nose, and his knife skittered out of his grasp. I did a fast survey of the danger points as I came up on my feet.

Höss was no problem. He sat with his knees up and his head down between them, continuing to hold his stomach and make that whining noise. Fritz and Laforge were rolling over and over, pounding away at each other. Jumbo was looking back and forth, uncertain whether he should help Laforge or take me first. The little skinhead raised his bleeding face and started using both hands to shove himself up.

I heel-kicked him in the ear, ending that problem, and began circling around him toward the fallen knife. That decided Jumbo. The knife was nearer to him than to me, but the hunched figure of the gut-shot Höss was between him and it. Jumbo jumped over him, startlingly nimble for his size, as I darted forward. I was bending for the knife when his huge hand closed like a vise around my right biceps and pulled me away from it.

I went with the pull and twisted in toward him, putting all I had into hitting him in that big belly. Using my left fist, with the brass knuckles on it.

It was like punching a fully inflated truck tire. No give at all. The brass knuckles hurt him, though. Enough for his grip on my arm to loosen. I broke free and hit him with another left—this one to his groin. He grunted with pain, but the brass knuckles hadn't gotten to his family jewels. His thighs were too close together, and thick as tree trunks.

The side of his fist clouted me across the forehead and knocked me spinning away from him—and away from that knife. He didn't bother going for the knife. Just came after me.

I tried to dance farther away—and staggered. My brain reeled and my balance was off. If he landed a couple more like that, it would be all over. He closed in on me. I went into a low crouch and feinted a right at his groin. Jumbo crouched to protect himself there with one hand while his other hand came around to clamp on the back of my neck and drag me forward. That left his face wide open. I raked the brass knuckles across it savagely, trying for his eyes.

I got his forehead instead, ripping it wide open all the way across. Blood spurted out of the deep gash and ran into his eyes, half-blinding him. He stumbled to the left, unable to see where he was going. Just trying to get away from me long enough to wipe his eyes clear. I drove my foot into the back of his knee. He went to both knees, leaning forward with his hands reaching down for support that he could use to shove himself back up at me.

But there was no support for him to find. He was kneeling on the dock's edge, with half of his huge body leaning out over the water, I bent and slammed the brass knuckles against the base of his spine. Jumbo went all the way over and hit the water with a tremendous splash, sinking out of sight under it.

I darted to the knife. When I got back to the dock edge with it, Jumbo's head had surfaced. Dripping oil and water and blood. But he could see clearly again. He reached up and grabbed the dock, ready to swing himself back onto it. I brought the knife up and back, holding it in perfect throwing position beside my ear. Poised to hurl it and send its blade plunging into his heart whenever his torso came up clear of the water.

I'd done some practice at knife throwing in the past, against a tree trunk. I never seemed to get it right. I could hit the tree every time, but much more often with the handle than the blade. When I did luck out and the knife hit the tree point-first, it was usually at a bad angle, with the blade not penetrating deep or bouncing away. The only thing I got down pat was the proper throwing position.

But Jumbo didn't know that. He shoved himself back down in the water and floundered away, hugging the side of the dock, heading toward the back of the U-boat pen.

I turned to Fritz. He was straddling Laforge's limply sprawled figure, punching away at his head. He was getting very tired. It took him longer each time to bring up a fist for the next punch. Laforge's head rolled inertly each time it was hit.

I walked over and put a hand between Fritz's hunched shoulders. "Are you sure you want him to die that quickly and painlessly? While he's unconscious?"

Fritz had a heavy fist raised for another blow. He held it up there for a few seconds, and then slowly lowered it. He was trembling a little, taking deep breaths, his chest heaving. I helped him to his feet. His left eye was swollen almost shut and there was blood dribbling from a cut across the side of his lower lip and he looked exhausted. But he was also looking very pleased with himself.

I glanced back along the dock. Jumbo had hauled himself onto it, a good distance away. He started running toward the back of the U-boat pen. To get help and a weapon.

He stopped suddenly—hearing the same thing I heard. Shouts and gunfire from some of the other pens.

The shooting was still going on, though diminishing in volume, when Thierry came into view out of the murk at the back of our dock. When he saw Jumbo, he brought up the pistol he was carrying and snapped an order. Jumbo turned wearily and leaned his forehead against the wall, crossing his wrists behind him.

Fabrice Pradel appeared behind Thierry, carrying a short-barreled shotgun in one hand. He took over with Jumbo, snapping cuffs on his wrists while Thierry came on toward me.

I tossed the switch knife into the water and walked to meet him. "You finally called in the local cops." I knew he wouldn't have left only three men to deal with the gang in the other sub pens.

Thierry nodded distractedly, his expression more anxiety-ridden than ever. "But we haven't found Laforge. Unless—" He looked past me, trying not to let himself hope too much.

I stepped aside and pointed to the sprawled figure at Fritz's feet. "There he is."

Thierry's whole face lit up. Visions of confidential kudos danced in his head. I could see it in his eyes when he went over to personally put the handcuffs on Laforge.

It wasn't until after full dark that the fishing boat came in—carrying high-grade cocaine off-loaded from a Venezuelan freighter a few miles off the Brittany coast. By then there were three different groups of cops waiting to grab boat, crew, and cargo. The local *police judiciaire*. A bunch of *stupes*, which is what everyone in France calls its narcotics agents. And a patrol boat manned by Saint-Nazaire's harbor police.

Well before that, Thierry had walked Fritz and me out of the U-boat base, past all those cops. Letting them suppose we were just another pair of his imported DGSE agents. Once we were back on the street, he begged us to fade away into the night and make like we'd never been there. We did so—after I called Rome and fulfilled my obligation to Major Diego Bandini.

Thierry was making his own phone call at the same time. To the director of the DGSE. Who promptly put through calls to both the president and the prime minister of France. Informing them that his secret service officers had captured France's most-wanted war criminal—and turned Laforge over to Saint-Nazaire's P.J., which was awaiting orders from Paris on where to send him. Apologizing for his officers having carried out their action on territory prohibited by the DGSE's charter. Explaining that they'd overstepped their authority out of urgent necessity. Pointing out that Laforge had dodged all attempts to find him for forty-five years—and that if the DGSE officers had simply passed their information on through channels, instead of acting immediately, Laforge might have had time to get away again.

Explanation accepted.

The news media were full of it the next day—and for months to come. The names of the DGSE agents involved in the capture of Laforge never reached the press, of course. But within the service, Thierry Gallion's exploit was duly noted. He wasn't going to have to remain a captain until he reached retirement, after all.

Major Bandini's government applied for the extradition of Max Höss when he was sufficiently recovered from his stomach wound to make the trip under guard. France let Italy have him. Italy's charge that he'd planted the car bomb that killed Lawrence Tuck was backed by three witnesses. The only thing the French could charge him with was being part of a criminal conspiracy to smuggle narcotics into the country. And it wasn't a strong case, because he'd been in no condition to either touch the drugs or fight the police. Not enough evidence to get him a heavy sentence.

Italy's case against him was strong enough to persuade Höss to sign a confession—in return for a sentence that held the possibility of his being released from prison, someday in the distant future.

Some of the disclosures in his confession soured Rudolph Gottfried Aumeier's relations with the German government, and induced his stockholders to remove him from his position as head of his company. The confession also implicated Laforge as the one for whom Höss had killed Tuck.

Italy applied for the extradition of Laforge. But France didn't buy that. France had a case involving much worse than a single murder that it was preparing against Laforge.

His trial—for "crimes against humanity"—didn't take place until midwinter. It was a long one. I visited the courtroom twice during its protracted course. Laforge looked another ten years older each time I saw him there.

His attorneys based his defense on the claim that everything Laforge had done during the Nazi occupation of Dijon had been done as a lawful citizen cooperating with the police—the police of that time.

The prosecutor didn't waste much time countering that. He concentrated on bringing in one witness after another from Dijon. People who had survived the reign of terror Laforge had spread through that city. Their testimony of what he had done to them and others went on for two weeks—and became too damning for the defense to stand against.

Laforge was found to be guilty as charged.

I went back to the court on the day he was to be sentenced. Helen Marsh was there, too. With Ferguson. That was no surprise. They had been there every day of the long trial. On this last day, Helen Marsh was dressed entirely in white. Like a bride—the thought struck me—a bride preparing to step into a different life. A crazy thought. Because there was nothing festive in her face. Her expression had a gravedigger's gravity.

Her gloves that day were white, too. She had worn gloves of one color or another throughout the trial, never taking them off.

My attention went to Laforge as the judge pronounced his sentence. Imprisonment for the rest of his life. In solitary confinement—for his own protection. Most of the normal run of criminals consider themselves patriots. When patriotism doesn't interfere with profit. Like most businessmen. There might be some among the prison's convicts who would get an impulse to administer a swifter punishment to Laforge.

The sentence was not unexpected. But I watched Laforge crumple before it. He didn't faint or stagger. But his formerly erect figure shrank as the energy drained out of it. The habitual arrogance of his expression gave way to an utter despair. A twitch that had developed in his left cheek as he listened to the testimony of the witnesses became more pronounced.

Helen Marsh stood up and walked toward him. There was nothing menacing in her approach, and nobody thought to stop her. When she was facing Laforge, she stopped and spoke to him. I couldn't hear her, but I knew what she was saying. She was telling him that she was the one who had done this to him.

Laforge frowned at her, puzzled. Not understanding. Most of his mind already locked inside that prison cell that was going to become all of his world until the day he died.

I watched Helen Marsh remove the glove from her mutilated hand. She held it up between them, and spoke again.

His eyes went to that hand. And then, very slowly, back to her face. His mouth sagging as he finally realized who she was.

She dropped the glove in front of him and turned away. He stared after her, still in shock, while she walked to the courtroom door. She began to smile as she went out.

About the Author

Ten of Marvin Albert's novels have been made into films. Several have been Literary Guild choices. He has been honored with a Special Award by the Mystery Writers of America.

In addition to being the author of books of fiction and non-fiction, he has been a Merchant Marine Officer, actor and theatrical road manager, newspaperman, magazine editor, and Hollywood scriptwriter.

Born in Philadelphia, he has lived in New York, Los Angeles, London, and Paris. He currently lives on the Riviera with his wife, the French artist Xenia Klar. He has two children, Jan and David.